"Of all Putney's heroes,
the Lost Lords are the most irresistible—
bad boys who are so very good."

—RT Book Reviews

"YOU'RE A GOOD MAN, LORD ROMAYNE, AND I'M A WICKED WOMAN!"

"I should be wearing scarlet, not widow's weeds, to warn men away from me!"

His gaze was searching. "Are you cruel? I've seen no signs of that. Are you a liar or profoundly self-ish? I've not observed that, either. How are you wicked?"

She wanted to spit at him. "I have no desire to re-veal my sordid past, my lord! I have done what I must to survive, and that includes deeds that the world would condemn." Not to mention the deed that could get her hanged. "I don't belong with a man who is almost a saint!"

His eyes flashed with real anger. "I am no saint!" He closed the distance between them in two steps, wrapped his arms around Jessie, and kissed her with a passion that seared her bones. . . .

Books by Mary Jo Putney

The Lost Lords series

Loving a Lost Lord
Never Less Than a Lady
Nowhere Near Respectable
No Longer a Gentleman
Sometimes a Rogue
Not Quite a Wife
Not Always a Saint

Other Titles

One Perfect Rose
The Bargain
The Rake
Mischief and Mistletoe
Dangerous Gifts

MARY JO PUTNEY

NOT ALWAYS A SAINT

ZEBRA BOOKS
KENSINGTON PUBLISHING CORP.
http://www.kensingtonbooks.com

ZEBRA BOOKS are published by

Kensington Publishing Corp.
119 West 40th Street
New York, NY 10018   •

All Kensington titles, imprints, and distributed lines are available
at special quantity discounts for bulk purchases for sales promo-
tion, premiums, fund-raising, educational, or institutional use.

Special book excerpts or customized printings can also be created to fit specific needs. For details, write or phone the office of
the Kensington Sales Manager: Attn. Sales Department. Kensington Publishing Corp., 119 West 40th Street, New York, NY 10018.
Phone: 1-800-221-2647.

Zebra and the Z logo Reg. U.S. Pat. & TM Off.

First Kensington Books Hardcover Printing: May 2015
First Zebra Books Mass-Market Paperback Printing: September
2015
ISBN-13: 978-1-4201-2717-1
ISBN-10: 1-4201-2717-9

eISBN-13: 978-1-4201-2720-1
eISBN-10: 1-4201-2720-9

10 9 8 7 6 5 4 3 2 1

Printed in the United States of America

To Marianne and Katy.
Just because.

Prologue

Bristol, Autumn 1806

The fleet was in, the moon was full, and business was booming at the Herbert free infirmary. Daniel Herbert didn't mind. He loved mending broken bodies and he loved the infirmary, which he'd designed with the able assistance of his sister, Laurel, who was his partner and best friend.

Nonetheless, by midnight he'd had enough of patching up drunken sailors injured in tavern brawls. The last one limped into the examination room dripping blood from a crudely bandaged left arm. Spotting the gin Daniel used for cleaning wounds, he lunged toward the bottle.

"Sit!" Daniel said firmly as he applied a nerve grip to the grizzled sailor's shoulder and forced him into a chair. "I need to get you fixed up so I can close the infirmary and get some sleep."

The sailor squawked and rubbed at the numbed arm. "Jus' want a li'l drink!" he said reproachfully.

"You won't find it here." With the skill of long practice, Daniel removed the filthy bandage to find a knife slash that was messy but shallow.

He deftly cleaned the slash, finishing with enough gin to make the sailor squawk. "Why'd you do that?" the sailor asked.

"I've found that gin helps wounds heal better so your arm is less likely to fall off," Daniel explained. "Now, off with you, and prepare for a terrible headache tomorrow."

"Not even one li'l sip from the bottle?"

"Go!" As the sailor thanked him and shuffled out, Daniel dropped his used surgical instruments into a basin of soapy water. As with the gin, he'd found that keeping instruments clean made for better results.

The door to his examination room swung open so hard that it banged the wall. He looked up to see his sister, who'd shoved the door open with one hand while her other arm was wrapped around the waist of a battered and bleeding young woman on the verge of collapse.

Imperturbable as always, Laurel said, "Don't put those instruments away yet, Daniel. We have a new customer." She helped the girl onto the examination table.

He hated seeing women who had been beaten, usually by the men who were supposed to protect them. As he studied the new patient, his fatigue vanished. She was hunched over, her face obscured by a tangle of dark hair that was matted with blood on the right side. She clutched a cloak tightly around her shoulders, and she was shaking from shock.

Voice gentle, he said, "I'm Dr. Herbert. What's your name?"

"J-J-J . . ."

She spoke clumsily, as if her mouth was having trouble forming words, so he prompted, "Jane?"

After a long moment, she whispered raggedly, "Yes, J-Jane."

"I'm going to examine you to find what needs fixing." He moistened a clean cloth. "Raise your head so I can clean the blood from your face."

She complied, revealing a face with one eye swollen shut and such massive bruising that her own mother wouldn't recognize her. Under the bruises she was very young, and he guessed that under normal circumstances she might be pretty. How could any man hurt a vulnerable young girl like this?

He buried his anger for later. What mattered now was patching her up. She winced several times as he washed the blood from her face, despite his being as gentle as possible. He was particularly careful around her eyes. "You're in luck," he said conversationally. "You'll have black eyes like a bare-knuckle boxer, but there's no serious damage."

As he cleaned the gash on her head, he asked, "Who beat you?"

She made a choked sound and cringed away from him. Noticing the glint of a wedding ring on her left hand, he asked, "Was it your husband?"

Jane stared down at her hand as if she'd forgotten the ring she wore. Then she wrenched off the narrow circlet of gold and hurled it across the examination room. The ring bounced from the wall and rattled across the floor.

"Sell it. Help . . . infirmary," she whispered hoarsely. Her uplifted face revealed her bruised throat. The brute had tried to strangle her.

Jane's movements caused her cloak to slide from her shoulders, revealing a bloody slash down her back. The jagged laceration ran from her left shoulder almost to her waist. She must have been stabbed as she tried to escape. The tip of the blade had skittered to the left when it hit the edge of her stays, then continued downward through the padded garment.

Keeping his voice calm, Daniel reached for his heavy scissors and cut away the stays. Her gown and corset were good quality, but the bodice was ruined and her thin shift was stuck to the laceration by dried blood. Dampening the shift allowed him to pull it gently from the wound, though Jane gasped as he peeled it away.

"Luckily this isn't deep, though I imagine it hurts like Hades." Particularly since he was now cleaning the wound with gin. Jane would probably carry the scars of this night for the rest of her life, but at least this one would be concealed.

He continued his soft stream of commentary to soothe her. Laurel assisted him, preserving Jane's modesty as much as possible.

When Daniel finished cleaning the wound, Laurel said, "You'll need new clothing, Jane. Daniel, could you bring some garments from our supply?"

Daniel might not be as adept at choosing female clothing as Laurel, but they had a standing rule that a woman who had just been battered wouldn't be left alone with a man, even him. He nodded and got to his feet, feeling the weight of the long day. "Do you have a place to go tonight? Family? Friends?"

Gaze still downcast, Jane whispered, "A . . . a friend will take me in."

"That's enough for tonight, but this can't be allowed to happen again," Laurel said firmly. "We'll summon the magistrate and you can bring charges against the man who beat you."

"No!" Jane clutched her ruined clothing close, her voice frantic. "The only way I can be safe is by leaving Bristol. A magistrate cannot help."

Daniel frowned. Jane seemed determined not to return to the brute, but too often women went back to the men who had injured them because they had no other choice. While he was out of the room, Laurel would counsel the girl.

Jane was not the first patient in need of clothing, so Laurel had filled two large wardrobes with garments for both sexes and all ages. Some were donated by local churches, others she'd found in rag shops. After patching and washing, the clothing was clean and respectable, if not fashionable.

The girl needed a loose smock that wouldn't hurt her injured back. Shoes? No, she was wearing sturdy, well-made half boots. Swiftly he collected what she needed and tucked everything into a simple canvas bag that she could carry easily. Lastly, he chose a deep bonnet and a cloak that would cover up her injuries and bandages.

After he delivered the garments, Laurel shooed him from the examination room so she could help Jane dress. He frowned as he closed the door behind him. He and Laurel offered services, not money. Almost all of the generous allowance provided by Laurel's estranged husband was spent running the infirmary, and cash was tight.

But sometimes exceptions must be made. His office was only a few steps away, so he unlocked the door and opened the hidden desk drawer where he kept money. Jane didn't look as if she had a penny to bless herself with. How much would it cost for her to run away and keep herself until she healed?

He couldn't bear to think of her returning to her violent husband. He collected twenty pounds' worth of coins and small bills, and tucked them into a cloth purse. It was a substantial sum, enough to get her away from Bristol and keep her for two or three months if she was careful. Then he returned to the examination room, reminding himself that he couldn't save everyone. Not even close.

Jane was bundled warmly in the old cloak, her bruised face and bandaged head concealed by the brim of the bonnet. Laurel was frowning. "You're sure you'll be all right? You can spend the rest of the night here in the infirmary."

"I can't," the girl said, her voice stronger now. "I will be fine, truly. I don't have to go far."

Daniel suspected she wouldn't stay because she feared she might be followed. He hoped she was telling the truth about having a friend who would take her in for the night. She might be planning to hide in a stable or church. That would do for one night if she was planning on leaving the next day. "You have some place to go if you leave Bristol? Family, by preference."

"There is no one, but I shall manage. I'm not afraid to work." She gave a brittle laugh. "Or to walk."

Daniel held out the purse. "Take this. It should

be enough to keep you until you can establish yourself elsewhere."

She gasped and tried to hand the money back. "I can't take this! You've already done so much for me."

He caught her hand, speaking slowly to emphasize his words. "We don't want to think of you leaving here and falling into a situation that's even worse."

Jane stared up into his face. The eye that wasn't swollen shut was a light, clear blue, and it held shadows that no young girl should have.

She bent and kissed his hand with her bruised lips. "Thank you," she said in a raw, husky voice.

She released his hand and tucked the purse inside her cloak, then turned to Laurel. "Thank you both so much. I shall never forget your kindness. If there is ever anything I can do to repay you . . ."

Daniel said firmly, "Make wise decisions. Be kind to others. That will suffice."

She ducked her head again, then turned and left the room. Daniel and Laurel followed her to the door, watching silently as the girl descended the few steps to the street and turned left. There was something heartbreakingly gallant about her slim figure as she disappeared into the night.

"The house behind us is for sale," Laurel said. "I want to buy it and create a sanctuary for women and children who need shelter from brutal men."

"I think that's an excellent idea," Daniel said immediately. A shelter for women like Jane would be a true godsend. "Do we have the money?"

"I'll *find* the money!" Laurel said with rare fierceness.

"Then we'll do it." Daniel put his arm around his

sister's shoulders and gave a comforting squeeze. "At the moment, though, we both need food and strong tea."

Laurel exhaled, relaxing under his arm. "What good advice, Doctor. There's a nice bean soup on the hob."

"Perfect." But before Daniel closed the door, he gazed at the shadows where Jane had vanished. As the back of his neck prickled, he had the uncanny feeling that he would someday see her again.

Chapter 1

Bristol, Autumn 1813

After burying his parents, Daniel Herbert returned to work, which had always been his passion and salvation. No matter how unquiet his own mind, his medical skills helped heal ailing bodies, and the occasional sermons he gave in the chapel he sponsored sometimes helped heal wounded souls.

To ensure that he was as busy as he needed to be, Daniel sent his junior doctor, Colin Holt, off on holiday with his new bride. Dispensing cough syrups and willow bark tea, and performing minor surgeries left Daniel tired enough to sleep. Exhaustion was preferable to thought. A fortnight had passed since the funerals and soon he must face the changes caused by their deaths; but for now, he preferred stitching up knife wounds in bawdy old sailors.

He was just finishing with a patient when Betsy Rivers, the infirmary manager, knocked and entered his treatment room. "Dr. Herbert, a gentleman is here to see you on what he says is important business."

"I doubt that his idea of important is the same as mine," Daniel said dryly. "But Red Rab here is just leaving, so send in the gentleman."

Betsy frowned at his blood-spattered apron but didn't try to talk him into changing out of his work clothing. "Yes, sir."

As Betsy left, Daniel tied the last suture on his grizzled patient. "Careful, Rab. One of these days someone might accidentally stab something vital."

"Naw, Doc," Red Rab chuckled as he stood. "We been fightin' each other so long, we know where it's safe to stick the blades." The sailor ambled out and Daniel began cleaning up the bloodstained rags and instruments.

Betsy returned, accompanied by a stocky, soberly dressed fellow with a keen gaze and a folio under his arm. "This is Mr. Hyatt, sir."

The visitor blinked at Daniel's rough and ready attire, then inclined his head courteously. "I'm Matthew Hyatt of the London law firm Hyatt and Sons. You are Daniel Herbert of Belmond Manor?"

Though Daniel hadn't lived there in years, the manor was definitely now his. "I am." He dropped his used surgical instruments into the waiting basin of soapy water.

"My sympathies on the loss of your parents, Mr. Herbert." The lawyer sighed. "The disease outbreak at Castle Romayne was a great tragedy."

"It struck with terrifying swiftness. Far too many of the people in the abbey and town died," Daniel said, his mouth tightening at the memory. His parents had been delighted to receive an invitation to a grand house party held by his father's distant cousin, Lord Romayne. They'd urged him to come, too, but he had no interest in such things. If he'd been there, might he have been able to suggest effective treatment in time? Drinking massive amounts of fluids could help dangerous fevers. Or would he have died as well?

He washed his hands briskly. "I have patients waiting, so perhaps you can tell me your reason for being here?"

The lawyer blinked at his bluntness. "Very well. It's my pleasure to inform you that you are heir to the honors and property of the Romayne barony."

Lord Romayne's other heirs had all died in that beastly outbreak of disease? Daniel froze, feeling the impact of the words like a fatal blow. The walls he'd built around his pain and guilt shattered and raw emotion scorched through him.

His life was over.

When James, Lord Kirkland, entered Daniel's office late the next day, Daniel was unsurprised. Kirkland was a shipping merchant and spymaster, as well as Daniel's brother-in-law and sometime friend. With his information sources, Kirkland usually knew what was happening before it actually happened. This evening he looked like a darkly elegant predator, but his eyes were compassionate.

Though Daniel had managed to paper over the internal cracks caused by having a barony fall in his lap, he was embarrassingly relieved to see Kirkland, who was also a master at fixing problems. Pushing aside his late, cold supper, Daniel offered his hand. "I assume you've heard the news? Because if Laurel was unwell, you'd be with her."

Kirkland smiled as he shook hands. "Laurel is at the stage of pregnancy where she has a terrifying amount of energy. I barely restrained her from coming with me."

Daniel's brows arched. "I assume she sent you to ensure that I don't put a period to my existence."

"Exactly," Kirkland said with dry amusement. "Inheriting wealth, influence, and a seat in the House of Lords is enough to drive any man to despair."

Daniel smiled reluctantly at how well Laurel and Kirkland knew him. He opened the bottom drawer of his desk and retrieved the flask of brandy he kept for unusually trying days. "I'm still reeling at the news. I'm only a third cousin once removed. But there were only a few intervening heirs, and all died at that damnable house party."

"A tragedy." Kirkland accepted the glass of brandy Daniel poured, then settled into the only other chair in the small office. "Not least for you."

Daniel sighed. "There's no way I can refuse the inheritance, is there?"

"Unfortunately not," Kirkland said. "The noble title and entailed property go to the nearest male heir of the Herbert bloodline, and that's you. You are now responsible for the estates and all the tenants who depend on them."

"I feel as if Atlas just dropped the world on my shoulders. You were raised knowing you were the Kirkland heir, but I barely knew Romayne existed, much less that I had any chance of inheriting." His father would have known, and would have been delighted if the inheritance had fallen to him.

Kirkland swirled the brandy in his glass thoughtfully. "A change of this magnitude is intimidating, but being a lord is well within your capabilities."

"No doubt." Daniel's face tightened at the thought of his greatest fear. Realizing Kirkland would understand, he added tersely, "But can I still be a doctor?"

"You will have more demands on your time," Kirkland admitted. "But you can hire good people to manage the properties. You're now a peer of the realm! Other lords spend large amounts of time collecting fossils or writing papers on mathematics or drinking themselves into a stupor. You can find time for your work."

"I hope so." Daniel tried to estimate how many hours would be consumed by managing people and property and his seat in Parliament. Too many. "I won't be able to help as many as I do now."

"I'll say the same to you as I did to Laurel. Your new honors are a burden, but also an opportunity, and a fortune makes it possible to help a great many more people." Kirkland smiled. "Your sister is spending my money with wild abandon as she helps open more women's shelters like Zion House. You can establish more infirmaries. Sponsor the education of promising young surgeons and physicians."

Oddly, Daniel hadn't thought about those possibilities. "I like those ideas, but I already have the life I want. Inheriting Romayne is a burden and a complication."

"Is it still the life you want?" Kirkland asked quietly. "Or is it time for a change?"

Daniel started to reply that of course his life was exactly right just as it was. Then he shut his mouth and reconsidered.

Damn Kirkland for being right! Here in Bristol, Daniel had valuable work and daily challenges, but he'd been lonely since his sister had reconciled with Kirkland and moved away. He needed more friends and different challenges.

"Perhaps it is time," he said slowly. "I've been in shock ever since the lawyer delivered the dread news. I need to think about what I want, and what is now possible."

"Come to London and stay with us," Kirkland suggested. "Laurel and I would love having you, and I can help you sort the practical and legal issues of your new position. You also need to be introduced to society. The little season will start soon, and the network of Westerfield Academy old boys will help you establish yourself to whatever extent you want."

Daniel's tension eased. London seemed more manageable if he stayed with Laurel and Kirkland. "I'd enjoy seeing old schoolmates, but I have my doubts about entering grand society."

"Wise of you to be wary," his friend said, amused. "Particularly in light of the dangers you'll face."

"I won't succumb to the lures of gambling and drink." Daniel regarded his empty glass, then poured himself more brandy. "Though you wouldn't know it to see me today."

"Difficult times call for stern measures." Kirkland held out his own glass for a refill. "But the danger I was referring to is the marriage mart. You are now the most desirable of commodities, a handsome, or at least presentable, peer in want of a wife." He grinned. "Perhaps you can find a pleasant, steady young widow who wants to manage your estates and leave you free to be a doctor."

Daniel found himself unexpectedly stirred by the idea of a wife. How many years had it been since Rose died? Too achingly many. She was a creature of sunshine and bubbling life, and she would never have wanted him to turn into the dour old bachelor he was now. If he was going to change, it was now or never.

He raised his glass in a mock salute. "Very well, then. I shall go to London and look for a wife."

Chapter 2

"Lord Kelham won't be with us much longer," the physician said quietly as Jessie Kelham returned to the sickroom carrying her sleepy four-year-old daughter.

She nodded acknowledgment. Philip had been failing for weeks, and it was clear the end was nigh. It was almost midnight, and she guessed he'd be gone by the dawn.

Beth yawned sleepily. "Is Papa better?"

Jessie stroked her daughter's soft toffee-colored hair. Though it was many shades lighter than her own dark tresses, anyone who saw the two together knew them for mother and daughter. Beth, the most precious being in Jessie's life. "No, sweetheart. Soon he'll be gone, but he wants to say good-bye to you first."

She carried her daughter to the massive bed, where Philip's frail figure lay peacefully in the soft lamplight. With his white hair and pale face, he almost disappeared against the crisp linen sheets. His manservant had made him presentable for this last meeting with Beth.

When they reached the bed, for a moment Jessie feared they were too late, but when she set her daughter on the mattress, Philip's eyes flickered open and he smiled with grave sweetness. "My little sunshine. I'm sorry I won't be here to see you all grown up, but I know you'll be beautiful."

Recognizing finality, Beth's eyes filled with tears. She leaned forward and kissed his grizzled cheek. "I don't want you to go, Papa," she said sadly.

He patted her hand where it rested beside his. "I'll never be very far away from you, sweetling. Just close your eyes and think of me and I'll be there."

"It would be better if I could hug you whenever I wanted!"

Philip smiled tiredly. "Indeed, but we can't always have what we want. Be good and do as your mother says. We'll meet again in heaven. A very long time from now, I hope." His breathing was becoming increasingly labored, so Jessie signaled Beth's nursemaid, who had followed them down from the nursery.

Lily lifted Beth with comforting arms. "Time for bed again, little finch. I'll sing to you until you sleep."

Beth went docilely, though her wistful gaze stayed on Philip as they left the room. Jessie was grateful that her daughter was old enough that she'd have some memories of how much her father had loved her.

When they were gone, Jessie perched on the edge of the bed and rested her hand on her husband's. The bones of his fingers seemed fragile as twigs. "My turn now. Like Beth, I don't want you to go."

"My time has come." He had a spate of coughs before continuing. "You and Beth gave me more years and more joy than I dreamed was possible after I lost Louise. I only wish she could have known you."

"I wish I'd known her, but if she hadn't died, we would never have met." Jessie squeezed his hand gently. "Perhaps she sent me to keep you happy until the two of you could be together again."

"What a splendid thought." He drew another labored breath. "You don't need to worry about your future, my dear. In fact, when the will is read, there will be a surprise for you and Beth." His lips curved into an impish smile. He'd always loved giving Jessie and Beth surprises.

"You've been a surprise from the beginning," she said with a nostalgic smile. "I couldn't believe that a fine gentleman like you would marry a trumpery minor actress."

He began coughing so hard that Jessie almost summoned the physician. When the coughing subsided, he whispered, "And I couldn't believe that the most beautiful woman in England would marry me even for money and a title."

"I didn't marry you for your money, and certainly not for your title," she said softly. "I married you for your kindness and wisdom."

They shared an intimate smile. Genteel society had been scandalized by the unequal marriage, but it had brought happiness to them both. When Philip died, she would lose her dearest friend.

Voice faded to a thread, he whispered, "Will Frederick reach here in time?"

"The roads are in bad condition after all the rain, so it's impossible to say," she replied. She didn't doubt that Frederick Kelham was on his way, but it would be for his inheritance, not because he loved his uncle. Frederick loved only himself.

As heir to the title and entailed property, Frederick had been waiting impatiently for his uncle's death for years. He'd been very unhappy with Jessie's pregnancy, and she'd prayed for a daughter who would not be an obstacle to Frederick's ambitions. Beth's birth had been a relief. Philip was delighted to have a little girl to dote on, and the tension eased.

She thought Philip had dozed off when he said in a surprisingly strong voice, "You must marry again, Jessie. You are too excellent a wife to waste in widowhood."

Her lips twisted. Philip, bless him, overrated her charms and her wifeliness. But now was not the time to disagree. She merely said, "If I find a man as kind as you, I shall consider it. But you will be a very hard man to live up to, Philip."

"You flatter me, wench," he said with amusement, his voice fading. "I trust you to choose well no matter what path you take." His faded blue eyes closed again and his labored breathing became slower and slower. The ticking of the mantel clock was unnaturally loud as it counted down the moments of his life.

She thought she heard him breathe, "Louise!" in a voice of soft wonder. Then he breathed no more.

She bent her head over their joined hands, silent tears flowing down her face. Philip Kelham had given her faith that men could be good. She didn't expect to meet another like him.

But she didn't want or need another man. As long as she had Beth and sufficient resources to support them both, it was enough.

After a long day of burying her husband and accepting condolences from neighbors who had mostly disapproved of her, Jessie would have been happy to postpone the reading of the will to the next day, but Frederick was eager for it to take place that very evening. He probably couldn't wait to learn the size of his inheritance.

Despite what Philip had said about a surprise, Jessie expected the reading to be straightforward. Philip had discussed his plans with her before revising his will a few months earlier, and Kelham Hall, this ancient barony in Kent, was entailed to the next Lord Kelham. Frederick would also receive a substantial amount of Philip's personal fortune, though he wouldn't be happy to learn that most of the money was tied up in legal trusts that would make it impossible for him to squander it.

Though earlier Kelhams hadn't achieved great fame, they'd traditionally used their resources wisely and cared well for their dependents. Jessie hoped Frederick wouldn't ruin that record, but she had her doubts.

A similar sum of money was left in trust for Beth, along with Philip's house in London. Jessie would receive a comfortable income for life even if she re-married, since Philip had said more than once that he hoped she would.

She would inherit outright a handsome house in Canterbury. The city had several good schools for girls, and it would be a fine place to raise Beth. They would have the London house for visits to town. Beth would be a considerable heiress, so it was im-portant that she learn to move in good society when she was older.

Wearily Jessie entered the library for the reading. Additional chairs had been brought in because there were numerous beneficiaries. The library was a favorite place since she and Philip often sat there together in the evening, sharing the fire, reading, and talking. Toward the end, when his sight began to fail, she'd read aloud to him.

Tonight the library was crowded and stuffy. The lawyer, Mr. Marcus Harkin, gave her a warm smile when she took a seat in front of the desk where he'd laid out his papers. Harkin had always been kind to her, even when she'd been a scandalous bride. For Philip's sake he'd given her the benefit of the doubt, and in time they'd become friends.

All the servants were present, the older ones sit-ting and younger ones standing in front of the walls of books. Even the newest servants received at least a modest sum, and the oldest were given annuities that would provide a comfortable old age.

The local vicar gave a sigh of relief at receiving a

sum designated to repair the bell tower, then smiled fondly when he learned he would also receive the carved ivory chess set upon which he and Philip had spent many happy hours in mock combat. No surprises here. Jessie was the one who'd suggested adding the chess set to the bell tower money so that the vicar would have a personal memento from his longtime friend.

Jessie hadn't had much sleep during the weeks of her husband's last illness, so after an hour she was dozing in the warm, overcrowded library. She came awake when Mr. Harkin cleared his throat portentously. "Lastly, to my beloved daughter, Elizabeth, heir to the honors of the barony of Kelham, I bequeath—"

"What?" Eyes blazing, Frederick Kelham surged to his feet. "*I* am the heir to the barony! What damnable nonsense is this?"

Mr. Harkin looked over his reading glasses, his tone level but a spark of wicked amusement in his eyes. "It's not nonsense, Mr. Kelham. Kelham is a most ancient barony of writ, created in Norman times. It can be passed through the female line."

"That's absurd!" Frederick sputtered. "All the heirs have been male!"

"Granted, it has been almost two centuries since the only direct heir was female, so the matter was largely forgotten," the lawyer agreed. "But your uncle recently came across this fact in the estate records. He had me research the matter, and it's quite true. Your young cousin, Elizabeth, is now Baroness Kelham in her own right."

Jessie gasped. So *this* was the surprise Philip had

promised! He would have been delighted to realize that his beloved only child would succeed him, but he hadn't realized how badly Frederick would react.

"*You!*" Raging, Frederick swung around to face Jessie. "This is all *your* doing! You forged evidence so your brat will inherit and you can plunder the estate!"

Mr. Harkin said sternly, "You quite mistake the matter, Mr. Kelham! Lady Kelham had no knowledge of this until today, and the 'evidence,' as you call it, is ancient and beyond any possible doubt. I've already drafted a letter to the College of Arms to authenticate the fact that Beth has inherited the title and the entailed property."

"So my uncle left me penniless," Frederick said viciously.

"Not at all. Lord Kelham had a considerable personal fortune, and the amount left after the lesser bequests is to be divided between you and his daughter. You will have more than enough to live in ease and comfort." The lawyer's voice turned dry. "It isn't as if you've shown any interest in running the estate."

"I planned to hire a good steward," Frederick snapped. "*I* should be Lord Kelham! My friends will laugh to hear I've been dispossessed by my uncle's brat!"

"They'll get over it," Harkin said even more dryly. "Be grateful that your uncle was so fond of you. He could easily have left his entire fortune to his daughter."

Frederick's eyes narrowed in fury as he glared

at Jessie. "The brat isn't Uncle Philip's child, but mine!"

Jessie felt the blood drain from her face. "How dare you say such a thing, Frederick!"

"The whole county knows how I brought you here to Kelham Hall as my mistress," he sneered. "And they know how you seduced my uncle because no man can resist you. You thought you had the best of both worlds, didn't you? The title and Uncle Philip's money and me to roger you whenever I visited. He never suspected, did he? I should have told him so he could have you thrown out like the slut you are!"

Jessie rose, her fists clenched and her voice shaking. "You are *disgusting!* I never betrayed my vows!"

Frederick smirked. "No one will believe the word of a lying, conniving actress."

Mr. Wicks, the butler, spoke up with cool dignity. "I keep a close eye on the comings and goings in this house. Her ladyship always shared his late lordship's bed until his final illness, while Master Frederick, on his rare visits, almost always slipped out of the house late at night."

One of the maids piped up helpfully, "He tups a cow maid in the village."

Frederick's face turned bright red as he teetered on the edge of explosion. Then his expression changed. "As Elizabeth's closest male relative," he spat out, "am I her legal guardian?"

Mr. Harkin frowned. "Her mother is, and I'm the chief financial trustee. You have no legal authority in respect to your cousin."

Frederick smiled, malice in his eyes. "But I owe it

to my uncle to see that my young cousin is raised properly as befits her new station in life. I'm sure that the courts will agree that the new Lady Kelham should be removed from her actress mother and raised by me."

Chapter 3

As collective gasps filled the room, Jessie froze. Could Frederick really take Beth away from her? She looked at Mr. Harkin, and saw that his shock matched hers.

She wanted to scream that Frederick would take Beth over her dead body, but she'd learned self-control in a hard school. "Feel free to spend your fortune on lawyers, Frederick. Given the speed at which the courts work, Beth will be grown, married, and a mother herself before the case is settled." Her eyes narrowed. "You are no longer welcome at Kelham Hall, and you will leave *now!* Mr. Wicks, see that Mr. Kelham is gone before the clock next strikes the hour."

The butler inclined his head. "As you wish, my lady." His gaze swept over the other servants. "The will has been read and it is time to return to your duties."

In other words, the show was over. Frederick stamped out of the library, followed by the servants, who buzzed with excitement. Many cast sympathetic glances at Jessie. Though there had been initial wariness about the master's young actress wife, Jessie had run the household with fairness and calm dignity, and gradually won the servants' allegiance. The butler's defense of her had been welcome proof.

But Frederick was Philip's nephew and considered a gentleman. That gave him power.

After he slammed from the room, Jessie folded, shaking, into her chair, her arms wrapped around her midriff. The lawyer asked quietly, "Are you all right, Jessie?"

Her mouth twisted. "My husband is dead and his nephew is threatening to take my daughter away from me. No, I'm not all right." But succumbing to panic would do no good. Forcing herself to relax, she asked, "Can he get custody of Beth, Marcus?"

The lawyer gave a troubled sigh. "I'd like to say you have nothing to worry about, but I can't. Though the legal ground for Beth's inheritance is sound, there are various ways that Mr. Frederick might cloud the issue. Chancery prefers that guardians not be men who would benefit by the demise of their wards, but because he is Philip's closest male relative, he might argue that as a baroness, Beth should be raised in accordance with her future responsibilities as a landowner, and he's best able to do that."

"So a male relative is automatically a better choice than a mere female," Jessie said bitterly. "A wastrel born to the beau monde is a better guide than a child's mother!"

"That is how many courts would see it," he agreed. "Particularly since you are not of aristocratic birth." There was a faint lift of the lawyer's voice at the end of the sentence, an invitation to tell him about her origins.

She ignored the implied question. Philip had known the general outlines of her past, but no one else. "My upbringing was respectable, but certainly not aristocratic, and I have no powerful family connections."

His lips pursed. "A pity. Family connections are invaluable in such cases."

"Can the title and entailed property be ceded to Frederick? He'll have no interest in Beth once he has what he wants."

Harkin shook his head. "The title is fixed in the blood. For as long as Beth lives, she's Baroness Kelham. But even if it were possible to disavow the title, you couldn't do it on Beth's behalf. The inheritance is hers, not yours."

Jessie's face tightened. "Well, Frederick will *not* get custody of my daughter! I'll run away with her before I allow that to happen."

"Jessie, don't even think about that!" Harkin exclaimed. "How would you live? Even if you somehow manage to conceal her safely, would you deprive her of her name and her inheritance? As you pointed out to Frederick, court proceedings take time. There is no immediate danger of your losing custody, but if you take a desperate action and fail, you *will* lose Elizabeth!"

Jessie took a slow, deep breath, knowing he was right, yet unable to suppress the cold fear in her heart. "Can court proceedings drag out until she's of legal age?"

Mr. Harkin sighed. "Not that long. Since the subject of the dispute is a child, Mr. Frederick's lawyers would ask for a swift resolution of the case."

"We can argue that giving custody of a vulnerable child to the man who will inherit her title and estate if she dies is a conflict of interest, to say the least!" Jessie snapped.

The lawyer frowned. "Surely you don't think that Mr. Frederick would actually try to physically harm her."

Jessie bit her lip. She had good reason not to trust Frederick, but without proof, she would sound like a hysterical female and be dismissed out of hand.

"Not that." Though she believed Frederick capable of that. "But no one can care for a child as well as its mother. Remember how ill Beth was two years ago, when she had lung fever? The doctor said she might not have survived if not for my care. If she fell ill again, Frederick would likely be in London carousing with his friends. You *know* she'll be better off with me!"

"I don't doubt it," Harkin agreed. "Philip had complete trust in you to care for his daughter. He wanted you to remarry, and if you do, your new husband can apply for guardianship. Philip knew you wouldn't choose a second husband unless the man would treat Beth as if she were his own."

Jessie bowed her head. "You cannot know how much I value Philip's trust," she whispered.

"No more than Philip valued your love," Harkin said quietly.

Guardianship of Beth could be transferred to a new husband. Jessie became very still. Philip had told her of that provision in his will, but she'd paid little attention to it because she couldn't imagine wanting to marry again. But if Frederick was going to try to take Beth away . . . "So if I remarry, Beth will be safe?"

"Assuming your new husband is a man of good character, yes." The lawyer's eyes narrowed thoughtfully. "It wouldn't be a bad thing if he's also well connected in a worldly sense, in case Frederick disputes the transfer of guardianship."

"He could do that despite Philip's explicit wishes?"

"Lawsuits can be brought for any and all reasons, no matter how foolish," Harkin said dryly. "Ideally, you would marry a duke or a bishop who has so much wealth and worldly status that he could crush any foolishness Frederick may come up with."

"I suspect there is a shortage of eligible dukes," she said with equal dryness. And she'd rather run off with Beth than marry a bishop. "But there are many men of less exalted rank who are vastly superior to Frederick."

"Indeed, there are. Though you'll have to wait until your mourning year is over, I'm sure you'll have no trouble finding a suitable husband who will please you and protect Beth." Harkin smiled. "Frederick was right that few men can resist you. If I didn't have my Helen, I'd be susceptible myself."

The fact that the lawyer was happily married had enabled them to become friends. But Harkin didn't fully understand how vulnerable women were, or what a curse beauty could be. She thought of the malice in Frederick's eyes. "Dare I wait a year? I can't help but feel the sooner Beth is out of his reach, the better. What if Frederick stole her away, claiming that as guardian, he has the right? Would I ever be able to get her back?"

The lawyer frowned. "You have loyal servants here. They would protect her."

"Yes, but most are old, and Frederick can be very persuasive." Jessie smiled humorlessly. "Perhaps I should take Beth to London and look for a husband immediately. A husband who can protect her better than I."

"Husband hunting when Philip is barely cold will give you exactly the sort of reputation that Frederick can use against you," Harkin said disapprovingly. "I do not advise it. Nor can you stay in Kelham House if you go to London since Frederick is living there and it would be difficult to dislodge him. You could hire a house, or take Beth to your house in Canterbury, but that won't necessarily be safer than staying here."

Jessie frowned. "I need a fortress and a powerful husband, neither of which I'll find in Kent. London has more possibilities."

Looking pained, the lawyer said, "I suppose so, but finding the right sort of husband will be difficult since you have few connections in society. Philip never took you to London and you say you have no powerful connections of your own. Unless you know some wealthy merchants? But I fear a judge might not look approvingly on a Cit for Beth's stepfather."

"I don't know any rich merchants and I've had very little contact with the beau monde." She caught her breath. "But I know a duchess and the daughter of a duchess."

Harkin blinked. "How?"

"Lady Julia Randall created the Sisters Foundation, which is devoted to providing sanctuaries for women and children who have been brutalized. I heard of her work and wrote her, offering what I could spare from my pin money. We continued writing since we enjoyed each other's thoughts. She also put me in touch with her good friend, the Duchess of Ashton, who is deeply involved with the foundation." Jessie smiled fondly. "Their letters were a bright spot during Philip's last illness."

"I've heard of both women," Harkin said, impressed. "They and their works are much admired. Can they help you when you are ready to consider remarrying?"

"They've already offered their aid and hospitality. Lady Julia's husband is a lifelong friend of the Duke of Ashton, so the Randalls have quarters at Ashton House. I was told there's ample space for Beth and me if we come to London."

"I've seen the outside of Ashton House. It is indeed a fortress," Harkin said thoughtfully. "Having such well-placed friends can only be a benefit, and I'm sure you and Beth will enjoy visiting London after these last difficult months."

Jessie nodded, her throat tight. Though not bluntly stated, it had been clear that the ladies were offering her a holiday as a respite after her husband's death.

The lawyer said quietly, "Philip told me a fortnight ago that he felt blessed to have such a devoted wife. I know that caring for him wasn't easy."

"Marriage vows are for sickness and in health,

Marcus. I was blessed to have such a kind husband."
She looked down to the knotted hands in her lap.
She could hardly bear the idea of marrying again.
But for Beth, she would do it.

It was either that or be prepared to kill Frederick
if the greedy devil threatened her daughter. "I must
look to the future for Beth's sake. I'll write Lady Julia
tonight to affirm that the invitation is still open."

Jessie must also force herself to accept the necessity of remarriage. She could do this. She just needed
to find a husband who was strong, and kind, and *safe*.

Chapter 4

It took only two days for Daniel to arrange matters at the infirmary so he could leave for London. That was the advantage of hiring good people and giving them opportunities to learn, but it was rather unnerving to realize that he was less essential than he'd thought.

Kirkland had stayed with him, using his time to attend to the business of his shipping line. They traveled to London in the splendidly sprung Kirkland carriage, which gave Daniel time to interrogate his brother-in-law about the responsibilities of a peer. Kirkland could always be counted on for an honest, insightful answer. Though nothing was beyond Daniel's abilities, most of his new duties didn't interest him.

But he'd have to learn anyhow. Sometimes he wished he hadn't been born with an overdeveloped sense of responsibility.

Despite London's noise and smells, his heart beat a little faster when they reached the city. It was an exciting place, where some of the best minds in Britain could be met.

Kirkland House was in fashionable Mayfair. Daniel had once made a brief visit, but because he'd arrived at night he hadn't paid much attention to the place's appearance. This time he arrived in the afternoon and he could appreciate the luxurious houses that faced the handsome park in the middle of Berkeley Square. Laurel had written of how much she enjoyed the trees and flowers of this urban garden.

As they entered Kirkland House, golden piano music spilled down the stairs in a rich flow of melody. Daniel smiled, his tension easing as he recognized his sister's playing. He'd been tense for quite some time, he realized.

"I'll take a quick look at these letters to see if there's anything urgent." Kirkland lifted the missives from a side table, but nodded toward the stairs. "Follow the music."

Daniel had once spoken the same words to Kirkland, and for the same reason: to find Laurel. Glad Kirkland was giving him time for a private greeting, he ascended the steps quietly, examining his surroundings.

On his brief previous visit, the house had seemed coolly elegant and unwelcoming, a place of mystery and secrets. Though the furnishings and decoration were little different, the atmosphere had changed. Now the house was warm and welcoming, and not only because afternoon light poured in the windows. The structure reflected its new mistress because Laurel created warmth wherever she went.

The music room door stood open to the upstairs corridor. He stepped inside and found Laurel at the keyboard of a magnificent Broadwood piano that was twin to the one in their Bristol house.

Laurel's eyes were closed as she played one of her favorite Beethoven sonatas from memory, her fingers sliding expertly over the keys. She didn't wear mourning black for their parents. Understandable, given that they'd disowned her.

When she finished the sonata, Daniel said softly, "I've missed having music flowing through the house."

"Daniel!" His sister spun on the bench and rose to greet him, glowing with Madonna warmth. She had never looked lovelier.

When she hugged him, she had to lean forward a little because of the expanding curve of her waistline. "I've missed you so much!"

"As I've missed you." His hug was swift but careful before he stepped back and scanned her with a physician's eyes. "You're feeling well?"

"Wonderful! I've passed the stage of feeling exhausted and ill. I suspect that I'm close to the end of the buoyant and energetic phase." Laurel grinned. "Soon I'll start waddling and counting the days till I meet this baby in the open air."

Daniel smiled fondly. "A joyous day indeed. Will Kirkland mind if it's a girl?"

Laurel spread her palm on her abdomen. "James swears all that matters is that the baby and I are healthy."

Daniel agreed. Childbirth was not without risks and Laurel was nearing thirty, rather old for a first child. "You have a good midwife?"

"Two of them! The wife of one of James's friends is an experienced midwife, and she's been very helpful. She probably won't be in London when the baby arrives, but she introduced me to a woman whom she recommends highly."

"I'd like to talk to the one who will be here when the baby arrives."

"Don't think you can intimidate Mrs. Granger," Laurel said with a laugh. "She knows her business as well as you know yours. But enough about me. How are you coping with your unwelcome ennoblement?"

Trust Laurel to understand. "I keep hoping there's been an error and that some other fellow who will appreciate the honor is the true heir," Daniel said ruefully.

"I fear not. Mr. Hyatt, the Romayne lawyer, visited me with the family tree in case I knew any other sprigs that might stand closer to the late Lord Romayne, but there was no one. You're trapped, Daniel. But once you become accustomed, you'll find there are advantages."

"Kirkland said as much," Daniel said dryly. "I haven't found them yet."

"You'll have more money for good works. I've been having a lovely time spending Kirkland's money on my favorite causes." She studied his expression thoughtfully. "Are you thinking of looking for a wife? This would be a good time to consider doing so."

He gave her a half smile. "You've always been good at reading my mind. A wife would indeed be convenient, especially if she's skilled at estate management."

His sister laughed. "Surely you have other requirements!"

"Reasonably attractive but not beautiful, because

beauties require too much attention," Daniel said promptly. "Mature and not addicted to London frivolity."

Laurel managed to avoid laughing again, barely. "That's a start, I suppose. We'll have to have a ball to introduce you to society."

Kirkland entered the room. "A ball in his honor will send Daniel flying back to Bristol in a heartbeat. Better to start with something less grand, like a musicale."

"You're right, of course," Laurel agreed. "But I do advise attending Lady Childe's rout three days from now. You won't enjoy it much, but you'll meet many people quickly so you'll start to receive invitations. Then you can choose events you like better."

"Let's hold a dinner party for the Westerfield Academy old boys who are in town," Kirkland suggested. "Some have wives who might have suitable friends."

"A fine idea." Laurel moved to Kirkland's side like a swallow returning to its nest.

"I'll enjoy seeing some of my other schoolmates." Daniel glanced away because viewing the deep tenderness between them seemed an invasion of privacy. He was no longer Laurel's best friend. Kirkland was, which was right and proper.

With sharp yearning, Daniel wanted that kind of closeness. He'd had it with Rose. After she died at age twenty, a few months before they'd planned to wed, his heart had closed down. He'd never looked for a potential wife, and he'd ignored the advances of women who thought a doctor would make a good husband. Or a good lover.

He hadn't recognized the extent to which Laurel had filled the empty places in his life until she reconciled with Kirkland and was no longer available for companionship. They'd been partners in their work and household for a decade, but no longer. Laurel had moved forward into her life, and he must do the same.

But he didn't know a blessed thing about courting a potential mate. Rose had grown up on the neighboring estate and they'd first met in the nursery. He couldn't remember a time when he hadn't known her, so no courtship had been required. Surely it would be possible to find a kind, sensible woman who would make his life easier?

Yes, such a marriage was possible. But given his ignorance about courtship, he'd better pray for good luck in his search.

Chapter 5

The Duchess of Ashton and Lady Julia Randall not only renewed their invitation to visit, but said they had a matter they'd like to discuss with Lady Kelham. Jessie wrote a grateful acceptance note, adding that she had something she wished to discuss with them also. When she sent the letter off, she prayed the two women would be as warm and understanding in person as they were on paper.

"Lady Kelham," the butler announced as he ushered Jessie into the small salon where she had been invited to join the duchess and Lady Julia after she'd settled Beth and her servants, and had a chance to freshen up. A good thing she'd had a guide, or she might have become lost in the vast sprawl of Ashton House.

She tried not to show her nervousness as she entered the room. So much depended on these women and whether they would help her!

Both were petite, though one was dark haired and had calm, wise eyes and the other was a vivacious blond beauty. Jessie was good at pretending confidence, so she stepped inside with a smile. "It's so lovely to finally meet you both face-to-face!" Her gaze moved to the blond woman. "You are surely the Golden Duchess."

"That's not a difficult guess since Julia is dark," the blonde said with a laugh as she rose to her feet and extended one hand. "It's a pleasure to meet you, Lady Kelham. I didn't know you were so shockingly beautiful. Do you often find that a burden?"

Jessie blinked as she took the other woman's hand. "I've never had anyone say that to me before, Your Grace. Clearly personal experience has taught you that being considered beautiful can be a nuisance. Even dangerous."

The duchess's mouth twisted. "When I was a mere nobody trailing around after my father, who was a perpetual houseguest in the homes of others, I learned early to fight for my virtue."

"As did I." As they exchanged rueful glances, Jessie continued. "I hope we'll be friends, Your Grace. But you may take an aversion to me in person!"

"I doubt that," the duchess said with a smile. "And among friends, I'm Mariah. I was not raised with high formality."

"Nor was I," Jessie confessed. "I'd like it if you'd both call me Jessie."

"And I'm Julia. 'Lady' is merely a courtesy title, not like the peerage titles you both have." Julia also rose and offered her hand. "You make me grateful that my appearance is merely passable!"

"A good deal more than passable, Julia," Jessie said firmly. It was the truth. As they clasped hands, she saw that while the other woman wasn't a striking beauty, she had a delicate prettiness and sweet serenity that surely attracted people as strongly as the duchess's beauty.

"A really good modiste helps greatly, but only my husband considers me beautiful, and that's the way I like it," Julia replied. "Now that the introductions are out of the way, we can relax and amuse ourselves till the tea and cakes arrive."

As they took seats, Mariah asked, "How was your journey?"

"The most comfortable I've ever taken," Jessie said fervently. "Thank you so much for sending one of your carriages. Though you may have spoiled me for all lesser forms of transportation!"

Mariah laughed. "The coachman was delighted to make the journey. He grew up near Canterbury, so he was able to pay a visit to his family before collecting you."

The fact that the duchess knew her servants as individuals and was considerate of them was confirmation that she was as kind as she'd seemed in her letters. The same was true of Julia, Jessie realized as they exchanged commonplaces. These were strong, confident, intelligent women who had experienced their share of life, and who were now at the center of London society. Exactly what Jessie needed.

But first, she must learn what they wanted from her. "Julia, you said in your last letter that you had something to discuss with me?"

"It is no small thing to ask, but you'll find the work very rewarding if you're willing to take it on," Julia replied. "You first wrote me because of your desire to support the sanctuaries established by the

Sisters Foundation, and your interest has continued."

"It's wonderful work you're doing," Jessie said warmly. "I'm glad that I can help in some small way."

"You should be wary of expressing such a wish in front of Julia or me," Mariah said with a grin, "because we'll take you up on it. We want to establish another Zion House in Canterbury. Since you live in that area, you'd be an ideal patroness if you have the time and inclination."

Jessie caught her breath. She hadn't known what to expect, but it wasn't this. "Why me? Surely there are others better suited."

"From your first letter, it was clear that you have a passionate belief in the work we do," Julia said. "The Sisters Foundation isn't merely another charity to you, and we need that kind of commitment."

Jessie's experiences had given her that passion, and she wondered if that was true for Julia and Mariah. But it wasn't the sort of question one could ask. "I would be honored to help, but I wouldn't know where to start."

"The initial organization and management will be done by a woman who has set up sanctuaries in Leicester and Norfolk," Mariah said. "She's a Methodist and works with local Methodist congregations to locate a suitable building and develop the program and facilities. But we've found it useful to have a local woman of rank become the public face for our work. As a baroness and a woman who is already involved with the Sisters Foundation, you would be perfect."

"I'm not sure my reputation will help you," Jessie

said uncertainly. "In some circles I'm considered a loose woman and a fortune hunter."

"Yet those who know you in Kent think of you as a devoted wife and mother who is loved and respected," Julia said quietly. "Any difficulties you had when you were younger have enhanced your compassion and understanding. Well-born women who have known only wealth and safety have trouble fully understanding what our clients have endured. We've made inquiries, and believe that you are uniquely qualified to represent the foundation in your area."

Jessie swallowed hard, fighting back an impulse to cry. "Thank you," she said, trying to keep her voice steady. "I seldom meet people who are inclined to believe the best about me rather than the worst. If you truly think I can do the job, I will accept your offer gladly."

Mariah raised her cup. "To our next Zion House sanctuary and its distinguished patroness!"

Smiling, Jessie toasted in tea, hoping that she could help other women as she'd been helped. "Now that we've established that, I would like to ask your aid in turn, though it's a less honorable matter. I shall understand if you prefer not to become involved." She swallowed hard. "After I ask, I'll also understand if you may wish to withdraw your request that I become a patroness."

"Ask away," Mariah said, her eyes shining. "You've aroused my curiosity!"

"I need to find a husband as quickly as possible," Jessie said bluntly. "A man who is kind, honorable, and powerful in his connections. And since I'm in mourning, I need to do it in a way that won't arouse a public scandal, since that will drive away the kind of man I want and reflect badly on my daughter."

"You don't appear to be the sort of woman who absolutely must have a man at all times," Julia said thoughtfully. "So you must have other reasons."

"To protect my child." Jessie explained succinctly, doing her best not to paint Frederick as a dangerous beast while making her fears believable.

When she was finished, Julia said, "So you need to meet the right kind of man under circumstances of utmost respectability. That can be arranged, I believe. Given your beauty, attracting men won't be a problem."

"Attracting males has never been a problem," Jessie said dryly. "It's attracting decent men with honorable intentions that is difficult."

Mariah gave an understanding nod. "We'll help sort out the undesirables. What are your other requirements for a potential husband? Young, handsome, titled?"

Jessie shook her head. "A title would be useful if it helps persuade Frederick not to try to wrest Beth away from me, but otherwise, I don't care. I want an older man, not a young one. Someone like Philip, who was kind and honorable. I need a husband who will cherish Beth as if she were his own child."

"Old, unhandsome, and delighted to acquire a beautiful, faithful young wife and adorable daughter," Mariah summed up. "I'll start thinking who might do."

"You're fortunate that it's the little season. The social round is less frenetic than the spring season, but there are enough entertainments of different sorts for you to meet people easily," Julia said. "If it becomes known that the Duchess of Ashton will accompany you, invitations will pour in."

"You're just as desirable a guest, Julia!" Mariah said. "We can attend as many events as you wish, Jessie. What kind might you particularly enjoy?"

Jessie blinked, surprised at how simple this was. "Anything with music. Lectures. I prefer small gatherings with good conversation, not great crushes."

"The sort that are acceptable for a woman in mourning," Julia said with a nod. "Those are my preference also."

"I'll need a suitable wardrobe," Jessie said as she ruefully indicated the gown she wore, which had never been fashionable and had been hastily dyed black after Philip's death. "Black mourning garments that are subtly alluring without being vulgar. Can you suggest a modiste?"

"Oh, yes!" Mariah chuckled. "This will be such fun. With your dark hair and fair skin, you look splendid in black. You will have your choice of kind, rich, older men with influence."

"One will do!" Jessie said as she returned the smile. A knot of tension began to unwind inside her. She had allies, women with power as well as understanding.

Even more, she thought, she now had friends.

Chapter 6

Daniel's brows arched as their carriage joined a line of coaches waiting to discharge passengers at the Mayfair townhouse. "Are you sure this rout is necessary?"

His sister laughed. "An hour spent here will simplify your life later. You'll have a chance to be seen and to meet others. Once it's known that you're an eligible lord, you'll be receiving invitations to every fashionable function in town."

"Kirkland warned me about that," Daniel said dourly as their carriage stopped in front of the townhouse. A footman opened the door and flipped down the steps. "I'm beginning to wish I'd refused Kirkland's excellent tailor and worn my unfashionable Bristol attire instead. Looking shabby might give some of the huntresses pause."

"Since you're titled and eligible, you could wear untanned bear skins and be considered delightfully original rather than unsuitable," Laurel said with amusement. "James and I will defend you if necessary, but I've seldom seen you lose your composure under any circumstances."

"You don't want to look shabby and provincial," Kirkland remarked. "Superb tailoring is a kind of armor because people see your surface, not the real you. Better to appear worldly and formidable rather than vulnerable."

Intrigued, Daniel asked, "Is that why you're always so impeccably turned out? Yes, of course it is. You're hiding in plain sight."

"And very effective it is." Kirkland climbed from the carriage, then turned to assist Laurel, who was graceful in a flowing green silk gown that only hinted at her pregnancy.

"I've learned to do the same," Laurel said seriously. "If I dress like a countess, few people will look more closely. Tonight you look intimidatingly grand and rather unapproachable. Not like easy prey."

Daniel's mouth twisted ruefully as he joined them at the entrance to the house. "You're making me feel like a sheep being tossed into the middle of a wolf pack."

"If so, you're a sheep with well-developed defenses," his sister said with a smile. "But it won't be that bad. You can eliminate the misses just out of the schoolroom right away since most would bore you senseless. But you'll meet young women who are more mature. Or you might find a suitable widow who knows more of the world."

"I'm keeping my expectations low," Daniel said as a footman admitted them to the crowded foyer. "If I meet a woman who can run the Romayne properties and leave me free to practice medicine, I may make her an offer on the spot."

Laurel shook her head. "I do hope that reality makes a hash of your sober intentions."

Kirkland laughed. "That so often happens. I was sure I wouldn't marry until I was old, over thirty, until I met you. But I think Daniel is more likely than most to keep his head despite the social whirl."

Daniel agreed. Low expectations. All he needed was a pleasant, honest, capable woman with whom he might have a family.

Children. He glanced at his sister's expanding waistline. He knew how much she wanted this baby, and he was startled to realize how intensely he wanted children himself. He'd been too busy to consider that in the past, but now—the time to start a family had arrived. If he didn't do it soon, he'd slide into permanent bachelorhood.

Daniel's tension increased as they joined the receiving line, the three of them one small part of a flowing mass of chattering people. Shyness wasn't part of his nature. In Bristol, he moved easily in every rank of society. But this was a new phase of life, one he wasn't yet reconciled to.

The couple ahead finished their greetings and moved on, so Kirkland stepped forward. Host and hostess were middle-aged, expensively dressed, and clearly accustomed to sailing the high seas of London society. As they smiled a welcome, Kirkland said, "Childe, Lady Childe, so good to see you again. You know my wife, of course, but allow me to present my brother-in-law, the new Lord Romayne."

The Childes instantly focused on Daniel. As he greeted his hosts, he could almost see wheels spinning in their minds as they searched for what they knew about the Romayne title and estate and calcu-

lated his potential value to them. From the approval
in their expressions, Kirkland had been right about
good tailoring being an essential form of armor.
Daniel looked as if he belonged in this glittering
throng.

"Good to meet you, Romayne," Lord Childe said
heartily as he extended his hand. "You're not a
member of White's yet, are you? I'd be delighted to
take you around the club to meet some of the chaps
you'll work with in the House of Lords."

Which was a not very subtle attempt to deter-
mine Daniel's political leanings. White's was the
unofficial headquarters of the Tories, while Brooks
was patronized by the great Whig lords. Kirkland,
typically enigmatic, was a member of both.

As he shook Childe's hand, Daniel said blandly,
"I don't know if I'll be joining any clubs since I've
no interest in gaming. I'm in London primarily to
sort out the legalities associated with the title and
estates."

Before Lord Childe could pursue the point, his
wife took over. "Lord Romayne, such a pleasure.
Let me offer my condolences on the loss of your
predecessor. Your . . . cousin, I think? I regret that I
didn't know him."

"A rather distant cousin. I had only the slightest
acquaintance with the late Lord Romayne myself."
Even that was overstating the case.

"I hope we shall see more of you than we did
your cousin," she said with a trill of laughter. "London can never have too many handsome young
gentlemen!" She gestured to her right. "My sons
are at school, but allow me to present my daugh-
ters, Miss Childe and Miss Mary Childe."

The two blond girls were pretty in unmemorable ways. Miss Childe, the elder sister, looked like a worldly twenty and she assessed him sharply before granting a smile. "Delighted to meet you, Lord Romayne. I hope we have a chance to talk properly later." She fluttered her lashes, clearly interested in him. He did not return her interest, sensing that she was the sort of female who would want a fashionable life. Not for him.

The younger daughter, Miss Mary, looked barely seventeen, and she was so shy that she couldn't even meet his gaze when she stammered, "A . . . a pleasure to meet you, my lord."

"The pleasure is mine." His voice softened when he replied. She was barely out of the schoolroom and far too young for him, but she needed kindness to emerge from her shell. She glanced up with a slight, grateful smile before her gaze dropped again.

They moved on so the next people in line could greet their hosts. The main drawing room was packed almost solid with chattering humanity. Elaborate chandeliers added to the heat, and the atmosphere was thick with the scents of bodies and perfumes. Laurel said grandly, "Daniel, welcome to the lion's den!"

He laughed. "The biblical Daniel survived, and so shall I. Though I'd prefer real lions. They're cats, after all, and I like cats."

"Lions are more benign than some of the guests here," Kirkland observed. "There are refreshments in the room to the right, but the tables will be mobbed and there's better food at home. I advise moving steadily toward the exit at the far end. Along the way, we'll introduce you to anyone we know. Once we reach the exit, we can escape."

"A good plan," Daniel replied as he wondered how long it would take to move through the crowd.

Unfortunately, Kirkland knew everyone, which made their progress slow. Daniel was impressed at how confidently his quiet, reserved sister moved among the chattering masses. She'd grown comfortable in her role as a countess.

She'd also been right that this crowded, noisy rout would be a good place to meet London society. Daniel was introduced to politicians, dandies, social leaders, and those who apparently cultivated eccentricity as a way of life.

As with Lord Childe, the politicians tried to discern his political leanings, and females evaluated him for his romantic potential, marital and otherwise. The eccentrics dismissed him as too dull to be competition for creating the next sensation and hence unworthy of attention.

Despite the noise and crowding, Daniel enjoyed it more than he had expected to. He found people endlessly fascinating, whether rich or poor, and this parade of humanity offered entertaining material for study.

But he didn't like being an eligible titled gentleman, which was indeed synonymous with "prey." He found himself automatically retreating into cool detachment. He was polite, but made sure he said nothing that could be construed as encouragement. For tonight, he'd concentrate on memorizing names and faces for future reference.

They were barely halfway across the room before

he began to cast longing glances toward the exit. At this rate, it would take another hour to reach it.

Repressing a sigh, he shook the hand of a man Kirkland had just introduced. The fellow was a member of Parliament from Yorkshire with a blunt, witty way of speaking. They exchanged a few words before moving in different directions, but Daniel was sure they'd meet again and speak at greater length. He mentally rated about 40 percent of the people he'd met as interesting and worth knowing better. This boded well for his future time in London.

During a brief lull while both Kirkland and Laurel were chatting with another couple, Daniel scanned the room. Though his height meant he regularly banged his head when he visited patients in cramped hovels, being tall was an advantage in these circumstances.

Was that Viscount Castlereagh, the foreign secretary, engaged in earnest conversation on the left side of the room? Kirkland would know, and would probably want to introduce them. Daniel was bemused by the fact that the most significant aspect of his unwanted inheritance was not money or property, but the political power that came with a seat in the House of Lords. In some circles, that was more valuable than rubies.

He repressed a sigh. Estate management could be delegated to capable stewards, but not his political responsibilities. Britain needed reforming in many areas, and it was being driven home to him that he was in a position to make a difference.

His gaze again shifted to the exit where people

were trickling out. Most were probably heading to another entertainment.

His eyes narrowed. Was that Alexander Randall from the Westerfield Academy? Randall had been a class ahead, but they'd sometimes been confused with each other because of similar height, build, and blond coloring.

Given the uneven lighting in the drawing room, Daniel wasn't sure of his identification, but if the man was Randall, he looked a lot happier now than in his student days. He'd planned to enter the army, and Daniel wondered how that had worked out. Kirkland was a classmate of Randall's and presumably would invite the other man to the promised Westerfield dinner. Daniel looked forward to catching up on the lives of men he'd known when they were all boys.

Daniel started to turn back to Laurel and Kirkland, then paused, his gaze caught by the profile of a woman standing near the exit, mostly surrounded by men. Her glossy dark hair was knotted up to reveal her graceful neck and the ivory perfection of her features. But there were other lovely women here. As he tried to analyze why she caught his attention, she turned a little, bringing her face into the warm light of a chandelier.

Coup de foudre. A lightning strike burned through him, paralyzing every fiber of his being. She was truly beautiful, with striking light eyes edged in darkness and a lithe figure that would shatter a stone saint, but what made her stunning was more than physical beauty. She radiated mystery, sensuality—and danger. She looked like original sin—and he craved that promise of reckless passion as intensely as Adam had craved Eve's apple.

As his heart hammered in his chest, he knew that he was officially insane. How could the sight of a woman he'd never met affect him so? Then she turned her head farther as if she felt his stare, and their gazes locked.

Lightning struck again, swift and fierce, setting his heart afire and searing through his veins. She was exactly the sort of flattered and cosseted woman he didn't need, yet he wanted her.

Insane.

Chapter 7

The woman's expression shuttered and she spun around to disappear into a group of people leaving the room. Only then did Daniel realize that he'd started forcing his way through the crowd toward her. He'd probably alarmed her with his blatant stare, though with her beauty, he couldn't be the first man to react in such a way.

"Is something wrong?" Kirkland's quiet voice said from behind his shoulder. "You look like you've seen a ghost."

Daniel took a deep breath and forced himself not to blurt out that he'd momentarily lost all claims to sanity. "I saw a woman who seemed familiar."

As he said the words, he realized they were true. Something about the lady was indeed familiar, though he'd be blessed if he knew what it was.

"What does she look like?" Laurel asked. "If she's from the Bristol area, perhaps I've met her."

"She looked like the kind of woman our parents warned us about," Daniel said with wry honesty.

"An interesting description, but not very specific."

Doing his best to sound sensible, Daniel said, "Her appearance was rather Welsh. Dark hair and a very fair complexion."

Which could describe at least a dozen women in this room. How could one be specific about "I did but see her passing by, And yet I love her till I die"?

"Not as tall as you, Laurel. Mid-twenties, perhaps, and quite staggeringly beautiful. If we've met, I ought to remember her, but instead, I had only a vague sense of familiarity."

"She doesn't sound familiar to me, but my idea of beautiful is probably different from a man's," Laurel observed. "Did you notice what she was wearing?"

"Black." Only now did he realize what that meant. "A mourning gown, I think. The cut was very modest, not evening décolleté like most of the female guests are wearing." And yet the effect had been profoundly alluring.

"Perhaps she's related to someone you know," Laurel said thoughtfully. "Someone who knows me would think you're familiar and vice versa."

"Perhaps that's it. I don't recall seeing any women who were staggeringly beautiful other than Laurel," Kirkland said with a fond glance at his wife. "But if she's part of the beau monde, you'll likely meet her in other places."

Daniel shrugged. "No matter. I was merely surprised by a brief sense of recognition." Which was considerably less than the truth, but he couldn't possibly explain that mad, flaring attraction. It meant nothing, and yet . . . *"I did but see her passing by . . ."*

Daniel gave his head a sharp shake. He'd never been much for poetry, but for the first time he understood the romantic fervor of the anonymous poet who'd written those words centuries before. The fellow had clearly been suffering from temporary madness.

If Daniel had actually met the woman in black, the reality of her would have had nothing to do with that brief fantasy. She would have been just a pretty woman, probably married, and not at all mysterious and dangerous. With her beauty, she might well be shallow and spoiled. The crowd of men surrounding her suggested as much. Better to bury that lightning bolt of reaction in the back of his mind. Even if she was unmarried, she did not look like wife material.

Kirkland's voice cut through his reverie. "Here's a lady you'll want to meet."

Daniel turned obediently and found himself face-to-face with Lady Agnes Westerfield, founder and headmistress of the Westerfield Academy. "Lady Agnes!" he exclaimed. "I had no idea you might be here!" He impulsively hugged her, remembering with a rush of affection how she'd shown him the tolerance and understanding that was so lacking in his parents.

"I'm in town to interview several potential students. It's about time you came to London, you rascal!" She laughed as she hugged back. "Best let me go now, though. People will think I've taken a young lover in my dotage."

"Dotage, indeed." He surveyed Lady Agnes, who looked as tall and strong and capable as always.

"Your students may have caused a few gray hairs in the last dozen years, but otherwise you haven't aged a day. I suspect you've made a pact with the devil."

"Then you'll just have to exorcise me." She glanced at Kirkland and Laurel. "I'm taking Daniel outside so we can talk properly. Look for us when you're ready to leave."

"Which won't be long." Laurel tucked her hand in the crook of her husband's arm. "I'm beginning to tire."

Kirkland patted her hand. "We'll go say hello to the Castlereaghs, then join you outside." Which would give Daniel and Lady Agnes time to talk.

Forceful as always, Lady Agnes took Daniel's arm and towed him toward the exit door. The noise dropped sharply when they stepped through into a corridor.

"Blessed relief," Lady Agnes said as she released Daniel's arm.

He'd locked memories of the Westerfield Academy away with so much of his youth, but now he remembered all the good times there. "I trust the school is flourishing? How are Miss Emily and the general?"

"Emily and the general are well, and so is the school. It gets a little larger each year, but we won't let it get so large that we can't give each student as much personal attention as he needs." She fixed him with a stern gaze. "Now explain to me how I sent you off to Oxford to train for holy orders, and now you've reappeared as the best surgeon in the West Country and a reluctant baron."

Startled and pleased, he asked, "How did you hear that?"

Her smile was warm. "I keep track of all my boys."

Should he tell her the short version, or the longer one that had all the important parts? After a moment of considering, he said, "It's a long story."

Her eyes twinkled. "Then you'd better get started."

When she saw him, Jessie barely managed to keep herself from bolting from the drawing room. Had Dr. Herbert recognized her? She didn't see how it was possible. She looked nothing like the way she had when they'd first met. But the way he'd stared . . .

She'd felt safe for years, but the old terror flared as quick and hot as ever despite the time that had passed, leaving her shaking. She'd known there was some danger in leaving her quiet life to move into society, but that danger had seemed remote. She hadn't expected to run into someone who could connect her with her past.

But her reasons for entering society and seeking a husband were as powerful as ever. It was too late to retreat.

As they walked down the quiet corridor that led to the street, Mariah said, "You look tired. Did you meet any good prospects among the men who flocked around you? If so, I'll see if I can arrange for you to meet him again in quieter circumstances."

"There were one or two gentlemen with potential," Jessie said, making her tone light. "But they tended to be crowded out by the young and randy. I hadn't thought that wearing mourning would actually attract men."

"Only those of the wrong sort," Julia said. "The kind who believe that a widow is in dire need of their services. Men can be such beasts." She slid a teasing glance at her husband, whose arm she held. "Present company excepted, of course."

"I'm gratified to hear that," Randall said, his tone dry but his eyes glinting with amusement. Since Mariah's husband, the Duke of Ashton, had been busy elsewhere, Randall was escorting all three ladies.

"Thank you for driving off the undesirables, Major Randall." Jessie smiled a little. "One stern look from you and they faded away."

"An advantage of a military past." He grinned. "I'm enough of a male beast that I enjoyed the envious glances from other men at my good fortune in escorting three such beautiful ladies."

Would his stern stare drive off Dr. Herbert? She doubted it. In his way, the good doctor was as formidable as the army officer.

Randall added, his tone apologetic, "You should probably know they're calling you the Black Widow."

She bit her lip. "Thank you for warning me. That doesn't sound very good."

"It was said with interest and admiration, not condemnation," Randall assured her.

"A nickname earned so quickly means you've been accepted into London society," Mariah said. "You may not have enjoyed the rout, but your dress and behavior were impeccable." Her tone became ironic. "Now you are one of *us*."

Jessie's companions were a better recommendation than the most impeccable gown, but Mariah and Julia had brushed aside her thanks since they assured her they were having a wonderful time. She asked, "What is our next social engagement?"

"Dinner with the Kirklands," Julia replied. "You'll enjoy that. Lord Kirkland was a classmate of Ashton and Alex, and he's inviting several Westerfield Academy graduates for a quiet evening. His wife is lovely, and very active with the Sisters Foundation. I doubt there will be any eligible older gentlemen, but I'm sure you'll enjoy yourself, and the Kirklands are good people to know."

"That sounds pleasant." Jessie wryly admitted that while her head said she needed a husband, her heart was more interested in quiet evenings with good company.

After returning to Ashton House, Jessie succumbed to temptation and climbed up to the nursery instead of retiring to her own room. Beth was her touchstone, the reason she was sailing in these uncharted waters. She needed to see her.

Silently Jessie eased open the door to her daughter's room. A dim lamp gave just enough light to reveal Beth's small form in the bed, her soft cloth doll in her arms. Jessie had made the doll, giving it toffee brown hair the same shade as her daughter's. Her little girl looked like a sleeping angel.

Resisting the desire to wake her daughter up, Jesse settled for feasting her eyes on her, then blowing a silent kiss before she headed to her room. Beth was worth any risk. Even the risk of stirring the dangers that lurked in Jessie's past.

Chapter 8

When they reached Kirkland House, Laurel and her husband retired to their rooms, though from the way they were looking at each other, Daniel suspected that they were not going to bed because his sister was overtired. What would it be like to retire to his own bedchamber with a wife who affected him like the woman in black . . . ?

Daniel shut off that train of thought immediately. He needed a good wife, not a dangerous siren.

Instead of heading to his room, he descended to the basement kitchen in search of a cup of tea. He liked knowing his way to the kitchen of any house he stayed in. One never knew when hunger might strike in the depths of night.

It wasn't particularly late, so he was unsurprised to find activity in the kitchen. A middle-aged woman with an air of authority glanced up from the dough she was kneading, her expression wary. "You'd be Lord Romayne." She brushed a lock of hair back, leaving a trail of flour on her cheek. "There's no need for you to come down here. You can ring for what you like."

The remark sounded like exasperation at having her territory invaded, but Daniel responded with a disarming smile. "I know. This household runs like a finely tuned clock. But I like kitchens, and I'm using the excuse of a cup of tea to explore. I think you must be Mrs. Simond? I've only been here a few days, but it's clear why Lord and Lady Kirkland value you so highly."

Expression mollified, the cook nodded. "Aye, that's me. Suzie, make his lordship a pot of tea. I could use a drop myself." The kitchen maid at the far end of the room nodded and set a kettle of water to heat.

Daniel said, "My sister says you have a very fine kitchen cat."

Mrs. Simond's expression softened even more. "That would be Badger. He's in that chair over there, hoping to benefit from me making beefsteak puddings."

Daniel followed her gesture and found Badger, a large black and white cat with huge green eyes and an expression of deep contentment on his furry face. He also had a rich, rumbling purr when his head was scratched.

"A very fine fellow indeed," Daniel said as the cat raised his chin to allow better neck scratching. "Every kitchen should have a cat."

"Your lady sister says the same," the cook said as her strong hands resumed kneading. "They keep the vermin away, they do."

Daniel was about to reply when a great clatter,

bang, and crash of breaking china sounded from behind a door at the other end of the kitchen. Suzie opened the door hastily to reveal a narrow servants' staircase and a young footman moaning with pain at the bottom of the steps, broken china scattered around him.

"Oh, Lester!" the cook exclaimed as she wiped flour from her hands. "Have you fallen over your feet again?"

Daniel covered the length of the kitchen in half a dozen strides before Mrs. Simond even finished speaking. Lester was sprawled on his side at the base of the stairs, his right arm twisted awkwardly and blood seeping from a cut on his forehead.

"Don't try to move yet." Daniel knelt by the young man and ran experienced fingers over his skull. "Do you think you broke anything? Your head? Bones?"

The questions helped Lester focus. "I'll have some bloody big bruises, sir, but otherwise . . ." He started to push himself to a sitting position and gave a cry of agony when he moved his right arm.

"Your right shoulder?" Daniel asked.

"Y-yes." Lester's face was pale. "Banged it into the wall when I fell."

Daniel guessed a broken or dislocated shoulder. "Let me help you up so I can examine it. I'm a surgeon, and I'll try not to make it feel worse than it already does."

He slid one arm around the young man's waist and hauled him to his feet. Suzie had pulled a solid wooden chair near so Daniel settled Lester into it. The forehead laceration mostly stopped bleeding after it was washed clean. "Mrs. Simond, do you have some salve for minor kitchen injuries?"

"I'll get it, my lord." Suzie scampered to a cabinet and brought back a small jar.

Daniel applied the ointment to the young man's forehead. Now for the arm. "Lester, I'll have to cut your coat off so I can take a closer look at your shoulder."

"Don't cut the coat!" Lester looked horrified. "It's new and Mrs. Stratton'll make me pay for another one!"

Daniel doubted that Kirkland would require that, but maybe the housekeeper would. "Then I'll take it off very carefully."

As Suzie swept up the broken china, Mrs. Simond returned to her kneading, but both kept a worried eye on the medical drama. Talking to distract Lester from his pain, Daniel remarked, "I see there's no railing on that staircase. I'll talk to Kirkland about having one installed."

Having peeled the coat off Lester's left arm, Daniel eased the other sleeve down the right arm. Lester gasped involuntarily before biting down on the sound.

As Daniel removed the footman's shirt, he continued, "Very useful things, railings. At my Bristol infirmary, I've treated any number of people who fell down steps. I can fix a broken arm, but a broken neck is quite another matter. Luckily, your neck is in fine shape and your head doesn't seem to have any serious damage. As for your shoulder . . ."

Lester's shoulder looked square, not round, a clear indicator of dislocation. The young man moaned as Daniel gently examined the damaged joint. A simple dislocation with no apparent damage to the humerus. The sooner the bone was back in its socket, the better. "You're fortunate. Your arm isn't broken, but the bone was knocked out of the shoulder socket. I'll move it back into place. This will hurt, but it will only take a couple of minutes and then the worst of the pain will go away. You'll have to lie down."

He took off his own expensively tailored coat and spread it on the floor. Suzie said, horrified, "Oh, don't do that, sir! I'll get a blanket from the laundry room."

"That will be more comfortable for Lester." Daniel tossed his coat over a chair. "While you're in the laundry, could you find a piece of fabric that will do for a sling?"

"Yes, sir." She darted off.

"Mrs. Simond, is there some brandy I could give Lester to help him relax?" Daniel asked.

The cook nodded toward the adjoining pantry. "The locked cabinet in there." She tossed him a ring with several keys. "The key with a red thread tied on it. Leave the bottle out. I'm thinking we'll all be in need of some by the time you're done."

"You are a jewel of a cook, Mrs. Simond." Daniel caught the key and opened the cabinet. Inside were several bottles of the kinds of alcohol used in cooking. He poured some brandy in a cup, then added water to reduce the kick.

"Drink slowly," he said as he placed the cup in the footman's shaking left hand. "You may not like the taste, but it should help you relax and numb the pain a little."

"Thank you, my lord." Lester sipped, made a face, then sipped more.

By the time he'd finished, Suzie was back from

the laundry room. She carried two faded but clean old quilts and a worn shawl that would be a good size for a sling. She was a clever girl.

After spreading the folded quilts out on the cold floor, she offered Lester a folded handkerchief. "This is clean if you want to bite on it."

His face was pale and beaded with sweat, but he nodded and accepted the handkerchief. Daniel helped him from the chair, then lowered him down onto the quilts. "This will look strange, but it works, and your shoulder will be fixed in just a few moments."

He pulled off his shoes, glad he hadn't worn boots, then sat on the floor on Lester's right side and set the sole of his foot against his patient's ribs. As he clasped Lester's hand, he said, "I'm going to slowly pull your arm up and back until the bone snaps back into the socket. Suzie, talk to him about anything that will distract him."

Suzie obeyed, standing where Lester could see her easily as she chatted about the fine weather and Mrs. Simond's wonderful pies and what a splendid mouser Badger was. Her comments were humorous, which helped hold Lester's attention as Daniel carefully raised the arm and manipulated the humerus back into place.

He felt a distinct *clunk* when the bone slipped back into the shoulder socket. Lester exhaled and spat out the folded handkerchief, which showed teeth marks. "I could use that cup of tea now, Suzie. And maybe add some brandy, if Mrs. Simond doesn't object." Despite his jaunty words, his face was pale and beaded with sweat.

Mrs. Simond finished shaping her dough and wiped her hands clean. "I wager we could all use some of that tea with brandy!"

Suzie poured four cups from the pot that had been steeping. Fixing Lester's shoulder had been so quick that the tea hadn't even cooled.

Daniel helped Lester to his feet, then guided him back into his chair. As he fashioned a sling to support the arm, he said, "Your shoulder will hurt for a while and you'll need to wear this sling. Only light duties around the household. I'll give you a dose of laudanum so you'll sleep well tonight." He draped Lester's coat over the young man's shoulders for warmth. "In a few days, when your shoulder is feeling better, I'll show you some simple exercises to keep the joint from getting stiff."

As Suzie handed him a cup of tea, she asked shyly, "How can a lord be a surgeon, sir? I've never heard of such a thing!"

Daniel realized that all three of the others were studying him with varying degrees of amazement. He hesitated, realizing that he'd surely be asked this question again in the future. "Being a lord is an accident of birth. A very unexpected one in my case." He took a deep swallow of tea. "Medicine is my true calling."

As the words resonated within him, he recognized how invigorated he felt after behaving like a doctor for the first time in days. Ever since learning of his inheritance, his life had been turned upside down. Kirkland and Laurel had been invaluable in helping him come to terms with his new status and responsibilities, but medicine kept him sane and gave meaning to his existence. He had to keep his work at the center of his life rather than allowing it to be eroded away by other demands on his time and energy.

If he was to continue to be a surgeon and physician, he must find a wife who would not only be able to manage the Romayne estate, but support him in his eccentric choice of career. Not to mention that she must be pleasant and trustworthy.

The task of wife hunting had just become much more difficult.

Daniel had been looking forward to Kirkland's dinner for Westerfield graduates, but even so, he was surprised by the pleasure he felt in seeing men he'd known when they were all young and life had been so much less complicated.

Daniel's classmate Damian Mackenzie was the first to arrive. He hadn't lost his wicked sense of humor, but he'd acquired a fashionable gambling club and a glorious, exotic wife who seemed as intelligent as she was beautiful. Justin Ballard, who had been a year ahead, appeared with tanned skin and sun-streaked hair because he lived in Portugal and managed his family's port wine business. He shook Daniel's hand warmly, saying he was returning to Oporto in the morning but was glad not to miss this reunion.

Lady Agnes Westerfield swept in grandly, as befitted a duke's daughter who hadn't lost her sense of style even though she worked with grubby boys. She was instantly surrounded by former students, like a favorite aunt bearing gifts.

Daniel smiled when she waved at him. As he

made his way across the room toward her, he realized that since starting to look for a wife, he'd begun to evaluate women for the qualities that he wanted to find. Lady Agnes had intelligence, originality, and great kindness, with a legendary skill at healing the spirits of troubled boys.

In his years at the academy, Daniel had only known her to fail once, and that was with a deeply troubled boy who was incorrigible. Perhaps he should ask if she had any available nieces who were cast in her mold?

No, she was one of a kind, but it might be worth consulting her to see if she knew any women who might be a good match. Even all these years after he'd left her school, he suspected she knew him better than almost anyone else in his life other than Laurel and perhaps Kirkland.

Behind him a babble of greetings arose as new guests arrived. Daniel turned and was delighted to see the Duke of Ashton. Intelligent and reserved, Adam Lawford had always had a faintly exotic air because of his half-Hindu heritage. He'd been the one who taught his classmates the Hindu fighting skills that had become a school tradition, passed down from class to class.

For the first time, it occurred to Daniel that Lady Agnes and her partners in the school had encouraged the study of Kalaripayattu not just because it helped students work off excess energy, but because it was a compelling form of discipline. One couldn't do Kalaripayattu well without self-mastery, which most of the students had needed.

Lessons and bouts were always monitored by

older students who were skilled in the fighting techniques. If a boy lost control and became dangerous, he was immediately pulled away and he wasn't allowed to participate for a week. Because the fighting lessons were so popular, the risk of suspension was another inducement to self-mastery. Clever Lady Agnes!

Ashton had a petite, laughing blond beauty on his arm. Laurel had told Daniel that Mariah was called the Golden Duchess, and it was easy to see why.

Behind Ashton was Alex Randall. He had a dark-haired woman on each side, all three smiling at some remark.

Daniel froze. One woman was petite and appealing—and the taller one was the woman in black. She was closer to him than when he'd seen her at the rout, and the light was better. She was even more shockingly beautiful than he'd thought, with an innate sensuality powerful enough to drop a normal man in his tracks.

Dear God, was she Randall's wife?

The stabbing pang he felt lasted only a moment. When the smaller woman tucked her hand around Randall's arm, Daniel saw the deep intimacy between them. She must be his wife, Lady Julia.

Again Daniel found himself moving involuntarily toward the woman in black. For an instant he checked his movement because this was a woman who was too glamorous, too social, for a man like him. Then he continued on because he must find out who she was before he drove himself mad.

Rather than addressing her, he extended his

hand to Randall. "It's a pleasure to see you again after all these years, Alex! I gather life has been treating you well?"

"Very well." Randall returned the handshake with a wide smile. "I survived the army, and persuaded the woman of my dreams to marry me." He gave the petite woman a warm glance. "Allow me to introduce my wife, Lady Julia. Julia, meet Daniel Herbert, the newly fledged Lord Romayne."

Randall's wife smiled. "Even without the introduction, I'd know you for Laurel's brother. I'm so glad to meet you, Lord Romayne."

Daniel returned the smile. "You're a midwife, aren't you? We shall have to have a professional discussion later."

Lady Julia laughed. "I fear we'd run out of conversation quickly. I'm a mere midwife while you are a physician, surgeon, bonesetter, apothecary, and now a lord!"

"And of those, being a lord is the least interesting," he said ruefully. "With medical work, I do what needs to be done, but I'm not equally skilled in all areas."

Lady Julia nodded with understanding. "It was much the same in the village where I lived for a number of years. There was no other medical help for miles around, so I treated wounds and set bones and did what I could."

Daniel thought wryly that it was a pity she was already married, for surely they would suit well. Though he'd still have to find an estate manager.

"Let me introduce our friend, Lady Kelham, as well," Randall said. "Jessie, the new Lord Romayne was a class behind me in school, and had the remarkably irritating habit of almost always being right."

"With age, I've realized that right and wrong are much harder to tell apart than I thought when I was younger," Daniel said as he turned to Lady Kelham.

Now that they'd been properly introduced, Daniel allowed himself to look directly into the eyes of his lady in black. And lightning shattered him again.

Chapter 9

Damn the man! When had he become a lord? Jessie had recognized him immediately at that cursed rout, but it had never occurred to her that a provincial doctor might turn up in this small, private gathering.

"Lady Kelham." His words and bow were polite and civilized, his voice rich and compelling, but his eyes blazed with desire. Though she was used to men being drawn to her appearance, she was jarred by her response. She hadn't felt so attracted to a man since she was a foolish, desperate sixteen-year-old. And look how badly that had turned out!

"Lord Romayne." She wanted to smile warmly and extend her hand, but he was not husband material. Too young, and they had met during a period of her life she'd done her best to forget. She returned his greeting with the cold courtesy she'd learned over the years. Ice was useful in suppressing a man's fire.

But her manner had no effect, for he continued to regard her with unsettling intensity. Odd that she remembered him clearly for his kindness, yet she'd forgotten how handsome he was. She didn't remember him as fashionable, either, but tonight his immaculately tailored black clothing and crisp white shirt and cravat would have done credit to Beau Brummell himself. The severity of his garments set off his blond good looks.

Instead of flirting, he said, "My condolences on your loss."

The sincerity in his voice threw her off balance. Belatedly she realized his clothing might also be mourning. But no matter. She could use her widowhood to keep him at a distance. "Thank you. My husband died quite recently." She swallowed back a genuine stab of grief. "He was quite possibly the best man who ever lived."

"Then your loss is even greater," he said quietly.

The sincerity was real, she could see it in his eyes, along with the knowledge of death that doctors had. But there was some other, subtler emotion visible, too. Regret that she might not be interested in a new husband, now or ever?

She reminded herself that she shouldn't be watching him so closely, but attraction could cloud sense, and he was unsettlingly attractive. Wanting to turn the conversation away from herself, she asked, "Are you also in mourning? It's harder to tell with men since they wear black more often."

His blue-gray eyes shadowed. "Both my parents died suddenly."

"I'm so sorry." She realized that Julia and Randall had moved on and were talking with others, leaving her and Lord Romayne with too much privacy.

She was about to excuse herself when he snagged two glasses of sparkling champagne from the tray of a passing footman. As he handed her a glass, he asked, "Forgive me, Lady Kelham, but you seem familiar. Have we met before?"

His fingers brushed hers as she accepted the champagne. Even through her gloves, she felt a sear of heat as if she'd touched a candle flame. Dear God, she must kill this curiosity and get away from him! She took a sip of champagne as she steadied her nerves. "I doubt it," she replied in her coolest tone. "I am new to London society."

"As am I," he said, unfazed by her coolness. "I'm from the West Country and I've lived in or near Bristol most of my life. Are you from that area?"

"My home is in Kent. It's unlikely our paths have crossed." Which wasn't quite a lie but should be enough to deter his questions.

Undeterred, he said, "I went to school in Kent. Perhaps I saw you there."

He'd have been well past his school days by the time she'd settled in Kent, but Jessie felt no need to tell him that. "Perhaps."

Even though she knew she should leave, she found that she didn't want to. Succumbing to curiosity instead, she asked, "Was Lady Julia serious when she said you have such a range of medical skills, Lord Romayne? Surely all the training required must have been very time-consuming."

"I didn't sleep much for a decade or so," he replied with an engaging chuckle. "The different medical disciplines are not unrelated, so separating them does patients no service. Physicians may be highly educated and considered gentlemen, but it's hard to diagnose disease from the opposite side of the room because they would consider it vulgar to actually touch human bodies."

She laughed, thinking of the more hidebound physicians she'd met. "Which is why you learned the ungentlemanly trade of surgery? That most certainly requires physical examination."

"Exactly. Healing requires understanding how bodies work, which comes more from clinical experience than theory." He shook his head. "There is so much we don't know. But good men are working constantly to increase our knowledge."

"And perhaps some good women as well," she pointed out. "Lady Julia told me that she was fascinated by all forms of medicine from the time she was a child, and she spent as many hours as she could with the local practitioners."

"Really? I did the same," he said, intrigued. "Medicine is a calling, I think, and very hard to deny. Lady Julia's patients are fortunate that she was called to midwifery. I've always suspected that a female midwife has a better respect and understanding for the territory."

"How remarkably enlightened you are," she said with admiration. His passion for his work was obvious, and it made him even more attractive. She shouldn't enjoy the growing warmth between them, but how dangerous could it be when they were in a room full of people? "Have you been successful at combining your various skills?"

He grinned, and she realized that he was younger

than she'd thought. Only a few years older than she was. "That depends on how you define success," he replied. "I never lack for patients, but since I run a free infirmary, that's not surprising."

She knew about his infirmary, but better to pretend she didn't. "I imagine all kinds of patients come seeking help."

"Exactly. I might not be as knowledgeable about midwifery as Lady Julia, but if I'm the only medical help available when a baby comes, I'll do my best. I haven't lost a mother yet," he said seriously. "I can also set bones and compound medications if necessary, though again, an experienced bonesetter or apothecary would be better."

The man was a saint in a world that could use more like him. "You are wasted as a lord," she said. "What do lords contribute to society, after all? While a good and versatile doctor like you saves lives. What is most challenging in your work?"

"Knowing when to do nothing," he said wryly. "Hippocrates said physicians should first do no harm, but it's difficult to know when it's best to act, and when it's best to step away."

"I've never thought of that," Jessie said slowly. "When seeing a person in distress, the first impulse is to help. But it's true that if left to its own devices, a body will often heal itself."

"And medical treatment will sometimes make a condition worse." His mouth twisted. "But often one doesn't know if that's the case until it's too late."

She wondered how many times he'd guessed wrong about a treatment and still felt guilty about the results. Even once would be too often. "I see that it takes courage to be a doctor."

"Courage or arrogance," he agreed with a self-deprecating smile.

"Are you involved with the Sisters Foundation? Mariah and Lady Julia told me that your sister is a valuable part of the organization."

"Laurel and I worked together, but Zion House, the women's sanctuary, was primarily hers," he explained. "I supported it and provided medical treatment, of course. I also did the pastoral work. Counseling, baptism, funerals, and even some weddings."

His words were like a splash of ice water on the warmth that had been growing between them. This was a man she shouldn't even be talking to. "You're a vicar as well as everything else?" she said coldly. "I'm surprised you sleep at all. If you'll excuse me, I want to meet Lady Agnes. I've heard so much about her."

She turned and walked away, but she could feel his gaze on her retreating back. With any luck, her rudeness would discourage him from pursuing a further acquaintance.

But she feared she wouldn't be so lucky. Not when so much unspoken tension had thrummed between them.

After the guests left, Daniel, Laurel, and Kirkland settled in the drawing room to unwind and discuss the evening. Accepting a glass of claret from Kirkland, Daniel said, "Thank you for having this dinner party, Kirkland. It was a real pleasure to see so many old schoolmates. They all seem to be doing well."

Laurel laughed. "Once or twice I caught Lady Agnes surveying the room with the satisfied expression of a farmer pleased with her crops."

Both men joined her laughter. "She has every reason to be pleased," Kirkland said. "In many cases her seed corn was unpromising."

"I think she succeeded because she was subversive," Daniel said. "On the surface, she was giving us a good, aristocratic education, but her real lessons were on how to fit into society's boxes while being true to ourselves. If not for her, I don't think I would have pursued a medical career since my parents were dead set against it."

Kirkland smiled reminiscently as he settled on the sofa by Laurel, his left hand clasping hers. "My aristocratic English relatives wanted me to develop a proper distaste for trade and for my low Scottish mercantile relations. Lady Agnes confirmed my belief in the worth of both."

"Which helped you prosper in so many commercial areas." Laurel smiled fondly at her husband. "The more money you make, the more I can plunder for my philanthropic projects."

"I live to be plundered by you, my love," Kirkland said with a gleam in his eyes.

To Daniel's relief, Laurel did not pursue the point. Some things were better said in private, especially when a man's sister was involved.

Unfortunately, the topic she chose next was worse. Eying her brother, she remarked, "You seemed to enjoy talking to Lady Kelham."

He sipped his claret as he decided what to say. His feelings for the lady were too powerful and confused for discussion. "She's the woman I saw at the rout that I thought I recognized."

"Oh? She didn't look familiar to me, so probably not from the Bristol area."

"She's from Kent. Perhaps I saw her in passing when I was at school."

Though he had trouble believing he could have seen her and not remembered. Hoping Laurel had learned more, he continued. "Lady Kelham is an intriguing woman. A new widow, I gather?"

"Mariah said it's only been a few weeks since her husband died," Laurel said. "Apparently they were devoted to each other."

Daniel said lightly, as if the subject was of no importance, "If her loss is recent, she's not likely to be interested in remarrying anytime soon. I'll have to look elsewhere."

Laurel's glance was shrewd. She knew him too well. "Actually, I believe she's in London to discreetly look for a new husband."

"That's rather sudden," Daniel said, surprised. "But with her beauty, she won't have any trouble securing wealth and a grander title."

"I'm sure she has her reasons for wanting to remarry so quickly." A hint of reproach sounded in his sister's voice. "And not necessarily obvious ones."

"I shouldn't make assumptions," Daniel said contritely. "But this proves that I'm not a prime marriage mart target, Kirkland, since it was clear that she had no interest in me. She couldn't wait to get away."

"I'm told she wants to find a kind, reliable, older man," Laurel said. "Which is how I learned all this.

Julia told me what Lady Kelham wants so I could keep my eyes open for possibilities."

Daniel felt a wave of deep compassion. "She'll never find a man who can be just like her husband. It's a mistake to try."

"She probably knows that, but perhaps on some level she feels that she can only be happy with a man who is similar." Kirkland looked thoughtful. "I only spoke with her briefly, but she seems intelligent and not easily known." He sipped at his wine. "I'm told they're calling her the Black Widow in the clubs."

Daniel frowned, feeling oddly protective of Lady Kelham. "Do they think she looks for rich old husbands so she can be widowed quickly?"

"I'm told that a sprig from the mighty Howard tree with delusions of poetry wrote some drivel to the effect that she sprang unheralded from nowhere, and so great is her beauty that a man could die happy for having once held her in his arms," Kirkland said wryly. "One of the caricaturists immediately drew a print illustrating her as an alluring black widow spider, if you can imagine. It's in his shop window now."

"That's revolting!" Laurel exclaimed. "And very quick. She hasn't been in London for long at all."

"Lady Kelham is a woman who is always noticed." Kirkland poured more claret. "She has my sympathies."

"Maybe that's why she wants another husband," Laurel speculated. "As protection against such harassment."

"Perhaps." Daniel considered their interaction. Usually he was very good at reading people, but he didn't know what to think of Lady Kelham. *Jessie.* She had seemed attracted to him at first and, realistically, he was prime husband material. Then she'd abruptly terminated what had been a mutually enjoyable conversation. Apparently she didn't like vicars, but her reaction had been extreme. "I have a feeling that her life has been more complicated than merely growing up in Kent and marrying a local man."

"Do you want me to see what more I can learn about her?" Kirkland offered. "Unlike Aphrodite, she can't have sprung full grown from nowhere."

Daniel hesitated. "I'll admit I'm curious about her, but I don't like asking you to use your special talents to spy on her."

"You might as well ask," Kirkland said with amusement. "Everyone else does."

Daniel laughed. "Very well, then. I still have the feeling that we've met before, and I'm curious."

"I'll see what I can learn."

Daniel nodded, then firmly turned his mind away from the lady in black. "Does your London women's sanctuary need a doctor a few days a week? I'm feeling restless."

"I'll ask Julia. I'm sure she'll welcome the offer."

"Good. I'm not cut out to be a gentleman of leisure." Any more than he was cut out to be a lord.

That night, the Black Widow came to bed with Daniel. His mind churned with visions of her lithe, feminine figure. He wanted to peel away her mourning black so he could see every glorious inch of her. He wanted to kiss her until they were both gasping for breath, yet unwilling to separate even for a moment. He wanted her to raise her arms and draw him close so they could join, body and soul. . . .

He woke gasping and sweaty, feeling a sinner's guilt without a sinner's satisfaction. He was no innocent. He'd spent his life working on human bodies, knew a great deal about how they worked, had heard all kinds of confessions and questions from patients. Yet now he was at the mercy of raw desire.

Closing his eyes, he relaxed his muscles one by one, starting with his forehead and working his way down his body to his toes. The exercise relaxed both body and mind to the point that he could pray. He couldn't pray for deliverance from his desires, because he didn't want to be free of them. But he could pray for the best possible outcome for himself and the woman who was becoming his obsession.

He was human enough to want that outcome to bring them together—and rational enough to recognize that might be a disaster for them both.

Chapter 10

Daniel and Kirkland were greeted with rippling music when they returned to Kirkland House after a long session with lawyers on an unseasonably warm day. Wordlessly they both climbed the stairs to the music room. Laurel glanced up from the piano without interrupting the liquid grace of her dancing fingers. "You both look rather limp. Is that from the weather or your ordeal by lawyer?"

As Kirkland brushed a kiss on his wife's head, Daniel said wryly, "Both. I would have bolted if Kirkland hadn't been there to block my escape. But Mr. Hyatt seems very capable. He has the legalities for confirming me in the barony well in hand, and informed me that our eccentric cousin Romayne left a substantial estate and fortune."

Laurel reached up and caught her husband's hand affectionately. "Since you're unable to escape the barony, it's good the finances are solid. Less work for you."

"And all boring." Daniel repressed a sigh. "I need

to visit the Romayne seat and some smaller properties as well."

"Here's something you'll like better," his sister said. "Lady Julia is very enthusiastic about your request to work at the London shelter. When can you start?"

"Today!" he said promptly. "Though tomorrow would be more sensible."

"Let's go over to Gunter's to celebrate," Laurel suggested. "Their ices are perfect for a warm day like this one."

Daniel's eyes narrowed. "This would be the Gunter's from which you and your maid were kidnapped?"

"It was only the one time," Laurel said with a laugh as she rose to her feet. "And the ices are divine. I'm particularly fond of the neroli flavor."

Kirkland offered her his arm, and the three of them headed downstairs and out into Berkeley Square. The large townhouses were built around a sizable treed park, and Gunter's was one of several shops on the other side. Daniel hadn't had time to venture into the square, but the grass and the shade cast by the tall plane trees were welcome.

As they approached the opposite side of the park, he saw that a number of fashionable carriages were parked along the street. Ladies ate inside the vehicles while their male escorts leaned casually against the railings as they ate ices from small bowls. A pair of waiters moved across the road to take and deliver orders, and several children were on the grass, eating or playing. Daniel smiled. "It looks rather like a village fair."

"Only better dressed." Laurel shaded her eyes

with one hand as she studied the carriages. "There's an Ashton House coach, I see. I imagine they also felt the need for cool refreshments."

Daniel went on alert. There was the carriage, and he saw that the Duchess of Ashton, Lady Julia Randall, and Lady Kelham had chosen to get out and stretch their legs rather than sit inside. "Then we must say hello."

"Of course." Laurel's voice was demure, but she gave him an amused glance. "We must be polite. Especially to Lady Kelham."

"I never could fool you," he said ruefully.

"I'm glad you've found a woman who takes your fancy," his sister said softly. "You need to become better acquainted."

"I'll try. I'm not sure if she's willing." Nor was he sure that it was wise.

As he spoke, the Ashton House party noticed them approaching. The duchess waved cheerfully, and the other two women turned as well.

Lady Julia smiled a welcome, but Lady Kelham gave a cool nod before turning to follow a small girl child across the grass. The child was applying herself industriously to a bowl of ice as she walked. Daniel hadn't known that Lady Kelham had a daughter, but this girl must be hers. Though her hair was lighter, her exquisite features mirrored those of her beautiful mother.

The night before he'd heard that Lady Kelham's given name was Jessie. He found himself calling her that mentally since it suited her. Despite the lady's coolness, he'd taken heart from Laurel's information that Jessie wanted another husband. Even though his rational mind said she was not the kind of woman he needed, he wanted to know her better to be sure. Maybe they were less different than he thought. A man could hope.

He ambled toward Jessie and the little girl. Raising his voice a little, he said, "Good day, Lady Kelham. I've been brought here to experience the wonders of Gunter's ices. I gather your hostesses decided you also needed to experience them?"

She couldn't courteously ignore him, so she paused and turned to reply. "I think Mariah and Julia were using me and my daughter as an excuse to stop by."

"May I be introduced to the young lady?"

He saw Jessie's hesitation, but it wasn't an unreasonable question. "Lord Romayne, allow me to present my daughter, Elizabeth, Lady Kelham. Beth, this is Lord Romayne."

As the little girl turned with her bowl in one hand and spoon in the other, he saw that Jessie was waiting for him to express shock or disbelief. There was only one way the child could hold such a title, and that was as heiress to a very ancient barony. Such things were rare, but not impossible.

He bowed deeply. "It's a pleasure to meet you, your ladyship. Is it confusing to have two Lady Kelhams in the house?"

The child giggled, a smear of bright pink ice on her lower lip. "I'm really Beth," she explained. "Are you a friend of my mama?"

"Not yet, but I hope to be."

"Then perhaps we shall meet again." She bobbed a very proper curtsy without dropping either bowl or spoon before her attention was caught by a yellow butterfly and she drifted after it as she took dainty little bites of her rapidly melting ice.

"I think one reason people have children is because responsible adults often need an excuse for pleasure." His gaze followed Beth as she drifted happily along the grass. "Children are far better at accepting joy."

"I don't ever remember being that young," she said wistfully.

"I'm not sure I do either," he admitted. "I see joy in children, but they don't recognize it themselves because they're busy being joyful."

"Living in the moment. Not worrying about health or safety or grief or loss . . ."

Her voice trailed off, and he guessed she was thinking of her late husband. Wanting to turn her to happier thoughts, he said, "You have a beautiful daughter. Though her coloring is different, she looks very like you."

"Her father had that same toffee-colored hair when he was young. By the time I met him, his hair was silver, and he was all the more handsome for it." She smiled at her playful child, and it was the first real smile he'd seen on her face. Breathtaking.

Would she ever smile at him with unreserved happiness? She might look dangerously mysterious and beautiful, but her love for her daughter was unmistakable.

He was about to say something inane because his wit vanished when he was around her, but his attention was jerked to a thunder of hooves. Horses traveling much too fast for this part of the city.

A fashionable curricle drawn by two sleek chestnuts harnessed in tandem burst from Bruton Street and swung around the corner onto Berkeley at a dangerous speed. The young driver wore the multi-caped cloak of a professional coachman, but that was mere affectation because his driving was disastrous. As he struggled to slow his horses to avoid plowing into the crowd of Gunter's customers, he lost control and the curricle careened wildly onto the grass of the park.

The vehicle skidded onto two wheels—and headed for little Beth Kelham like a cannonball. Jessie screamed and darted toward her daughter. Dear God, she was putting herself in harm's way with no chance of saving Beth!

Other screams sounded as people scattered out of the path of the oncoming carriage. Kirkland swept Laurel back behind a plane tree and the Ashton ladies dodged behind their heavy coach.

Without conscious thought, Daniel raced after Jessie, calculating speed and angles. His longer legs covered the ground much faster than hers and he reached Jessie just as she caught up to Beth, but the lead horse was only yards away. With his left arm he scooped up the child as his right arm locked around Jessie's waist. Using his momentum, he spun away to the left, wrenching all three of them from the path of the onrushing horses.

As he hit the ground rolling away from the road, hooves smashed down inches away and chunks of turf pelted him. He wrapped himself protectively around mother and child till he came to a sliding halt with Jessie sprawled on top of him. His right arm was still wrapped around her waist and Beth was tucked under his left arm.

The curricle swung wildly into a plane tree, sending the driver flying and jerking the horses to a panicked stop. But Daniel was barely aware of that because all his attention was on Jessie, whose shocked eyes were mere inches away. Her legs bracketed his and her soft breasts and hips pressed against him with shocking intimacy.

Time was suspended. The fear and rush to save Beth and Jessie were transmuted into a fierce, unexpected arousal that blazed through every fiber of his being. Shockingly, there was a startled response in Jessie's eyes as if her body recognized and craved his, too. He wanted to meld with her, bury himself in her irresistible femininity. . . .

The mad moment shattered when Beth began to wail with distress. Jessie shoved away from Daniel and reached for her daughter. "Beth!"

Daniel's fears for the child evaporated when she wailed, "Mama! My ice dish fell and broke! I wasn't finished!"

He extricated himself from the tangle of skirts and limbs as Jessie pulled her daughter onto her lap in a crushing embrace. They were rumpled and grass stained and they'd lost their bonnets, but Daniel didn't see obvious signs of damage or pain. He asked, "Are you both all right?"

"Nothing that matters." Jessie ran frantic hands over her daughter's limbs. "Beth, do you hurt anywhere?"

Only seconds had passed since the accident. As Daniel got to his feet, he saw that no one seemed to have been injured other than perhaps the driver, who'd been thrown from his vehicle. A man was soothing the wild-eyed horses while most of Gunter's customers were gathering in small clumps, talking excitedly about the accident and their near miss.

Jessie was still sitting on the ground with Beth in her arms, so he asked, "Do you want me to help you up?"

"I . . . just want to sit here and shake for a while," she said unsteadily, keeping her eyes down as she cuddled her daughter against her.

Recovering quickly, Beth turned to study the scene. "That man was a very bad driver," she said disapprovingly.

"Very true," Daniel agreed. He wondered if the blasted young fool had broken his neck when he was thrown from the curricle. Though Daniel wasn't feeling very charitable toward the fellow, he'd better take a look at him.

The Ashton ladies appeared, a little ruffled but undamaged. "Do you want me to take Beth?" Lady Julia asked.

Jessie drew a deep breath. "Not yet, thank you, but could you get another ice for her? The bowl dropped when . . ." She swallowed hard, then glanced up at Daniel, her aquamarine eyes stark. "When Lord Romayne pulled us to safety. I haven't thanked you yet, my lord. When I think of what almost happened . . ." She shuddered.

"If you had been a little slower, all three of you would have been gravely injured or worse," Lady Julia said quietly. "Well done, sir."

He gave her a twisted smile. "I'm just glad I was fast enough. Now to see if the driver has survived his idiocy."

"I'll stay with Jessie and Beth and leave him to

you," Lady Julia replied. "He rolled softly, like a drunk, so he might not be badly hurt."

"I'll get Beth her ice," the duchess said. "Would you like one, Jessie?"

Jessie managed a smile. "No, but I would dearly love a cup of tea!"

"It shall be done." The duchess moved toward the shop, and in one swift gesture collected a waiter and gave the order.

Daniel was reluctant to leave Jessie, but duty called. He crossed the stretch of grass to where the curricle driver lay in a muddy lump. The fellow was moaning and blood was dripping into his face, but at least he wasn't dead. Lady Julia had been right about both the soft landing and the drinking; the boy smelled like a bottle of brandy had been poured over him.

Daniel knelt beside him and started a swift examination. "Congratulations," he said dryly as he used a handkerchief to wipe the blood from what turned out to be a messy but shallow laceration of the skull. "You're not as dead as you should be. Does anything seem broken?"

The driver blinked. "Don-don't think so."

"Mr. Shelton," said a disgusted voice. It was Kirkland, who'd turned the horses over to another man and come to investigate. "You are not only a fool, but a dangerous fool. I shall suggest to your father that he take your horses away. By the mercy of the god of horses, it appears that they won't need to be put down, but your curricle is fit for nothing but firewood." He continued with a tongue-lashing that surely peeled the fellow down to raw, twitching nerves.

Daniel listened admiringly as he finished his examination and used his handkerchief to put a crude bandage on Shelton's head. An older man joined them. "I'll take you home, lad, and my footman will lead the horses after us. You were lucky."

Shelton pushed himself to a sitting position dizzily. "Luckier than I deserved," he muttered, his voice shaking. He glanced toward Beth and shuddered. Daniel suspected that the young man wouldn't drive so recklessly anytime soon.

Having done what was necessary, he rose and looked over to Jessie. She was on her feet now, her composure restored and looking quite achingly beautiful as she sipped a steaming cup of tea. Beside her, a grass-stained Beth was happily digging into another ice. Daniel gave silent thanks that the accident had caused no serious injuries.

Except, perhaps, to his heart or possibly his brain. He no longer cared about the fact that Jessie, Lady Kelham, was utterly wrong for him. Despite their differences, he saw only one possible course of action.

He'd just have to ask her to marry him.

Chapter 11

"**Y**ou have a visitor, Lady Kelham." The Ashton footman presented a silver tray with a card set neatly in the middle. "He's in the small salon. Will you receive him?"

Jessie took the card, wondering if it was one of the two older gentlemen who had been calling on her assiduously. But they came in the afternoon, not the morning, and eyed each other like wary cats when they visited at the same time.

LORD ROMAYNE. A mere two words that made her pulse jump with an alarming mix of emotions. Her mind had been churning since the near-disastrous visit to Gunter's the day before, and his lordship had been far too present in her thoughts. It would be easier to say she wasn't at home, but she owed him too much to hide. "I'll see him."

After the footman withdrew, she checked her appearance in the mirror that hung above the mantel in her small sitting room. Black gown, firmly restrained hair, a very proper widow. But her eyes. How could she control her eyes?

Should she ask Julia or Mariah to join her? But they were both in the nursery with their babies, a time of day they loved. She shouldn't interrupt.

Realizing she couldn't delay any longer, she descended to the ground floor. Mariah had told her how much drama the small salon had witnessed over the years. Jessie hoped there would be no more today.

Dr. Herbert—Lord Romayne—was gazing out the window when she entered. He was his usual composed self, but there was tension visible in his lean, muscular body. He turned as she entered, his expression grave.

"Good day, Lord Romayne," she said lightly. "Has no one mentioned to you that morning calls shouldn't be made in the morning but in the afternoon? It's an important mark of society's basically irrational nature."

He smiled a little. "I actually had the rules explained to me, but I wanted to see how you and Beth were doing after the unfortunate incident at Gunter's."

She chuckled. "You mean almost being killed by a drunken young fool who shouldn't be allowed near a carriage? Beth is fine. She's been asking when we can go back to Gunter's for more ices. She and I have bruises and her dress was ruined, but that was all."

"She might not appreciate the danger she was in, but you do," he said quietly. "Did you have nightmares last night?" Seeing her flinch, he swiftly said, "I'm sorry. I didn't mean to upset you again."

Jessie swallowed hard. "I've been upset ever since it happened. When I remember that carriage bearing down on Beth . . ." She shuddered. "I knew I couldn't move fast enough to save her, but I had to try. If . . . if she was killed, there would be no reason for me to live."

She struggled for composure, but the horrifying vision of the carriage rushing toward her daughter seared across her mind again. Beth's sweet, small, vulnerable body. The crashing hooves of frantic horses and a wildly out of control carriage . . .

She began to sob uncontrollably. Remembered fear was drowning her, until warm arms came around her. She buried her face in the doctor's elegant coat. He said nothing, just stroked her back and held her as she shook.

As her paroxysms of fear subsided, she realized just how right it felt to be in his arms. He was warm and strong and kind. She closed her eyes and allowed herself to relax, until she remembered her acute physical awareness the day before when she was sprawled on top of him. For a mad moment, desire had been as intense as fear.

Once again desire flared, intimate and disturbing. She forced herself to step away, smiling apologetically. "I'm sorry. I haven't allowed myself to cry because I knew I'd fall to pieces. But if you needed proof of how powerful my gratitude is, I believe I've just demonstrated it."

His breath had quickened, but his voice was calm when he said, "I hope that you'll have fewer nightmares tonight."

"One may hope." Her smile was lopsided. "Please take a seat. I'll ring for tea?"

"No need." He hesitated. "I have another purpose for calling on you. One reason I'm in London is to look for a wife. I've heard that you're also looking for a husband. I would be greatly honored if you would allow me to court you."

She gasped and pressed one hand to her mouth. She had not expected *this*!

"Is the idea so absurd?" he asked. "This must be difficult when you're so recently bereaved, but I'll wait until you're ready."

Mariah or Julia must have told his sister, Laurel, that Jessie was looking for a husband. She muttered a silent oath that she hadn't known at first about the close connections between Ashton House and the Kirklands. Perhaps she should have been more discreet about her goals, but she'd needed the ladies' help. "You are well-informed, but . . . forgive me for being blunt, Lord Romayne. You are not the sort of husband I seek."

His gaze was probing. "You may prefer an older man, Lady Kelham, but you can never replace your late husband. Though I can't make myself older, in other ways, I think you'd find me a reasonable choice. I have my share of eccentricities, I suppose, but I've recently come into a substantial fortune, I have no terrible vices, and my reputation is sound. You can make inquiries if you wish."

"Choosing a mate is not a simple matter of logic, my lord," she said helplessly. "While you're a very desirable potential husband and I owe you a debt that can never be repaid, that doesn't mean we should marry."

"You owe me nothing. Trying to save a child is every decent person's obligation, not a way of keeping score." Refusing to back down, he asked, "Do you dislike me? I've thought there was a certain harmony of mind as well as a powerful attraction between us, but perhaps that's wishful thinking on my part."

She bit her lip. She was a good liar when necessary, but she didn't want to lie to this man. "You're not wrong, but attraction isn't a sound basis for a marriage."

"Isn't it a start?" he asked quizzically. "Shouldn't we at least try to discover if we'd suit?"

"Didn't anyone ever tell you it's ungentlemanly to ask a lady why she doesn't accept you?" Jessie said with sudden exasperation. "A simple 'no' should suffice!"

His mouth curved wryly. "As with the rule about morning calls, I'm aware of that, but I don't choose to comply. This is too important. *You're* too important."

"Then I shall have to be even more blunt," she said flatly. "You are a good man, Lord Romayne. You do indeed have an impeccable reputation as a physician, a surgeon, and a man whose life is devoted to helping others. You're held up as an example of good Christian values. You're even a vicar, for heaven's sake! But that alone is reason enough to decline your flattering offer."

"I noticed before that you don't seem to like vicars," he said thoughtfully.

"My father was a vicar," she retorted. "I want nothing to do with another one!"

He didn't flinch, but his expression became unreadable. "Though I've been ordained, I'm not a practicing cleric," he said in a mild voice. "I founded a chapel in Bristol where nonconformists meet and hold services. I sometimes give a sermon myself, but medicine has always come first with me. If you intend to despise me for my low occupation, it should be surgery, not the church."

"I don't despise you." She paced across the room, her steps taut. "I simply don't want you for a husband. I shouldn't have to explain why!"

"But I need to understand." He took a few steps toward her, moving into the sunshine that poured through the window, making his hair shine like polished golden oak. "The best way to get rid of me entirely is to make it very clear what your objections are. Having been trained in medicine, I need reasons. Evidence."

She swung around, her hands knotted into fists. "Because you're a good man, Lord Romayne, and I'm a wicked woman! I should be wearing scarlet, not widow's weeds, to warn men away from me!"

His gaze was searching. "Are you cruel? I've seen no signs of that. Are you a liar or profoundly selfish? I've not observed that either. How are you wicked?"

She wanted to spit at him. "I have no desire to reveal my sordid past, my lord! I have done what I must to survive, and that includes deeds that the world would condemn." Not to mention the deed that could get her hanged. "I don't belong with a man who is almost a saint!"

His eyes flashed with real anger. "I am no saint!" He closed the distance between them in two steps, wrapped his arms around Jessie, and kissed her with an urgency that seared her bones.

Desire might not be a solid foundation for marriage, but it overwhelmed her stunned senses. Her

arms slid around him and she tilted her face up to
his warm, vital mouth. His quickening heartbeat
mirrored hers as her breasts pressed against his
chest.

Her lips opened under his and their tongues
touched in mutual hunger. She wanted to con-
sume, or be consumed. *Both.* It had been so long
since she'd experienced passion, and never had it
been so fierce. Her pelvis ground against him and
he hardened, his hands sliding down to cup her
buttocks and pull her even tighter.

Desire flared still higher. She felt like melting
wax, her existence dependent on him. . . .

The horror of that imminent surrender slammed
her back to her senses. Dear God, what was *wrong*
with her? The last thing she needed was mindless
passion leading her into an abyss.

She shoved away from him. "You kiss very well for
a saint," she gasped. "But it's time for you to go!"

"Saints are so often celibate. That does not appeal to me." He caught her hand, his warmth and
intensity weakening her resolve. "How can you
deny what's between us?" he said, his deep voice
compelling. "Marry me, Jessie Kelham! I swear you
won't regret it."

Her mouth twisted bitterly and she yanked her
hand free. "Perhaps, perhaps not. But you would,
Lord Romayne! This is only lust, as swift and de-
structive as a summer storm. After it passed, you'd
curse the day you met me. And then you'd despise
me for ruining your life."

He blanched. "You have a low opinion of me and
an even lower opinion of yourself if you believe
that. Passion isn't everything, but it can be a vital el-

ement of a good marriage. Please, give us a chance to find what else we have in common!"

Her exasperation with him faded, replaced by sadness. She'd think his earnestness romantic if she didn't know how wrong he was.

But dear God, he was mesmerizing in his passion and sincerity! Wanton woman that she was, she yearned to lie with him. She wanted to taste the forbidden apple in a way that would damage neither of them. It had been so long, so long, since she felt vibrant desire beating through her.

Perhaps it was worth risking a brief, mad satisfaction. She swallowed hard, unnerved by the thought of her own brazenness. More likely, she'd drive him away, and that would be good. But she needed to try.

Catching his gaze, she said, "If passion is unhinging your mind, I have a solution. Let us have an affair. Wild and wanton but very discreet, because I don't want a reputation that will reflect badly on my daughter. We'd both enjoy it greatly, and in a few days or weeks you'll come to your senses. You'll thank me then for my wisdom, and we can go our separate ways, cured of this unruly desire."

The intensity that had lit him up like a candle vanished as his desire and hope drained away, leaving him older and grayer. "I think not, my lady."

She released her breath in a sigh, knowing he was wise, but bitterly regretting the loss of this rare, sweet connection. Because it was real, and powerful—but utterly wrong for both of them.

After a half-dozen beats of silence, he said in a colorless voice, "If your plan was to drive me away, you've succeeded." He bowed ironically. "I thank you for your honesty and wisdom. Perhaps someday I'll be grateful that you refused me. But . . . not today."

He turned and left the salon, his hand fumbling blindly before he found the knob. The door closed behind him very gently.

Shaking, she sank into a chair and wrapped her arms around herself. She'd been right to destroy their budding relationship.

But why did being right have to hurt so much?

Chapter 12

Instead of heading for the exit of Ashton House, Daniel quietly stepped into another receiving room and closed the door behind him. Then he leaned back against it, knowing he couldn't face anyone until he'd mastered himself. Assuming that was possible. He felt . . . gutted. A hollow man, now broken.

He supposed he should feel relieved that Jessie's brazen honesty had prevented their relationship from developing any further. It wasn't even a relationship, merely lust, as she'd pointed out so firmly.

The lower side of his nature had wanted desperately to accept her offer of an affair. He was still so aroused that his brain was barely managing to function.

But agreeing would have been wrong in so many ways. She'd acted as if a few afternoons of mad coupling would take the edge off their inconvenient desire, after which they'd cheerfully go their separate ways. But he couldn't imagine any good end to such an affair, because he could not imagine a day when he wouldn't want her.

How long had he been a hollow man? Certainly since Rose had died, but the seeds had been sown earlier by his parents, who wanted to be proud of their son without understanding him. Or wanting to understand. They doted as long as he did exactly what they wanted. He'd learned early how to get their approval.

His relationship with them nearly shattered when they disowned Laurel because she'd left her husband. They didn't care how justified she might have been. The only thing she'd ever done that they really approved of was marry an earl, and they couldn't forgive her for the breakdown of the marriage.

Nor had they really forgiven Daniel for taking Laurel's side, though they hadn't disowned him. They'd needed their image of their perfect son even if they were privately furious with him.

His relationship with them had continued dutifully, but inside it was . . . hollow. When they died, he'd felt sadness and regret, but not true grief.

For whatever mad reason, Jessie Kelham had seemed like a woman who could fill his emptiness. That had proved to be only his desperate imagination. But imagination had been sweet while it lasted. . . .

Closing his eyes, he prayed for peace. Then he forced stillness on himself, limb by limb, muscle by muscle, until he was in a fit state to be in public. Fortunately he was now scheduled to drive to the East End to work at Zion House's small infirmary. Treating patients would require his full attention, so he could begin to put the Black Widow behind him. He had survived worse than being rejected by a woman he scarcely knew, and he would survive this.

But he wondered how long it would be before his heart stopped bleeding.

It was late by the time Daniel returned to Kirkland House. He had a key, so he let himself in quietly, not expecting to see anyone. But before he could head up to his room, Kirkland emerged from his study. He was coatless and bootless and held a glass of some dark amber liquid in one hand. The fashionable spymaster relaxing at home.

"I assume that's not your blood on your shirt," Kirkland said mildly.

Daniel glanced down to see reddish brown stains smudged across his once immaculate shirt front. "I was able to do some surgery. It was quite invigorating."

Kirkland smiled. "It has to be more interesting than the financial papers I've been working on. I'm ready to call it a night before I fall asleep in my chair. Care to join me for some brandy? Or food?"

"I ate at a tavern with several staff members so we could discuss future plans. Very good people." Daniel dropped his hat on a table, feeling weary. But the work had driven off the worst of the demons. "I wouldn't object to some brandy, though."

Kirkland led the way into his study and opened a well-stocked cabinet. As he poured another glass of brandy, he remarked, "It sounds as if you're expanding your original idea for the Zion House infirmary?"

"There's a great need in that area. A young surgeon from Bart's has been volunteering at Zion House when he has the time. He's capable and versatile, so I'm going to provide a salary that will allow him to work there half-time."

Daniel settled wearily into a wing chair and stretched out his legs. It had been a long day. Was it just this morning that Jessie Kelham had refused his offer? "There's a building for lease on the other side of the street from the Zion House shelter, so I'll have Hyatt get that for the infirmary. Any extra space can be used by Zion House for more shelter areas."

Kirkland smiled as he took the opposite chair. "You're finding the advantages of wealth and lawyers who will instantly do your bidding?"

"Indeed." Daniel sipped his brandy, resisting the desire to toss it back in one gulp. "One of the women at the shelter is an apothecary's widow. Very knowledgeable. She's ready and willing to set up a dispensary if I'll provide the materials."

"It sounds as if you've had a very productive day." Kirkland sipped at his brandy, his gaze shrewd. "Is that why you look as if you were run over by a mail coach?"

Daniel grimaced. His first impulse was to deny that there was anything wrong beyond simple fatigue. But he felt the need to talk, and because he didn't want to upset his sister, Kirkland was the only choice. "This morning I asked Lady Kelham for permission to court her. She turned me down. Very firmly."

Kirkland went still, his brandy glass halfway to his mouth. After a long moment, he said quietly, "I'm sorry. I presume you wouldn't have asked her without considerable thought."

Daniel's mouth twisted. "On the contrary. When I'm around her, I can't seem to think at all."

His brother-in-law blinked. "That's . . . unexpected."

"I've found it so, given that I've never had a problem keeping my head where women are concerned." Daniel managed a halfway genuine smile. "I believe the lady is divine punishment for my lack of understanding of how you and Laurel fell in love at first sight."

Kirkland swallowed all of his remaining brandy and poured more for both of them. "*Very* unexpected. I never blamed you for not understanding how we felt. You were right that we were too young and what we felt might have been mere infatuation. As it happens, the love was real, but it took ten years for us to rebuild our marriage after it broke. Love at first sight is more likely to be a shooting star than enduring love."

It was easy to think of Jessie as a shooting star, swift and brilliant and impossible to capture. "She and I are older and perhaps wiser. She was quite clear about why we wouldn't suit, and it wasn't just that we don't know each other well."

"Is it because she's looking for an older man, like her late husband? If that's the case, perhaps she might change her mind."

"That's not why she rejected me." Daniel toyed with his glass, watching the lamplight refract through the rich, dark brandy. "She says that I'm a good man and she's a wicked woman, and once the initial attraction wore off, it would be a disaster."

Kirkland's brows furrowed. "That's very blunt, but she might be right."

"Perhaps she is." Daniel closed his eyes as pain flared again. "But I wish she'd allowed more time before closing the door so firmly."

"She may have thought a quick amputation was best."

Daniel snorted. "Medical metaphors are my province, not yours." A thought struck him. "I'd asked you to look into her past. Have you discovered why she thinks of herself as a wicked woman?"

"A thorough investigation would require sending people to places she's lived, and there hasn't been time or the necessity to do that. But her beauty attracts attention, so anyone who has known her in the past has been gossiping since she arrived in London," Kirkland explained. "Which means confusion, exaggerations, and outright lies, which are impossible to evaluate properly."

"I understand the limitations of gossip, but tell me what you've heard," Daniel said, his voice flat. "Perhaps that will make me grateful for her rejection."

"As you wish, but there's not much hard data. No one seems to know where she was born or what her family background is."

"She told me her father was a vicar. I gather that explains part of her distaste for the breed."

Kirkland's brows arched. "That's more than anyone else has known. It makes sense, though. She's always been considered well-spoken and well-bred. She first entered public view as an actress in Yorkshire. She was young and inexperienced, but her striking looks kept her well employed in ingénue roles. As an actress, she was the target of considerable gossip in York. It's said that she had many lovers, but the number is probably exaggerated."

"No smoke without a fire?" Daniel murmured.

"Very small sparks can be blown up to appear like major fires," Kirkland said dryly. "The actresses I've known say that reports of their profligate behavior are greatly exaggerated. Acting is hard work and most of them don't follow conventional morality, but they don't have the time or energy to bed every lout who considers them fair game. So they tend to be selective."

Feeling sick, Daniel wondered just how profligate Jessie had been. "How did she get from a Yorkshire theater to a good marriage in Kent?"

"She had at least one serious lover, Frederick Kelham. He took her to visit his uncle, Lord Kelham."

Daniel frowned. "Is it plausible that the heir to a barony would take his mistress to visit a respectable old gentleman?"

"Not very," Kirkland agreed. "Though I suppose it could happen. It's said that when she saw Lord Kelham's wealth, she seduced him into marriage. There's a theory that Frederick was complicit in that since he's been telling everyone that he and the lady continued as lovers and her daughter is his, not her husband's."

Daniel winced. "Ugly if true."

"Which it may or may not be. Lady Kelham has been a model of decorum, and she may not be aware of the gossip. Those who knew her in Kent say that she was a gracious hostess and respectable wife who was devoted to her husband and daughter."

"So which is the real woman?" Daniel mused. "The scandalous actress or the modest, demure wife and mother?"

"Both might be true," Kirkland pointed out. "We simply don't have enough good information to judge. Young men often sow wild oats before settling down to their responsibilities, and such things are viewed with indulgence. For a female to do the same is less common and more hazardous because she'll be judged much more harshly. But recklessness is not the same as wickedness."

True, but Daniel was still unnerved by the outlines of Jessie's past. A moot point, given that she'd refused even to consider him as a possible husband. "Thank you. Knowing more of her background makes it easy to understand why she thinks we wouldn't suit."

What a pity that knowing she was all wrong for him didn't stop him from wanting her.

Chapter 13

"We won't have many days more like this." Mariah took a sip of lemonade as she gazed from the Ashton House gazebo to the sunny lawn where Beth and several other children were playing with shrieks of delight. "We'll be heading home to Ralston Abbey soon. You can stay on if you wish, though. Heaven knows the house is large enough."

Jessie felt a pang. She'd loved living under the same roof as Mariah and Julia, who had become the best female friends she'd ever had. Writing letters wouldn't be the same. "No need. We've had a wonderful visit, but it's time to return to Kent."

Mariah had been idly shuffling through a small stack of invitations that had been delivered to her earlier. She pulled one out to study more closely. "The Dunhavens are having a harvest ball next week, so stay until then. That will be a nice ending to the little season. Any fashionable folk still in town will be there, so we can say our good-byes. The Dunhavens are splendid hosts."

"I'm not sure I should go to a ball," Jessie said half seriously. "My resolve to behave might dissolve and I'll disgrace myself by waltzing."

"The world wouldn't end if that happened." Mariah set the invitation aside to be answered later. "But how goes your quest for a husband? You haven't said much about that lately."

"Well, I've received indecent propositions from several men anxious to comfort a lonely widow. Most of them married." She made a face. "One was from Sir Harold Truscott."

"Isn't he one of the widowers you considered to be a good husband prospect? Rich, agreeable, and elderly?"

"He seemed a good choice, but alas! It was not to be. When he propositioned me, I told him I'd consider marriage, but not an illicit affair." Jessie chuckled. "He suggested that he might be willing to marry me, but first he would have to try the goods to be sure of what he was getting. I told him I wasn't going to lower my market value by giving away free samples. It was all dreadfully mercantile."

Mariah laughed. "Were you tempted to continue negotiations in hopes of striking an acceptable bargain?"

"Not really. His hands were clammy." Jessie suspected that she might have been able to charm Sir Harold into an offer of marriage, but she really didn't want to marry him. She couldn't help but compare him to Lord Romayne. Though Sir Harold was an easygoing man with a good reputation and good connections, he was boring, and the more she saw of him, the more boring he became.

"I'm surprised that you haven't received at least

one offer," Mariah mused. "You've enchanted any number of gentlemen just by stepping into a room."

"I don't count the very young men who offer their hearts and bad poetry," Jessie said. "There were several of those. I invoke my recent bereavement and refuse very gently but very, very firmly. There's only been one remotely plausible offer, but that one wouldn't have worked."

"Oh?" Mariah gave Jessie a bright-eyed glance. "Who was plausible but wrong?"

Jessie hesitated. She shouldn't have said anything, but she realized she wanted to talk about him. "Lord Romayne asked permission to court me. I declined, of course."

"What?" Mariah stared at her. "What do you mean, 'of course'? Daniel is a lovely, intelligent, charming fellow, and as Laurel's brother and a long-term friend of Adam, Randall, and Kirkland, he's a known quantity, not an unreliable stranger. Apart from his age, he fits your conditions perfectly. I've seen him at the Zion House infirmary and he's wonderful with children. He'd be a marvelous stepfather for Beth. He also has a title and powerful connections to help keep you and your daughter safe from the loathsome Frederick. How could you say no?"

Daniel. His name was Daniel. "I was very tempted," Jessie admitted. "But I don't think we would suit, and I . . . like him too well to burden him with a wife he'll soon regret."

Mariah pursed her lips. "I have the feeling that this is much more complicated than you wish to discuss."

Jessie's smile was crooked. "You're right, and I appreciate your tact in not asking more questions."

"I can be tactful when there's no other choice," Mariah said dryly. "Apparently you're no longer as worried about your nephew as when you first arrived in London?"

Jessie nodded. "I haven't heard a word from him, and now I think I reacted too strongly to his threats. He was furious, but he's also rather lazy. After he got over the initial shock of not inheriting the title, he must have realized that he'll have a very handsome fortune with none of the responsibilities of running the estate. That should suit him perfectly, considering how averse he is to anything resembling work."

"As a mother, of course you reacted strongly to a possible threat to Beth," Mariah said sympathetically. "But if the danger has passed, no need to rush choosing a new husband. It shouldn't be hard to find a man you like who doesn't have clammy hands."

They both laughed. Mariah was right. Now that Jessie's fears had subsided, there was no need to rush into marriage. In truth, she'd rather not marry at all. Her gaze went to her daughter, who was giggling with the butler's daughter. While she had her doubts about marriage, she'd love to have more children.

Maybe someday . . .

The Dunhaven ball proved to be worth waiting for. After an initial round of greetings, Jessie found a position by the wall where she could enjoy the music and elegant guests spinning across the polished floor. In her mourning, she felt like a raven at the feast, but even if she couldn't dance, she could enjoy. Surely tapping her foot to the music wasn't a serious violation of mourning customs.

The ballroom was less crowded than Jessie's first rout, and there was a relaxed air as people came to bid farewell to friends they wouldn't see for months. Mariah and Julia were dancing with their husbands, and very happy all four of them looked. Jessie smiled wistfully. She loved to dance, but Philip hadn't, so it had been far too long since she'd attended even a simple country assembly.

But next year she could return to London, and she'd no longer be in mourning. Mariah had given her an open invitation to Ashton House, and Jessie looked forward to future visits, not least because Beth needed to grow up as part of this sophisticated world.

She was about to join a group of older women who'd taken possession of one corner of the ballroom when her attention was caught by new arrivals. Lord and Lady Kirkland and their guest, Lord Romayne.

Jessie felt as if she'd been kicked in the stomach. She hadn't seen him since their last meeting almost a fortnight earlier, and she'd hoped to keep it that way.

Since he hadn't yet seen her, she retreated through a pair of French doors to a balcony overlooking the extensive Dunhaven gardens. The early autumn air was brisk, but it steadied her nerves. She shouldn't have been surprised to see Lord Romayne when most of fashionable London was in attendance tonight, but she'd tried not to think about him.

She rested her hands on the wooden railing, thinking of her time in London. Though she was profoundly grateful for the friends she'd made, she was ready to return to the quiet of Kent. London had taken the edge off of her grief over Philip, and now that she wasn't worried about Beth, she could begin building her new life as a modest widow who didn't need a husband.

The next time she saw Lord Romayne, he'd probably be happily married to a woman of impeccable reputation. Jessie hoped his wife would also be kind because kindness mattered, and he deserved it.

She was ready to return to the ball when the doors opened behind her, releasing warmth and merriment into the night. Before she could turn, a large male hand trapped the gloved fingers of her right hand where it rested on the balcony railing. She tried to pull her hand free, but the man kept her pinned to the railing.

Thinking it was another lout who wanted to comfort a poor widow, she turned—and was appalled to see Frederick Kelham.

Outraged, she freed her hand with a powerful yank, giving thanks for gloves that meant their bare fingers hadn't touched. "How *dare* you! Get away from me!"

He moved a step back, raising his hands placatingly. "Don't take on so, Jessie! I just need to speak with you in private." He was a handsome man, and quite charming when he smiled at her as he did now. He had blue eyes and the toffee-colored Kelham hair, and looked rather like a youthful version of Philip.

Best of all, he looked reasonable tonight. Perhaps he wanted to apologize for his outrageous tantrum when he'd learned that he wasn't heir to the title. "Very well," she said warily. "Did you want to tell me that you've come to terms with Philip's will?"

His mouth thinned before he replied. "Now that I've had time to think about it, I've come up with a perfect solution."

She frowned. "There's nothing that needs solving. The situation is quite straightforward, and I think Philip handled it very fairly."

"I was robbed of my inheritance!" Frederick snapped. "No one knew that the title came from a damned barony of writ, and there was no need to bring it up! Beth would still be an heiress and she'd never have missed being Lady Kelham."

So Frederick had not recovered from his tantrum. "Perhaps not, but it gave Philip great joy that she was his heir," Jessie said icily.

"My uncle is beyond caring," Frederick retorted. "But as I said, I have a solution. Marry me, Jessie. Then we can be a family together at Kelham Hall."

She stared at him, shocked. "Have you run mad? I'd never marry you after all you've done!"

"I haven't always behaved well, Jessie," he said with an apologetic little-boy smile that didn't suit him. "But you wanted to marry me once, and we had a great time together. There's no one like you, and I was a fool to let you go."

Her mouth tightened at his disingenuous description of how their affair had ended. "I am honored by your regard, sir," she said with deep sarcasm, "but I must refuse, for I fear we would not suit." She frowned. "I'm not sure it would even be legal since you're Philip's nephew."

He shrugged that aside. "We're not blood kin, so that's no barrier. And think of the advantages, Jessie!"

Ignoring her flinch, he cupped her chin, and said huskily, "You're a passionate woman, Jessie, and you need a man. I know how to make you happy, eh?"

Revolted, she retreated out of touching distance. "Why the devil would I put myself and my daughter under your control? Kelham Hall and the title belong to Beth, and marrying me won't change that, Frederick! You've inherited a comfortable fortune and you needn't worry about running an estate or sitting in Parliament or any of the other boring responsibilities that go with the title. So enjoy your life and *leave us alone!*"

His handsome face turned ugly. "My damned uncle tied up my fortune in a trust so that I'm living on a quarterly allowance like a bloody pauper! I'm Kelham of Kelham Hall and I deserve better!"

Her stomach knotted as he revealed his weakness and greed. Those traits hadn't been visible when they'd first met. She'd been too young and foolish to see beneath his amusing surface.

As she edged slowly back to the far end of the balcony, she had horrific visions of what it would be like to be his wife. He would take over Kelham Hall and invite hordes of his drinking and gambling friends. He'd find ways to skim money from the estate, not caring if he destroyed what had taken generations to build. And he'd surely continue his quest to have Beth declared his illegitimate daughter rather than Philip's legitimate heir so the title would come to him.

His voice coaxing again, he followed her, keeping too close for comfort. "You're a smart girl, Jessie. When you think about it, you'll see what a fine plan this is. We'll rule at Kelham together and you'll have a real man in your bed. Philip was a good old fellow, but you can't claim that he was much of a lover."

Her fear changed to swift rage. "You weak, contemptible swine! Philip was a hundred times the man you are, both in and out of bed!"

Frederick laughed. "I've always liked your spirit, Jess. It's why you were such a great mistress. But sheathe your pretty claws and accept the inevitable, because if you don't marry me, you'll regret it."

"Rot in *hell*, Frederick!" she said in a low, dangerous voice. "I'll never marry you. Stay away from us, and do not *ever* set foot at Kelham Hall again! I have powerful friends and I won't hesitate to ask for their aid if you try to cause us trouble."

"How long will they be your friends if they know the truth about you?" he sneered. "That you're a whore and Beth is my daughter. Anyone seeing us together will recognize the truth. She looks like me and she was born barely nine months after you and I parted. I've made all the preparations to file a suit to gain custody of the brat. I've already talked to a Chancery judge, and he said it won't be difficult to be declared her legal guardian." His voice dropped to a hiss. "Accept my generous proposal, Jessie, or I'll ruin you and take your daughter. I swear it!"

She tried to dart around him to escape, but he grabbed her into a hard embrace. "Damn, I've missed you," he breathed before his mouth crushed down on hers, his tongue hot and wet as he tried to force it between her lips.

Revolted, she managed to twist her head away, but he laughed again. Catching her left hand, he pressed it against his hard erection. "Remember how much you liked that? Show me again."

Furious, she shoved her hand lower and grabbed his testicles, squeezing with all her strength. He gave an agonized squawk and fell back toward the railing. She bolted around him toward escape, but she couldn't outrun his furious words. "You *bitch!*" he swore. "You and your brat will pay for this!"

Before he could say more, Jessie darted through the doors into the ballroom. The laughter and music were jarring, as if she'd fallen into a different, happier world.

She closed the doors behind her and leaned back against them for a moment, bending her head as she fought the desire to vomit. She must collect herself before anyone noticed that she looked like a madwoman.

Relax your expression. Smile. Stop panting like a frightened hare. As her heart slowed to a more normal rate, she cursed herself for making a bad situation worse. Believing that Frederick had accepted Beth's inheritance had been foolish on her part. He cared only for himself, and she feared that a desire for revenge might overcome his natural sloth.

Would he be able to convince a court that he was Beth's father and should have custody of her? Marcus Harkin hadn't thought so, but he hadn't said it was impossible either. Dear God, how long would Beth survive if she was in Frederick's hands?

Jessie wanted to seize her daughter and run so far and fast they'd never be found, but Marcus had been right about the dangers of that. Jessie should have continued with her plan to marry a man of power and influence who would protect Beth. Might she be able to convince Sir Harold Truscott that he needed her for a wife? She'd consider that later when she wasn't so upset.

She raised her head and brushed down her skirts, then moved away from the French doors. She needed to disappear before Frederick returned to the ballroom. Would the Ashtons mind if she asked to have their coachman take her home? She would settle for waiting quietly in the coach until her friends were ready to leave.

Her restless gaze searched the room—and stopped when it reached the tall, compelling figure of Lord Romayne.

Chapter 14

Jessie caught her breath when Lord Romayne turned and their gazes struck and held. As Mariah had said, the saintly Dr. Herbert fit her requirements perfectly, except for age, and that was hardly his fault. For Beth's sake, she'd overlook his saintly tendencies, and the dangers of him coming to know more about her.

His eyes narrowed as they stared at each other, intensity pulsing across the width of the ballroom. He didn't look pleased to see her, but neither did he look as if he despised her.

She'd been attracted to him from the beginning, and abruptly she recognized that her attraction had counted against him because her judgment in men had always been terrible when desire was aroused. But she was older and wiser now, and he was very different from the men who'd given her grief in the past. He was much more like Philip than like Frederick. Besides being a lord in his own right, he was friends with Kirkland and Ashton and

Randall, all powerful men who could help protect Beth if necessary.

It was time to risk all. Hands shaking, she started across the ballroom, dodging dancers doing a reel. He watched, his face coolly impassive, only his eyes sharp with curiosity. And wariness, too, she suspected. She couldn't blame him for that.

She halted within touching distance, her pulse hammering. "Lord Romayne." She moistened her dry lips. "May I speak with you? In private?"

He frowned, but said courteously, "As you wish, Lady Kelham. I believe there are some quieter rooms off that corridor."

"Thank you." She tucked her hand in his elbow and felt a shiver run through him. Or perhaps that was her own reaction to touching him.

The second door on the corridor was open and revealed a small, empty reception room. Jessie gave thanks that most of the guests were dancing or demolishing the buffet in the supper room, so they had this place to themselves. Lord Romayne detached himself and turned to her. His impassive face showed none of the warmth she'd seen on earlier occasions. "How may I be of service, Lady Kelham?"

"This is . . . difficult to say." She'd rejected his offer of courtship, and he'd rejected her suggestion of an affair, yet the reason for both offers smoldered between them, mindless and urgent.

"Do you have an ailment you'd like advice about?" he asked in the helpful but neutral tones of a doctor.

He thought she wanted free medical advice? "Nothing of that sort," she replied. "This is quite a different matter." And it was going to be even harder than she'd expected.

Nervously she brushed at her hair, loosening a dark glossy strand to fall along her throat. It was unintended, but she was gratified to see how his gaze became riveted on that untamed lock of hair. This could only work if he desired her enough to overcome all the reasons he should run in the opposite direction.

"I wish to invoke a woman's right to change my mind." She began pacing around the room with small, tense steps. "A fortnight ago, you expressed an interest in courting me. I refused, saying that I didn't think we would suit."

"I was there," he said dryly. "I remember. I thought you covered our differences quite thoroughly. What changed your mind?"

She smiled crookedly. "My head was trying to be wise, but my heart has drowned it out. I've been thinking of you ever since we met. I would be deeply honored by your courtship, and should you offer for me, I swear I would do my best to be the kind of wife you want and need."

Her words visibly rocked him, but he said coolly, "Perhaps we should stay with heads ruling our hearts. We barely know each other, and what we know doesn't suggest that marriage would be wise."

"I've never been particularly wise," she said wryly. "Except for choosing my late husband, Philip. Marrying him was the wisest thing I've ever done. I believe marrying you would also be wise."

"But would it be wise for me to marry you?" His mouth twisted. "That was your objection before."

"That part hasn't changed," she said honestly. "But you were right that we should take the time to know each other better."

"So we can hurt each other more?" he asked in an edged voice.

She inhaled sharply. "I hope not. Isn't the fact that we can hurt each other a sign of caring?"

"Perhaps. But not a very encouraging sign."

Despairing, she wondered if she'd already destroyed her chance with him. She must play her only trump card. "There is one thing we undeniably have in common, and it's powerful and very real."

She closed the distance between them. When she was only a step away, she halted and raised a tentative hand. "I suspect desire is why we've been feeling each other's sharp edges up until now."

Her fingers skimmed his high cheekbone and drifted through his bronze-blond hair while he stood rigid. Strong bones and deep-set gray eyes formed a handsome face where lines of seriousness were balanced by lines of laughter. If a man's character was written on his face, this man was strong and intelligent and kind.

"Daniel," she whispered, and her hand curved around his nape as she drew his head down for a gentle, exploratory kiss.

When he'd kissed her the first time, it had been fire and frustration and had driven them both half-mad. Now she offered softness and promise, the better parts of herself. She drifted forward until her breasts pressed against his chest. He had a wonderful strong body, one she wanted to explore. But first she must persuade him.

"Jessie." He made a choked sound and his arms came hard around her, one at her back, the other circling her waist. He locked her tight against him as if he were a dying man and she was the water of life. "You drown my senses and my wits!"

His lips opened and the kiss deepened. After a wave of weak-kneed relief, she fell into their embrace, savoring his strength and warmth and the uniqueness that was neither doctor nor lord, but quintessentially Daniel.

She loved the feel of his quickening heartbeat and the slow caress of one hand over her hip. Why had she resisted him when this was so clearly right? The question faded away as she let him drown her senses and wits in turn. She wanted this embrace to last forever. . . .

"Merciful heavens!"

The shocked exclamation in a woman's voice jarred Jessie like an ice-water plunge. Dear God, how could she have forgotten where they were?

She jerked away from Daniel and spun toward the door. A stiff, white-haired woman with an expression of malicious outrage was glaring at them through a diamond-studded lorgnette. "*She's* no better than she should be," the woman spat out, "but I would have expected better of you, Lord Romayne." Her disdainful gaze rested on Jessie. "Though men are so weak. Easy prey for trollops."

Other guests were gathering behind the woman and were watching with expressions of shock or distaste. Dear God, there was Frederick, a vicious smirk on his face! He was surely contemplating Jessie's ruin and an easy grant of custody because Beth's mother was a slut.

The thought galvanized Jessie's petrified brain. "I'm so very sorry!" she said in a breathless voice. "We meant no offense. But Lord Romayne and I rather forgot ourselves because we've just agreed to wed."

What? Daniel stared at Jessie, wondering if he'd heard correctly. She was gazing up at him, a frantic plea in her mesmerizing eyes. Whatever was going on with her was not trivial.

This must be sorted out, but not in public. He wrapped an arm around her shoulders. "Indeed, we owe you all an apology. Our betrothal is such an unexpected joy." He did his best to keep any hint of sarcasm from his voice.

Kirkland appeared at the back of the gathering throng, clearing a path by sheer force of personality. Laurel was on his arm, looking thoroughly bemused.

The pair of them entered the room and Kirkland offered Daniel his hand. "Congratulations! Ever since you spoke to me of Lady Kelham, I've been hoping for your success." He gave Jessie a glance that was ironic but not unkind.

Laurel stepped forward and gave Jessie a light kiss. "I am so glad that we are going to be sisters, Jessie," she said warmly. As always, her presence spread peace.

With family acceptance of the betrothal, the mood changed from condemnation to best wishes. Daniel endured it as long as he could before saying, "Pray excuse us. I'm going to take Lady Kelham for a walk in your garden, Lady Dunhaven. We have much to discuss."

Jessie looked justly wary, but she fluttered her

lashes appropriately. "What a lovely idea, my dear! The gardens look so romantic."

She certainly could act. How the devil was he going to learn the truth from her? Assuming there was truth to be found.

Laurel tugged off her wrap, a soft Indian shawl in rich shades of gold and dark red, and offered it to Jessie. "Take this. It's cool out and I don't want my brother's bride to take a chill."

Jessie accepted the shawl, her expression surprised and moved. "Thank you so much. I look forward to getting to know you better, Lady Kirkland."

"Laurel." She smiled warmly; then she and Kirkland left the room.

Daniel draped the shawl around Jessie's shoulders with a proper show of solicitude. The rich pattern and colors contrasted dramatically with her black mourning gown. Then he took a firm grip on her elbow and maneuvered them from the reception room and downstairs into the night.

The cool air was bracing. As they followed the crushed oyster shell path that led into the gardens, Daniel released his hold on Jessie's elbow. When she gave him an inquiring glance, he explained, "This may be the most important conversation of my life, and it's best if I try to be rational. When I'm touching you, reason goes out the window."

"I tend to feel the same about you, and heaven knows that we need to be rational!" She looked back at the house, where lights shone from many of the windows and figures could be seen peering out. "I wonder how many people are watching us."

"Anyone who can find a suitable window, I imagine. We'll be a source of exciting gossip for at least a day, maybe even two," he said cynically. "Lady Dunhaven is surely happy for the spice we've added to her ball."

Jessie sighed. "I would have preferred not to be so interesting a guest."

A stone archway led into the main gardens. The waxing moon cast enough light to see dimly and made it easy to follow the light-colored oyster shell pathways. The lush, faintly decadent scents of late-season flowers and bushes couldn't mask the misleading innocence of Jessie's delicate violet perfume.

Daniel's head said he should walk away and repudiate their alleged betrothal in the morning, but his heart—and other parts of his body—weren't convinced. As they moved through the geometrical pattern of the parterre, he said, "In darkness, it's easier to speak the truth. Will you tell me what that was all about? I don't think you were trying to trap me into marriage, though if that was your intention, you won't succeed. I'm perfectly willing to be ungentlemanly and jilt you if we can't come to an understanding."

"I like that you won't be a prisoner to social expectations," she said seriously. "I've always thought it mad that two people should be forced into matrimony if they're caught in a compromising situation. Though since I'm a widow, I don't suppose that was likely here. Your reputation is good enough that you'd be forgiven if you announce that we're not betrothed, and I'll be considered the villain of the piece."

"Because you're a wicked woman?"

"Exactly." She shrugged and turned a corner, the oyster shells crunching softly under her evening slippers. "I've never even met the woman who was denouncing me, yet she was quite sure what I am."

"I need to know just how wicked you are, Jessie. Assuming you are wicked. So far, that's only hearsay." Strange how directly he could speak to her. Was that an aspect of the physical attraction between them, or something else entirely? "We must take this time to learn about each other. I need the truth about you, just as you need it about me."

They'd walked half a dozen more steps before she said soberly, "There are things I will not discuss, but I swear I won't lie. Where do you want me to start?"

Learning about her past might remove some of her tantalizing aura of mystery, he thought, allowing reason to return. "Where are you from?"

"Like you, I'm from the West Country. I've been in Bristol, so if you think I look familiar, that's why." She glanced up at him, her heart-shaped face ivory pale in the moonlight. "I didn't live in Kent until I married Philip. You would have been long gone from the Westerfield Academy by then."

He nodded at the confirmation of his guesses. "What about your family? You said your father was a vicar. Was that true?"

"Yes," she said reluctantly. "Apart from Philip, you're the only person I've ever told. I wonder why I did? I try not to think of my father. Ever."

"People tend to talk to me," he replied. "It's a function of both my callings, I suppose."

"I think it has more to do with you personally than the fact that you're an ordained clergyman. My father was revered for his public piety, but a meaner, more intolerant representative of the

Church would be impossible to find," she said bluntly. "He gave God a very bad name. My mother died when I was young. I have few memories of her, but my father told me often how much I looked like her, and that was proof of my wicked nature."

He winced at the vivid pain in her voice. "No wonder you despise vicars. Most are not like him."

"They can't be, or no one would ever set foot in a church," she said tartly.

"Did you run away and become an actress to get away from him?"

She hesitated, and he guessed she was deciding how much to tell him. "It wasn't a direct path. I ran away from home to marry my lover."

So Philip wasn't her first husband. "Was that an improvement on living under your father's roof?"

"Not really. I was glad to be away from my father, but the marriage was a great mistake. I was much too young and innocent." She bent and picked a pale flower beside the path, twirling the stem gently. "My husband was young, and . . . not innocent. After his death, I was penniless and I had to find a way to support myself. In desperation, I walked into the Theatre Royal in York and asked for work. Because of my looks, I was taken on and given minor parts, particularly ones that showed off my legs."

Daniel's gaze dropped involuntarily to her legs, which were completely covered by heavy folds of black fabric. But he suspected that they were as perfect as the rest of her. "I'm sure you were good for the theater's business, and you received the kind of offers actresses routinely receive."

"Oh, yes. But I was fortunate because the theater owner put me under his personal protection."

His mouth tightened. Well, he'd wanted the truth. "I see."

"Actually, you don't." Their path opened into a hedged square with a fountain splashing softly in the center. Jessie sat on one of the benches facing the fountain, her skirts drifting gracefully around her ankles. "The owner preferred men to women. It was an open secret among theater people, but as you know, such behavior is against the law."

"A hanging offense," Daniel said as he sat beside her, as far from her as the bench would allow. Darkness was good for speaking truths, and it also paradoxically made him even more aware of her intoxicating physical presence. "Though mercifully that's seldom invoked. So he flaunted you as his mistress to conceal his true preferences."

"He was kind and amusing, so the arrangement worked well for some time."

Darkness might encourage truth, but there was also dangerous intimacy in the night air. Unable to see her clearly, he'd become acutely aware of her scent, of the richness of her low voice. "What happened then?"

"I met Frederick Kelham at the theater," she said in a flat voice. "He was a charming, handsome young gentleman, owner of a manor near York, heir to a barony, and he seemed to dote on me. I . . . I very much wanted a man to dote on me."

"So you became his mistress." Daniel's voice was quiet, without condemnation.

"He asked me to marry him, and I accepted." Her voice was bitter. "I was older, I should have been wiser, but once again, passion scrambled my wits.

We were betrothed and I was a widow, not a young maiden. I behaved . . . foolishly."

"So you anticipated your vows. That's not terribly wicked."

"It was wickedly *stupid!*" she retorted. "He said he was going to take me to meet his uncle. I thought Frederick wanted Philip's blessing on our marriage. Instead then . . ." Her voice choked off.

He wanted to draw her into his arms to soothe that raw pain, but that would shatter his fragile control. He settled for taking her hand, warming her cold fingers in his clasp. "Frederick did something unforgivable?"

In a low, strained voice, she whispered, "He ordered me to seduce Philip."

Chapter 15

Daniel stared at Jessie's bent head, appalled that she'd been treated like a whore by a man she trusted and wanted to marry. "Why did he ask you to do such a thing?"

"He hoped his uncle would increase his allowance," she said wearily. "Frederick was extravagant, and the income from his estate and a modest quarterly allowance from Philip weren't enough for him. I realized then that he'd never really wanted to marry me. He just wanted to use me to get more money from his uncle."

Daniel shook his head. "Frederick sounds incredibly stupid. Lord Kelham had the reputation of an honorable man. Surely he would be appalled if his nephew's betrothed tried to seduce him."

"Frederick claimed no man could resist me, so of course I'd succeed." Her hand tightened on Daniel's. "His thinking was very muddled, but I think he planned to cast me as a wicked, faithless woman in the hopes that his uncle would pay him to end the engagement or buy me off or some such. He didn't know Philip at all."

"Those without integrity don't usually understand those who have it," Daniel observed. "Obviously his plan didn't succeed."

"I was horrified when Frederick told me what he wanted to do. Philip was so kind and dignified, and he'd welcomed me as his future niece even though I was an actress with no background. He was a gentleman, and Frederick was a *pimp*."

"You ended your betrothal then?"

She nodded. "I told him he disgusted me and I ran away. Philip found me sobbing in the garden. One rather like this, actually. Strange how life works."

"Did you tell him what Frederick had planned?"

"I was tempted, but . . . Philip loved his nephew almost like a son. I didn't want him to know how vile Frederick could be. Assuming he believed me, which he might not have since I was just a wicked woman." Her fingers clenched Daniel's hand. "So I just said Frederick had come to believe we wouldn't suit, and I'd released him from our betrothal because I knew he was right, but naturally I was sad. It was the best explanation I could come up with on a moment's notice."

She'd been wise not to slander Frederick to his uncle. Had she realized how her dignified behavior would appeal to a man like Philip Kelham? "So Philip comforted you, and it turned out to be true that no man could resist you."

Her head shot up. "Do you think I planned that?" she asked, anger in her voice.

"No, though perhaps that's more proof of your magical power over men," he said wryly. "But from what I've heard about Frederick Kelham, it's easy to believe he was both stupid and venal. Did you know he's been going around London telling people that he's the father of your daughter as well as the true heir to the barony?"

Jessie made a sound like a hiss. "He has been claiming that since Philip's will was read. He's another guest at this ball, and earlier in the evening he cornered me on the balcony and said that if I didn't marry him, he'd file suit to get himself declared Beth's father and her guardian." Her voice broke. "He wants to take Beth away from me!"

Daniel gave a low whistle. "I think I understand the events of this evening a good deal better now. Is this why you sought me out and asked me to renew my courtship offer?"

"Yes," she whispered. "I hope you don't hate me. I came to London to find a husband who will love Beth like she was his own, and who has the power to protect her from Frederick."

"And surely to protect you as well?"

"Beth matters much more. She is the joy of my life, as she was of Philip's. I would do anything to protect her."

"Including marry a man you don't care for?" Daniel said dryly. This conversation was straining his tolerance and understanding to the limit.

"Of course it must be a man I care for, and one who cares for Beth, but I wanted a husband who is older and wiser. Less prone to anger and jealousy," she said, her tone wry. "My experiences with younger men haven't been good. That's why I wouldn't consider you as a possibility before."

"But tonight you were desperate enough to reconsider." His mouth curved. "I don't think of myself as overly proud, which is good, because what pride I have is taking a beating."

"You wanted the truth," she reminded him. "When I escaped Frederick's clutches back into the ballroom, I saw you and realized that you were the right man in all ways. I also realized that you probably despised me, but . . . I had to see if I could change your mind. Which brings us here."

"Your claiming we were betrothed was an interesting surprise," he remarked. "Though I suppose it was the only thing that could save us both from scandal when we were caught kissing."

"I was terrified because Frederick was in the group that gathered at the door. He was gloating because I'd just given him ammunition to gain custody of Beth."

"*Is* he her father?"

Jessie hesitated. "Almost certainly not."

He tried to see her face more clearly in the darkness. "That's an interesting answer. I would expect a flat denial."

"I promised you honesty." She drew a shuddering breath. "When I broke things off with Frederick, he . . . he raped me before I could get away. Since it was unexpected, I hadn't taken any precautions to prevent pregnancy. I suppose that gives him some grounds for thinking he might be Beth's father."

Daniel sucked in his breath, hating the thought of Jessie being assaulted by a vicious brute. "The devil you say! And you didn't tell his uncle?"

"I could see no point to it. If Philip believed me, he would have been devastated, and if he didn't believe me, everything would have become much, much worse. Instead, he said that Frederick was a fool not to marry me, but Philip was no fool, and he'd be greatly honored if I would consider an offer from him. I'd liked him from the moment I met him, and he seemed like a . . . a safe harbor." She drew a shuddering breath. "I wanted so much to be *safe*."

"You married very quickly?"

"A week later, by special license." She looked away, embarrassed. "But I had my courses in that week, so I don't think it's possible that Frederick could be Beth's father. She was born a little early, though, which clouds the issue. She looks like Philip, but he and Frederick share a family resemblance." Her hand knotted around Daniel's.

"She is surely Philip's daughter," he said firmly. "Born in wedlock a reasonable interval after your marriage, and fully acknowledged by Lord Kelham. It sounds as if Frederick was trying to intimidate you into marriage because he knows he can't win on the facts. Particularly since you've demonstrated that you have powerful friends."

"I hope to heaven you're right," she whispered. "I daren't take risks with Beth."

"I'm right." He squeezed her hand, again controlling the impulse to draw her into a comforting embrace. "I'm sorry to have asked you so many painful questions. What I see here in the darkness is not a wicked woman, but a brave woman and a passionately devoted mother."

"More desperate than brave. But enough about me. You came to London in search of a wife, you said. What sort of woman are you seeking?"

He tried to remember what he'd said to Laurel. That seemed a lifetime ago. Now Jessie filled his imagination. "I wanted a mature woman, not a giggling girl. Sense is more important than beauty. In fact, I specifically did not want a beauty since such women can be demanding."

"Well, I'm no giggling girl. That's something," she observed. "And I don't believe I'm particularly demanding. What other requirements do you have?"

"A woman capable of overseeing my properties, since I'm more interested in being a surgeon than in breeding sheep or raising crops." He studied her pure, pale profile. "I don't suppose you've had experience as a land steward."

"Actually, I have," Jessie replied. "I'm interested in everything, and because Philip loved Kelham Hall, he was happy to teach me about estate management. As his health failed, I took over more and more of the work. I don't claim to be an expert, but I know what needs to be done and what questions to ask."

"That would be really helpful," he said, surprised and pleased. "Would you object to a husband who continued in the low, ungentlemanly profession of surgery?"

"Why would I object to a husband who helps people? Such behavior should be encouraged." She chuckled. "Plus, if you're busy, it keeps you out from underfoot. But what of you, my lord Romayne? I've done most of the talking, Now it's your turn. What has shaped you into a saint?"

He frowned. "I wish you wouldn't call me that. I'm no saint. Helping those in need is very rewarding. I don't deserve special credit."

"Careful," she warned. "You're adding humility to your other virtues."

He had to laugh. "That wasn't my intention. My life has been mercifully less dramatic than yours. I was born with an interest in medicine and healing, and I spent as much time as I could with the area physicians and bonesetters and surgeons. My father was the local squire, so they were willing to let me trail around behind them."

"The doctors and midwives I've known seem to share that early passion," Jessie said thoughtfully. "Born to heal."

"I've found the same. Doctoring is hard work, sometimes heartbreaking, and occasionally dangerous," Daniel mused. "It's a calling, not a mere job. It's also quite unfashionable. My parents were appalled when I said at quite a tender age that I wanted to go to Edinburgh to study surgery."

"Is that how you came to attend the Westerfield Academy?"

"Oh, no," he said with amusement. "They didn't believe I was seriously interested in medicine. They were far more worried by my interest in religion. Naturally my parents encouraged a proper belief in the Church of England, with regular attendance and donations to the deserving poor.

"But there was a Methodist chapel in the village,

and I liked the congregation there much better. They improved lives in practical ways, like teaching reading and writing, and they didn't worry about whether the poor were deserving or undeserving. I taught some classes myself, though I don't think my parents ever learned that. It's a pleasure to teach those who hunger to learn."

"So you were packed off to Lady Agnes to be turned into a proper, boring English gentleman." There was a smile in her voice. "I'm glad it didn't work."

"So am I." At first he'd resented being sent there instead of a larger school, but it hadn't taken him long to realize how well Lady Agnes and her students suited him.

"Now it's your turn to answer painful questions, my lord," Jessie said, her amusement vanishing. "What should I know about you? What joys and tragedies have shaped you into the man you are today?"

He owed her the kind of honesty she'd given him. "Though I'm an ordained minister, I've never been a proper cleric. To please my parents, I was willing to go to Oxford to study for the Church since philosophy and theology interested me. They thought that would keep me busy and respectable until it was time to take over my father's duties at Belmond Manor." He'd drifted along comfortably for several years. He hadn't even realized he was drifting. "Then everything changed."

"In what ways?"

"I brought my good friend Kirkland home for a visit and he and my little sister went mad and married, which was unsettling in several ways." He fell silent, battling old pain. "And . . . not long after, my fiancée, Rose, died suddenly when I was up at Oxford."

"I'm so sorry," Jessie said with genuine sympathy. "That must have been devastating. What was she like?"

"Sweet and golden and sunny-natured." Her image seared through his mind, a laughing young girl who would never grow old. "Our family estates adjoined and we grew up together. It was the most natural thing in the world to imagine that we'd marry and live the same comfortable country life of our parents. But then she died."

He fell silent so long that Jessie prompted, "And?"

"I've never told this to anyone, even Laurel," he said slowly, "but I've always wondered if I could have saved Rose if I'd been there. She died of a fierce, sudden fever. There are things that could have been done that weren't. Perhaps . . ." His voice ran down.

Jessie drew their clasped hands to her heart. "And ever since, you've been trying to save as many people as possible because you couldn't save her?"

He sighed. "Perhaps. I might not have been able to help her, but I'll never know. Yet the biggest change came when Laurel left Kirkland. She refused to say why. For the first and only time in my life, I was tempted to murder someone, even though Kirkland and I had been the closest of friends. What made it infinitely worse was when my parents disowned Laurel and refused to let her come home."

Jessie gasped. "How could they do such a thing to their own daughter?"

"I couldn't believe it either." He grimaced. "I've since realized they were very self-absorbed, and didn't see either of their children as individuals. They were proud of me because I reflected well on them. They didn't have much interest in Laurel, but were delighted when she secured an earl as a husband. Which made it all the worse when she left him, even though he made a point of saying it was all his fault."

"And was it?" Jessie asked, intrigued.

"Yes, though I didn't find out the cause of their separation until years later. At the time, though, what mattered was how furious I was with my parents for disowning Laurel. She'd been the sweetest and most loving daughter imaginable, and then to be abandoned!" Even now, it made his blood boil.

"So you opened an infirmary together?"

"Eventually. First we set up a joint household. I had a modest inheritance and she had a generous income from Kirkland, which made that easy. She ran the household while I studied medicine and surgery until I'd learned enough not to be a menace to my patients. Zion House was her particular project, but we worked together on whatever needed doing. The fact that I'm ordained means that I'm able to perform christenings and weddings and funerals, which has been convenient."

"How did your parents feel about that?" Jessie asked curiously. "Did they disown you also?"

"No, though the relationship was strained nearly

to the breaking point." And was never the same again. Daniel regretted his parents' premature deaths, but he didn't mourn them. Which wasn't very Christian of him, but pretending otherwise would be a lie. Yet in a curious way, his parents' intolerance had benefited him because it led to his decision to study medicine, and laid the foundation for his close relationship with his sister. "They wanted me to be a respectable landowner. I learned the basic skills growing up at Belmond Manor, but the prospect is like being thrown in prison."

"And now you're responsible for not only your family estate, but all Romayne properties. No wonder you want a really good manager to oversee them all. Luckily, such people can be hired."

"Or married, perhaps." His brows arched. "Do you enjoy estate management?"

"I do," she admitted. "I rather like giving orders, and I like the satisfactions of a well-run farm with prosperous people living on it. But a marriage is more than working well together." She turned and raised a hand to his face, her fingers lightly brushing his lips. "It's also trust. Intimacy. Passion."

He kissed her fingertips. "Do we trust each other, my lady?"

"I trust that you will look out for Beth, and that is my most important requirement." She twined her fingers into his hair. "I hope you trust that I was telling you the truth when I said I'll do my best to be a good and faithful wife."

"I do." He touched her cheek, unable to resist her smooth, sumptuous skin.

"Intimacy comes with time and talk." She pressed

her cheek against his hand. "Sharing bed and board and passion."

"Passion, my lady, is easy." No longer able to resist, he swooped her onto his lap. Her warm, feminine softness intoxicated him.

Passion was *very* easy.

Chapter 16

Calm reason dissolved as Jessie settled in Daniel's lap. His embrace warmed her as no Indian shawl could. Silently he buried his face in the angle between her head and neck, his pulse pounding. She closed her eyes with a sigh of relief, feeling like a sailing ship that had found a safe harbor as she learned the strength and shape of his muscular male body. Powerful, uniquely himself.

"I love holding and being held by you. Did we need all that rational talk?" she breathed. "We keep coming back to passion, which is more honest than mere words can ever be."

He exhaled, his breath warmly tickling her ear. "I'd like to think the talk has helped build a bridge between us. I've wanted you since we met, but marriage requires more."

She exhaled softly at his words. "Are we to marry, then?"

His caressing hands stilled. After a dozen heartbeats, he said more soberly, "If you truly want to marry, yes. But I really don't think Frederick Kelham can harm you and Beth legally, so perhaps you don't need a powerful protector after all."

Chilled, she lifted her head and tried to make out his expression in the dark. "Does this mean you'd rather not marry me? I put you in an impossible situation tonight, but if we let a few weeks go by without an announcement, we can then tell anyone interested that we decided we wouldn't suit. That shouldn't be too scandalous."

"Perhaps we're not as ill-suited as I thought. Certainly we've learned more about each other in the last hour than we would in a whole season of balls and routs and Venetian breakfasts," he said thoughtfully. "You're not the pampered beauty I assumed you were, and I do hope you've stopped thinking of me as saintly. Whether we share enough common ground, I don't know. I think that marriage is always the triumph of hope over fear. But I do want to marry you, if you're sure for both yourself and Beth's sake."

She drew a somewhat shaky breath. "I'm as sure as I can be. Granted, I would never have considered marriage so soon if not for Frederick's threats. But having met you, I don't want to lose you because the timing isn't ideal."

"In that case . . ." His mouth found her, intimate and commanding.

Jessie had almost forgotten how wondrous passion could be. Now that they'd decided to marry, she let her early doubts dissolve so she could be swept along by the rare mutual passion they'd been granted. Lips and tongue and touch, and hot, hard demand in an endless, luxuriant kiss.

He held her crosswise on his lap with one of his arms around her back for support. That left his other hand free to caress. His hand slid under the shawl to cup her breast. As he thumbed the peak, she made a purring sound in her throat and pressed into his palm, wishing the layers of corset and petticoat and gown would magically vanish so they could be skin-to-skin.

His hand stroked down across her abdomen, warm and enthralling, along her hip, coming to rest on her knee. Feverishly she rolled her hips in his lap. Every fiber of her body was in motion, urgently alive.

His hand slid under the hem of her gown and found her bare knee, his thumb stroking her inner thigh. She gasped and pulled her mouth away to say, "The ground. Now! It will be better."

He froze and she felt tension vibrating through him. Then he dropped her hem and immobilized her in his embrace. "I've waited this long," he said, his voice shaking. "I intend to wait for a proper bed."

Jarred into remembering where they were, she swallowed hard and did her best to leash her desire. "I suppose you're right, but how long do we have to wait?"

"We're in London, so a special license will be easy to obtain." He stood and extended his hand to help her to her feet. "Three days? Before our friends all leave London."

"I think I can survive three days without going up in flames," she said wryly.

"It will be a long three days." He helped her brush down her skirts and straighten her gown. "I need to spend some time with Beth so she can get used to me. Shall I call in the morning and the three of us can take a drive in the park?"

"Beth will like that. We can also decide basic issues, such as where we'll live."

He placed a warm hand on the small of her back and guided her toward the house, oyster shells crunching beneath their feet. "That's a complicated question. You have Kelham Hall, I have Belmond Manor and several Romayne properties I've not even visited yet. I thought about going to Castle Romayne when I left London since it's the family seat. Would you be willing to consider that as a wedding trip?"

"That would be interesting, but let's put aside all practical thoughts till tomorrow." She squeezed his arm. "Tonight I just want to *be*."

Further tidying was required when they entered the house. Luckily no one was in the foyer. She brushed crushed grass from her skirt. "Good that we're both wearing black. It shows less of what we've been doing."

"I think most of the other guests will be indulgent since we're just betrothed." He crooked his elbow so she could take it. "The ball must be almost over. Shall we ascend and show all those interested people that we've come to terms?"

She tucked her hand around his arm. "In particular the loathsome Frederick. Perhaps now he'll accept that it's time to give up."

"We may hope." Daniel's tone was not convinced. Neither was Jessie, but she couldn't help but hope.

The musicians were striking up a waltz when they entered the ballroom. Mischief in his voice, Daniel said, "Shall we announce that we're in harmony by dancing this waltz?"

Jessie's first thought was for her state of mourning. Dancing would be scandalous.

Her second thought was *yes*! "Please! I love dancing, my lord Romayne."

Smiling, Daniel drew her into waltz position and they swung into the music. His expression was positively lighthearted. She'd seen him smile and even occasionally laugh, but his underlying seriousness was always present.

Not tonight. He was happy, and it showed. A lock of dark blond hair fell across his forehead and he looked almost boyish. Yet with his height and broad shoulders, he was all desirable male. The passion they'd suppressed in the garden thrummed between them, deep and intoxicating. Only a few more days . . .

He was a superb dancer, with a skill born of practice, not just childhood lessons. Had he loved dancing with his lost Rose, then put it aside in favor of more serious pursuits after her death? That seemed like something he'd do. Saints weren't usually known for being lighthearted.

She hadn't been very lighthearted for a while herself, but tonight, she'd enjoy the magic of hope. She was putting herself and her daughter into the hands of a good man. Heavens, he'd be her third husband! She should have learned a few things by now.

Only her first marriage was the result of fervent declarations of love, and that had been a disaster. Philip had taught her that it was better to start with liking, respect, and a mutual desire to marry. That would give love a chance to grow. She and Daniel weren't in love, but they liked each other, and there was certainly attraction. That was enough.

Daniel spun her around and she caught a glimpse of Lady Julia watching with a bright, approving expression. There were indulgent smiles on most other faces, but there were exceptions. The woman who had discovered them kissing was purse-mouthed and furious. No sign of Frederick, which was a relief.

Mariah gave Jessie a mischievous thumbs-up behind her husband's back. Jessie threw her head back and laughed, held secure in Daniel's strong arms as the ballroom lights spun around her. Tomorrow she'd worry about the changes and challenges of her life. But tonight, she *danced*.

Frederick Kelham managed to control his furious curses until the bitch and her latest gull had gone back into the house. It had been clear to anyone with eyes that when she'd claimed Romayne was going to marry her, it was the first Romayne had heard of it.

When he'd hauled Jezebel outside to talk to her, Frederick had shadowed them, sure that Romayne would denounce her. But no, the fool was another to fall for the bitch's wiles. He really was going to marry her. The first thing she'd make him do was apply for guardianship of the brat. Romayne had powerful friends, too. Every time Frederick saw him, he was with a duke or an earl. Worse, his sister was married to Kirkland, who was known as a dangerous bastard.

Fighting down his fury, Frederick considered

what else he'd heard. Interesting that she'd been married even before she'd come to York. She'd never told *him* that. Tonight she'd been vague about the first husband. Maybe he hadn't died. Maybe she'd just run away and left her legal husband behind, which would mean her marriage to Uncle Philip was invalid and the brat was illegitimate.

That was probably too much to hope for, but it was worth investigating. He needed to know more about her than that she came from the West Country, though. Had she given Frederick her real name back in York when he'd asked her to marry him? Or had that been another lie? Hard to say, but the name was unusual enough that maybe he could track it down. Worth a try.

Mouth tight, Frederick left the garden and headed for home. He could and would learn more about the scheming slut who'd married his uncle. And when he did, there might be a way to take back what was his.

Laurel waited till the three of them were alone in the Kirkland coach before she pounced. "So you're really going to marry Lady Kelham?"

Daniel settled in the backward-facing seat opposite his sister and her husband. "Apparently." He couldn't help himself, a broad grin spread over his face.

"Is that wise when you've only known her such a short time?"

"How long did you and Kirkland know each other before you were betrothed?" he countered.

Kirkland laughed as he clasped his wife's hand.

"About four hours, as I recall. I might have asked sooner, but I didn't want to look too hasty."

Laurel joined in the laughter. "Point taken. When one feels as we did, the usual measure of time doesn't count. Love isn't very patient."

What would his romantic sister say if Daniel told her that his marriage was not based on love the way hers was? He suspected that one had to be very young to fall in love with that kind of absolute clarity and commitment. He'd loved Rose like that. Laurel and Kirkland had that kind of love also, or it wouldn't have survived their ten-year estrangement.

But that was not a discussion he wanted to have with her. Laurel would be genuinely shocked. She'd probably also lecture him. Better to answer obliquely. "We are old enough to know our own minds, so there's no reason to wait."

Laurel didn't notice what Daniel wasn't saying, but Kirkland gave him a narrow-eyed glance. He noticed, but was less likely to lecture. Probably.

Laurel said, "Lady Kelham seems very down to earth even though she's so amazingly beautiful."

"Her beauty has been more bane than blessing," Daniel said seriously. "That's made her practical."

"You were quite sure you didn't want to marry a beautiful woman," Laurel said mischievously. "Is it rational to change your mind?"

"How often have you known me to be irrational?" he asked, amused.

Laurel's brows drew together. "I can't think of any occasions offhand."

"Sadly true," Daniel said with self-deprecating humor. "Blameless rectitude is rather dull. I think it's time I did something deeply irrational."

"Marriage is a high-stakes game for experimenting with irrationality," Kirkland said dryly. "Have you learned more about Lady Kelham's origins?"

"Enough. There's still much I don't know, but we covered the important points." At least, he hoped so.

"I find a certain sisterly pleasure in seeing how you ignored your original list of requirements for a wife," Laurel said. "You didn't insist on a woman of average looks, so I presume you also abandoned your plan to marry a land steward."

"Not true. As her husband's health declined, Jessie began helping with the estate management. Not only is she knowledgeable, but she actually enjoys such work."

"You really did find your dream woman!" Laurel said admiringly. "And she has an adorable daughter as a bonus. When do you plan to marry?"

"Very soon. There's no point in waiting, so I'll get a special license. Kirkland, will you stand up with me?"

"I'd be honored. I presume you'd prefer a church rather than a service here or at Ashton House." Kirkland chuckled. "You're both currently residing in the parish of St. George's, Hanover Square, which you might find alarmingly fashionable, but there are other parishes nearby."

Daniel hadn't even thought about that yet. "I'll put that on the list of things Jessie and I need to discuss tomorrow morning."

"Milton Manor might be a pleasant place for a honeymoon," Laurel said. "Since James's seat is in Scotland, he bought the manor as an easy country escape. It's only about an hour from London. Wonderfully private."

"That's a good thought," Kirkland said. "You've both been very busy in London. Milton Manor is peaceful. A place where you can relax and enjoy each other's company without interruption."

"Something else to discuss with Jessie." Daniel frowned. "Does one take a child on one's honeymoon? Marriage is becoming more complicated by the minute!"

"I'd be happy to have Beth for a few days, but I'd have to fight Mariah and Julia for the privilege. They both dote on her." Laurel rested her hand on her expanding abdomen. "I like that our baby will have a sweet girl cousin to look up to."

It was a sharp reminder that marriage wasn't just two people, but two families coming together. If Daniel was making a mistake to marry a woman who still held too many mysteries, the damage would go beyond him and Jessie.

Which was a rational thought. And he still didn't feel the least bit rational where Jessie Kelham was involved.

Chapter 17

Daniel said his good nights and retired to his chamber as soon as they returned to Kirkland House, but he was too excited to sleep. After stripping off his jacket and cravat, he poured a glass of claret and paced the room as he took occasional sips.

His life was about to change drastically. But with Jessie part of it, he was now contemplating his future with anticipation, not dread. Where they'd spend most of their time would be the biggest challenge since Jessie had responsibilities in Kent as he did in Bristol. Not to mention Castle Romayne.

He'd have to establish an infirmary or cottage hospital in each place where he'd spend much time. Most towns and villages needed better medical facilities, so doing that would be a good deed as well as giving him a place to work when he was in residence. The idea was absurd, possible, and invigorating.

After an hour or two of pacing and a second glass

of claret, he was relaxed enough to consider going to bed. Yet after years of being a doctor, he wasn't surprised when a quiet knock sounded on the door. He opened it to find Kirkland, still fully dressed. "Is Laurel unwell?" Daniel asked immediately.

"She's fine, but some midnight medicine is required if you're not too distracted."

"Of course." Daniel reached for his coat. "Where?"

"The patient is here in our kitchen."

"Convenient." Daniel changed his aim from his coat to his medical bag. "How fortunate I am that my brother-in-law lays on medical amusements for the entertainment of his guests. How serious is it?"

"A bullet in the upper arm. Not life-threatening if it doesn't become inflamed, but it needs treatment."

"Do you regularly have wounded men in your kitchen?"

"Not regularly, but it's not unknown." Kirkland led the way down the back stairs to the kitchen. The room was well-lit and a kettle was steaming on the hob. A man with white-blond hair was slumped over in a chair by the scrubbed deal table. His coat had been tossed over another chair and his left shirt sleeve was saturated with blood. A crude bandage had been tied around his upper arm.

Daniel's pace quickened as he crossed the kitchen. The man looked up. He was pale under a tanned complexion, and he had a familiar face. Kirkland said, "I think you'll remember Captain Gordon, though under another name."

Lady Agnes's one failure, alive and relatively well in Kirkland's kitchen. This was possibly the most interesting day of Daniel's life, though he much preferred Jessie's company to Gordon's. "Gordon is actually one of your long string of names, isn't it?" He set his medical bag on the table and pulled out a pair of sharp-edged scissors. "I assumed that if I ever saw you again, it would be on the gallows, but a bullet wound will do."

Gordon gave a crack of laughter. "Trust you to remember all those names, Herbert. Kirkland says you're Romayne now. Now you can be righteous on a larger scale. At school, you did your best to treat me with Christian forbearance while I did my best to make you lose your temper and behave badly."

"Kirkland, I need two basins, one filled with warm water and the other empty. Then some clean rags or towels and some brandy." Daniel carefully cut off the rough bandage. "You didn't quite manage that, Gordon, but you came close. Dare I ask how you came to be here?"

"A while back I ran into our noble schoolmate, the Duke of Ashton, which gave him an opportunity to practice charity." Gordon gasped as the bandage was peeled away.

"By which he means Ashton made him captain of his latest steamship, the *Britannia*," Kirkland said dryly as he poured boiling water into a teapot. "A fact for which I'm very grateful."

Gordon shrugged, then winced at the pain. "I know a fair bit of engineering and have some seagoing experience. It's not a common pair of skills, so I took charge of the ship until he found a better qualified captain."

Kirkland's eyes glinted with amusement. "Ashton said he wanted you to stay, but you told him you preferred working alone rather than having to give orders to a crew of scurvy, worthless sailors."

"That, too," Gordon muttered as Daniel cut away the shirt sleeve.

Kirkland set the basins and a short stack of clean clothes on the table by the medical bag. The speed with which he produced them suggested that this might not be the first time the kitchen had been used as an infirmary.

Daniel washed the entrance to the wound, which was still seeping blood. "The ball missed the bone, which is good, but it's still in your arm, which is not so good. It shouldn't be too difficult to remove, but it will hurt. Is that tea ready? A cup of it with sizable amounts of sugar and brandy will help."

"That's the best suggestion I've heard all night." With his free hand, Gordon accepted the steaming mug Kirkland prepared and swallowed deeply. He screwed his eyes shut as Daniel probed for the lead ball.

The ball wasn't hard to find, but it took several attempts to wrench it out. As Daniel clinked it into the basin holding the bloody rags, he asked conversationally, "How did you end up here with a pistol ball in your arm?"

Since Gordon's eyes were closed and his face was beaded with sweat, Kirkland answered. "He's been doing some work for me. It has the advantage of allowing him to work alone, and the disadvantage of sometimes being dangerous."

"I got the job done, didn't I?" Gordon snapped.

"Indeed you did, and you'll be well compensated," Kirkland replied. "If you need any discreet investigations done, Daniel, Gordon is your man."

"Oddly enough, that isn't something I usually need. Hang on, this is going to hurt even more."

He pulled a flask of gin from his bag and began thoroughly cleaning the wound. Gordon flinched but didn't make a sound.

As Daniel bandaged the arm again, he said, "I'll fashion a sling for you. Take it easy, and change the dressing every couple of days."

Gordon nodded understanding. "Thanks, Doc. I owe you."

Daniel shrugged as he began cleaning his instruments. "Don't worry about it. I don't keep score."

"I do." Gordon's gray eyes glinted like steel.

"Some of my patients pay in chickens. Or maybe a nice bag of potatoes or apples," Daniel suggested, amused.

Gordon's only reply was a snort. He was sagging and white faced, but on the whole, he'd been lucky. If the bullet had struck a few inches to one side, it would have hit his heart.

As Kirkland helped Gordon to his feet, Daniel was struck with the thought that now that he was going to marry Jessie, he might need the services of a discreet investigator. No, she might not have told him everything, but she'd revealed the important facts about her past.

At least, he thought she had.

Jessie's friends were delighted by her betrothal to Lord Romayne. She suspected that *his* friends were less pleased by the news.

She had her own doubts as she tried to sleep later that night. She'd kept her distance from Daniel to keep him from knowing too much about her. Her reasons were still powerful, and marrying him put her onto very thin ice. But he'd accepted the portion of truth she'd offered, and perhaps that would be enough. She hoped so, since that distant past had nothing to do with the woman she'd become.

As she tossed and turned, she told herself that in time they'd grow closer. That might soften his judgment if the whole truth came out. Too late to change her mind . . .

Morning came too early. When Lily brought Beth down to share breakfast in Jessie's rooms, the little girl's bright cheerfulness made Jessie feel old. Philip had also been an early riser, which proved that even he wasn't a perfect husband.

Food and strong tea revived her. As Jessie spread marmalade on Beth's toast, she said, "This morning we're going on a drive with Lord Romayne. Remember him, from Gunter's?"

Beth frowned. "The man who broke my dish of ice before I finished."

"He also saved you from being crushed by that carriage," Jessie reminded her. "And you did get a replacement ice from the duchess."

"Mmmmmm." Mollified, Beth accepted the marmalade toast.

Jessie considered telling her daughter that she was going to marry the gentleman in question, then decided to wait for Daniel so they could present a united front.

They had just finished breakfast when a footman came to announce that Lord Romayne had arrived. Pulse accelerating, Jessie washed marmalade from her daughter's cheek, helped her into a handsome new green velvet cloak, then led her downstairs.

Daniel bowed when they entered the small salon. He'd given up mourning black in favor of a dark navy coat and buckskins, and he looked quite appallingly handsome. "Lady Kelham and Lady Kelham," he said. "It's a pleasure to see you both."

Beth giggled. Being called Lady Kelham still seemed more game than reality. She dropped a neat little curtsy. "Mama said you're taking us for a drive?"

"Indeed, I am, and the weather is very pleasant." He had the gift of speaking as directly to a child as to an adult. "I thought we could go to the park and feed the ducks."

"Oh, yes!"

Daniel's glance at Jessie silently asked if Beth had been informed of their plans yet. She gave a small shake of her head. It was time now. "Beth, besides a drive, we have a surprise for you," she said. "Lord Romayne and I are going to get married, so you'll have a new father."

Beth's small jaw dropped. "I have a father!"

Daniel went down on one knee in front of Beth so he wasn't looming over her. "Yes, and he loved you very much. He'll always be with you in your heart." He touched a gentle finger to the middle of Beth's chest. "But when a father can't stay, sometimes he sends a stepfather to look out for his child. It's a great honor for me that your mother is willing to accept me as your stepfather."

Frowning, Beth retreated and took Jessie's hand. Judging that it would be best not to give Beth time to brood, Jessie said, "Now it's time for that drive."

Beth retained her grip on Jessie's hand, regarding Daniel warily. He was relaxed, not trying to ingratiate himself, as he held the door and guided them outside.

He had a handsome curricle with a liveried groom perched on the back. Courtesy of Kirkland, Jessie guessed. She and Daniel were fortunate in their friends.

Jessie helped Beth into the carriage; then Daniel assisted Jessie. The bench seat was wide enough for all three of them, but Beth climbed into Jessie's lap, her expression wary. Daniel swung up into the curricle, then produced a folded blanket from behind the seat. "The sunshine is lovely, but the air is brisk so we can use this blanket."

"Like a cocoon with three butterflies," Jessie observed as she tucked the blanket over herself and her daughter. Beth giggled at that.

After they were settled in, Daniel expertly guided the curricle from the Ashton House grounds and along the street to Hyde Park. As they passed other vehicles, he asked casually, "Beth, do you like horses?"

She eyed him suspiciously. "I'm Lady Kelham. If you call me Beth, I should call you by your given name."

"Beth!" Jessie said reprovingly. Sometimes her clever little daughter was just too precocious.

Daniel only laughed. "That's fair. My name is Daniel. You may call me that if I am permitted to call you Beth."

Beth gave a victorious nod. "I shall permit it, Daniel."

"Thank you. Now, about horses . . ."

"I love horses!" Beth straightened up alertly in

Jessie's lap. "I want a pony, but Mama won't let me."
It was an old grievance.

"A pony might be too strong for you now," he
said, "but perhaps later?"

Jessie said, "When you're older and larger, Beth."

"I'm older and larger today than I was when we
came to London!" Beth said with irrefutable logic.

"And you'll be older and larger again tomorrow,"
Daniel said equably. "Your mama will decide when
you're ready. What kind of pony would you like?"

"Nice," she said decisively.

"Would you like a bay like that fine fellow there?"
He gestured with his whip.

"A chestnut." Beth wriggled off Jessie's lap into
the space between the two adults. "Or gray. Not a
bay."

"My first pony was a chestnut," Daniel said. "He
had two white socks and a blaze on his forehead."

"What was his name?" Beth demanded.

"Rascal. He had a bit of mischief in him, but he
was a grand pony," Daniel said nostalgically.

"Did he die?"

"Yes, but not for many, many years. I outgrew
him and then he became my sister's pony."

"I'd like a sister," Beth said thoughtfully.

"That is one of the advantages of your mother
and I marrying." Daniel glanced at Jessie with heat
in his eyes. "You may well get a little brother or sister."

"I want a sister, not a brother!"

"We don't get to choose, darling," Jessie said, impressed at how quickly Daniel was winning her
daughter over. "But as the oldest, you would rule

the nursery until you became a young lady and left any brothers or sisters behind."

Beth clearly liked the idea of that. Jessie would have enjoyed having a sister. Mariah and Julia had showed her how splendid sisters could be. Women often disliked Jessie, perhaps fearing she would try to lure their husbands away. It was wonderful to be with women who were secure enough in themselves and their marriages that they didn't regard Jessie as a threat.

She'd loved Philip and their quiet country life, but now her life was opening up in numerous ways. She couldn't decide if she was more excited or alarmed.

Chapter 18

They entered Hyde Park and Daniel drove along to the Serpentine, the long, curved lake that was one of the park's chief features. When the road was at its closest approach to the water, he halted the curricle and climbed out, passing the reins to the groom who'd been riding on the back of the vehicle.

He asked Beth, "Would you like to fly like a duck?"

"Yes!"

"Fly, little duck, fly!" He caught her around the waist and swooped her twice around before setting her on the ground. She squeaked with pleasure.

With Jessie, Daniel took more time, gazing into her eyes and clasping her hand warmly as he helped her to the ground. She smiled. "I can see you're well experienced with small people."

"Practice. When a child has fallen and gashed his head and is bleeding copiously, a certain tact is required." He reached behind the curricle seat and produced a small canvas bag, then left the groom to walk the horses back and forth to keep them from cooling off. "Now for the ducks!" he announced as he handed the bag to Beth. "There are pieces of bread in here for them and any swans who might come by."

"*Quack!*" Beth took off for the lake as fast as her short legs would carry her.

"Your daughter may have a future as a race-horse," Daniel observed.

Jessie laughed as she took Daniel's arm and they followed Beth at a more sedate pace. "At some point, I'll need to explain the concept of 'ladylike' to her, but I hate to quell all that exuberance."

"I'm sure she can become a charmingly exuber-ant young lady." He chuckled. "But it won't happen overnight."

Walking along the edge of the water was a blond girl about Beth's age, accompanied by a young woman dressed as a nursemaid. Beth trotted up to the other girl and produced a handful of bread chunks from her bag. "I am Beth, Lady Kelham. Would you like to help me feed the ducks?"

The blond girl brightened. "I am Lady Lydia Hambly, and yes!" She belatedly glanced at her nurse for permission. "Please?"

The nurse studied Jessie and Daniel as she con-sidered. Then the two women exchanged a nod of mutual approval. "You may, Lady Lydia."

As the nurse settled on a bench to watch, the chat-tering girls scooted to the water's edge and started tearing the chunks of bread into small pieces. Lady Lydia tossed her bread one piece at a time while Beth inclined to flinging several pieces at once. Ducks seemed to appear out of nowhere, quacking in a gathering throng.

"The girls both have a nice sense of equity," Daniel observed. "See how they try to make sure that all the ducks get some bread?"

"Beth always wants to share with other children." Jessie chuckled. "It looked as if she and Lady Lydia may be striking up a lifelong friendship here. I think Beth will make a wonderful big sister when the time comes."

Daniel looked down at her, and she was suddenly, acutely aware of just how that new sibling would be created. Blushing, she said, "We were going to discuss practicalities this morning, weren't we?"

"Ducks and practicalities," Daniel agreed. "This afternoon I'll go to Doctors Commons for a special license. I'll need your full name and your place of birth. Is Jessie your Christian name, or is it a nickname for Jessica or Jessamine or Janet?"

Jessie sighed, some of her good humor fading. "It's short for Jezebel."

"Seriously?" Daniel said, shocked.

"I told you my father hated females. Jezebel, the wicked woman who tried to turn her devout husband from the true God," she said bitterly. "The name is inscribed right there in the family Bible."

"Jezebel also means 'princess,' " Daniel said quietly as he rested his hand over hers where she clasped his arm. "That suits you much better."

"Thank you." She swallowed hard, thinking that she'd wanted a husband who was kind, and she had found one.

"Given your feelings about your father, would

you be willing to marry in a church, or would you prefer a private ceremony?" he asked. "With a special license, we can marry when and where we wish."

She hesitated. Her father had made her deeply wary of the Church, but kindness worked both ways. She suspected that marrying in a church would matter more to Daniel than not marrying in one would matter to her. "As long as you and our friends are present, a church is a fine and proper place to wed."

"Thank you." He smiled apologetically. "It wouldn't seem real to me if we were married in a parlor."

Her first wedding had been in a parlor, her second in a church. The second marriage had worked much better. Maybe that was an endorsement of church weddings.

"You'll need my married names as well as my birth name." She didn't like revealing so much of her past, even to Daniel. But this was her third marriage with a special license, so she was something of an expert. My full legal name is Jezebel Elizabeth Braxton Trevane Kelham. I'd better write that all down for you."

"That would be helpful," he agreed, tactfully not mentioning the number of married names. "Is Elizabeth a family name?"

"Yes, my mother was Elizabeth. I hated being called Jezebel and my mother didn't approve, so when I was little, I was often called Lisbet." Though she had few memories of her mother, the ones she had were good. She wondered sometimes how different her life would have been if her mother hadn't died. "When I moved to York, I needed a new name, so I decided to use Jessie as a nickname for Jezebel."

"I'm sure your mother would be honored to know that the family name is being continued," he said. "Now, for a different practical topic. The Kirklands have offered the use of a manor house they own that's only about an hour from London if we want to have a quiet honeymoon before we travel to Castle Romayne. Would you like that?"

"After all the rush of my time in London, that sounds wonderful." Her brow furrowed. "Though having Beth there will make it less quiet."

"Laurel has offered to take her, and says that the duchess and Lady Julia would happily do the same. Would you be comfortable leaving Beth with one of them? If not, of course she should come with us."

"I've never been apart from her." Jessie hesitated. Though Beth was part of her, a husband should be equally important in a different way. "But a few days just for us is a good way to start a marriage."

As she spoke, she realized that she wanted that private time, too. She was uncertain how well they'd suit in the long run, but given the degree of attraction between them, the honeymoon should be splendid.

Daniel glanced at the girls, who were still tossing bread and chattering like magpies. A pair of stately white swans had joined the throng and were honking greedily. "The decision is yours."

"Beth is so friendly and outgoing that she'll be fine staying with friends," Jessie said decisively. "The Ashtons and the Randalls are about to leave town, but they both live to the west. Since we'll be traveling in that direction anyhow, we can collect Beth on the way to Castle Romayne."

"That will work." He smiled sympathetically. "Being separated will be harder on you than Beth, I suspect."

Her return smile was uneven. "I'm sure you're right. But I really do like the idea of a week or so of quiet time just with you."

"Good," he said, heat deep in his eyes.

She blushed again, exasperated with herself for acting like a nervous virgin.

Apparently reading her mind, Daniel murmured, "You blush most charmingly even though you're not an innocent girl from the schoolroom."

His words were casual, but she realized this was a topic that needed to be aired. "Does it bother you that you'll be my third husband? That seems so *extreme* on my part!"

Daniel's brows arched. "I don't mind being the third husband as long as I'm your *last* husband."

She laughed, relieved not to see signs of jealousy. That had been the worst failing of her first husband, Ivo—and he'd had no shortage of failings. "You will be! I would have stopped at two if not for practical reasons."

His eyes cooled a little. Perhaps she should not have been quite so honest. She was wondering what to say when out of the corner of her eye, she saw a man walk purposefully to the edge of the Serpentine. He was carrying something in one hand. When he reached the water's edge, he tossed a small sack into the water as far as he could. A high feline wail came from the sack before it splashed into the lake.

Lady Lydia shrieked. Beth—dear God, Beth plunged right into the water! She was splashing her way toward the sinking sack when the bottom dropped away under her feet. Suddenly Beth was in over her head, splashing and yelping frantically.

As Jessie gasped with horror, Daniel bolted from her side and straight into the water. Though the Serpentine looked placid, it was formed from the Westbourne River and a slow, steady current was pulling Beth away from the shore.

When the bottom dropped away, Daniel began swimming toward Beth with powerful strokes. He overtook her quickly, but she was weeping and kicking. To Jessie's surprise, he didn't return immediately to shore but kept swimming, Beth under one arm.

The cat in the sack. He grabbed it with one hand and gave it to Beth, who clutched it as Daniel began side-stroking back to shore, moving more slowly since he could use only one arm.

Freed of her paralysis, Jessie ran for the curricle and grabbed the blanket that had been tucked behind the seat again. "Turn the carriage around," she ordered the groom. "We're going to need to return to Ashton House immediately."

As he complied, she raced back to the waterside, where Daniel was emerging with Beth in his arms and water streaming from both of them. He looked like a river god, gloriously powerful and protective. The tenderness in his face as he cradled Beth to his chest twisted Jessie's heart.

Beth was clutching the drenched sack. "The *kitty!*" she wept. "That bad man tried to drown the kitty."

"I'll take a look at it," Daniel said in the soothing tones of a doctor. "First we get you wrapped up in a blanket."

Jessie opened the blanket in her arms. "I'll take her."

Daniel laid Beth into Jessie's embrace, deftly took the wet sack, then wrapped the folds of the blanket around the little girl. As Jessie gathered her shivering daughter close, she realized just how chilly the air was. "You must be freezing," she said to Daniel.

He shrugged. "I'll do." He produced a folding pocketknife and cut the cord that tied the sack shut. Inside was a half-grown gray tabby that looked like a drowned rat.

"Kitty!" Beth reached for the cat.

"Just a moment." Daniel stretched the tabby out on his left arm and gently pressed on its back for a few seconds. Press, release. Press, release. The little cat coughed up water and raised its head to look around in terror. Then it scrabbled up Daniel's chest to his shoulder with little needle claws, crying frantically.

"You've had a hard day, haven't you?" he crooned as he pulled it from the shoulder of his expensive, ruined coat. He tucked it under his coat to protect it from the cutting wind. It huddled close to him, only the small striped face and bristling whiskers visible. Daniel stroked its head with one finger.

Beth's bonnet had disappeared, so Jessie kissed her daughter's wet curls. Jessie was shaking, she realized. Forcing her voice to sound calm, she said, "Beth, you were very brave, but also very foolish. Don't ever, *ever* just run into the water like that!"

Beth looked up with a sunny smile. "But kitty and I are both well."

"You could have drowned if the current had been stronger or if there wasn't someone around to pull you out of the water," Daniel said, his voice stern. "Do *not* do such a foolish thing again."

Beth looked up with wide, innocent, manipulative eyes. "No, Dandy," she said earnestly. "May I have Smoky?"

His brows arched. "Dandy?"

"For Daniel Daddy," she explained as she held her hands out for the little cat.

From his amused gaze, Daniel recognized that he was being manipulated by a master, but he brought the little cat out from under his coat, petted it a couple of times to ensure that it had calmed down, then placed it into Beth's eager hands. "Hold Smoky carefully with your arm underneath for support," he ordered.

Clearly Daniel saw that trying to separate a child from a kitten would be both cruel and impossible. Especially a kitten that had already been named. Jessie said, "We need to get both of you warm and fed. The poor little puss looks like he's starving."

"He can have the bread." Lady Lydia had joined them, and she solemnly produced a handful of broken bread crumbs from the bread bag.

"That's very thoughtful of you," Daniel said as he put the crumbs on his flat palm and held them in front of Smoky. The little cat dived at them ferociously. He might not be a bread eater by choice, but just now, he'd take what he could get.

A hesitant voice said, "Sir? Lady Lydia asked me to get our carriage robe for you." It was the nursemaid, a dark green woolen carriage blanket in her hands.

"Thank you." Daniel opened the blanket and pulled it around his shoulders. "You are both very kind. Where shall I return this blanket later?"

"Hambly House, sir. On Mount Street."

Mount Street wasn't far from Ashton House. "Perhaps you and Beth can play together in the future," Jessie said. "Would you like that?"

Both girls piped up, "Yes!"

Daniel gave the nursemaid his card. The Hamblys were also leaving London soon, but there would be future seasons.

"Now that we're all sorted, time to go home," Daniel announced. "Good day to you both."

As they headed back to their waiting curricle, Jessie said, "You ruined your clothing."

Daniel shrugged. "I told Kirkland his attempts to make me look fashionable were doomed to failure. Do you want me to take Beth? She must be getting heavy."

She was, indeed. At four going on five, Beth was a substantial armful. Luckily, the cat didn't add much weight. Jessie was glad to transfer her daughter to Daniel.

They felt so much like a family. Jessie wished she could believe that the future would continue this smoothly.

Chapter 19

St. George's, Hanover Square, was an impressive church. It was relatively new, less than a hundred years old, and had a grand portico supported by six massive columns. Daniel wasn't sure if it was intended to celebrate the glory of God, or the wealthy Mayfair district it served.

As the groom's party climbed from their carriage outside, Kirkland observed, "You look ready to bolt."

Laurel patted Daniel's arm. "It's only nerves. This is an important day, after all."

A day in which he was to marry a woman he'd known for only a few weeks. "When you two married, you had such absolute certainty. I wish I had that."

"It's easy to be certain when one is young and hasn't seen the many ways things can go wrong," Laurel said wryly. "Since you're older and wiser, you're more aware of the possibilities and risks."

"But you're also better prepared to deal with any

problems that arise." Kirkland gave Daniel a searching look. "If you have doubts about marrying Lady Kelham, it's not too late to change your mind."

No! "I want to marry her," Daniel said tersely. "I'm wondering if she might have changed her mind about marrying *me*." It was said that a second marriage was the triumph of hope over experience. What did that make a third marriage?

"Apparently she hasn't reconsidered," Laurel said. "I see two Ashton carriages over there, so the bridal party has arrived."

Daniel tried not to show his relief. Given their mutual uncertainties, she might easily have decided that she wasn't ready to marry again.

The interior was both simple and grand, with more columns and an arching barrel vault ceiling high above. Rather daunting for mere mortals. Seeing Laurel glance up at the west gallery, which contained the organ and organist, Daniel asked, "Are you wishing you were the one playing the organ?"

She chuckled. "I was tempted, but I want to see the wedding of my only brother rather than merely being in the church with my back turned."

While she joined the small cluster of guests in the front pews, Daniel and Kirkland took up their positions in front of the altar. There were perhaps two dozen of their friends. On his side, they were mostly old schoolmates and wives.

Even Gordon had come, looking quite respectable in his pew at the back of the church. Daniel should probably have asked Gordon to be the groomsman since the position was supposed to go to a single man and Gordon was the only old friend present who wasn't married. But Kirkland was his closest friend, and Gordon would probably have been horrified to be so visible.

Farther back were a handful of women he didn't recognize, but he suspected they just liked weddings. Since a church was open to all, most congregations had members who regularly attended wedding ceremonies so they could admire clothing and flowers, and speculate on the chances of a happy marriage. This particular wedding had generated a fair amount of talk, so it was no surprise to see strangers.

"Steady on," Kirkland murmured. "She'll be here soon."

"It's not too late for her to bolt," Daniel murmured back wryly.

The music changed and the wedding party entered the nave. A beaming Beth led the way clutching a bouquet of flowers. Rumor had it that she'd wanted to bring Smoky, and only firm orders from her mother had prevented it.

Lady Julia and the Duchess of Ashton were attendants. Both were attractive women. In fact, the duchess was considered one of the great beauties of the beau monde. Yet they paled next to Jessie, who followed on the arm of the Duke of Ashton. She carried a nosegay of white roses and surely was the most beautiful woman in England, quite possibly in the world. Daniel's heart hammered with wonder.

She wore a quietly elegant dove gray gown, which was a color of half mourning. The color suited her fair skin and made her look ethereally lovely. Her shining dark hair was swept up and held in place with a chaplet of flowers, and a pale lace veil fell behind all the way to the hem of her gown.

Their gazes locked as she walked toward him. Her light clear eyes showed both anxiety and determination. Proof that they had things in common.

Then she was there beside him. Almost his.

The ceremony was oddly blurred, perhaps because Daniel had married many couples himself. The only unusual element was that they exchanged rings. Jessie had told him that both Mariah and Julia had given their husbands rings, and she liked the idea if he didn't mind. He hadn't minded; it seemed only fair. If she was his, he was also hers.

During these days of preparation, they'd been so unnaturally polite to each other, like the near strangers they were in many ways. He wondered how long that would last.

In a rolling voice, the vicar intoned, "I pronounce that you be man and wife together!"

Done. Married past redemption. He exhaled with relief and lifted her hand to his lips for a kiss, saying in a whisper, "Thank you for marrying me, my lady."

Her return smile was shaky. "My lord," she said deferentially.

The music changed to a joyous march. Jessie took his arm and they headed down the aisle. He suspected that he was beaming like a fool. This marriage might be the worst mistake of his life, and he didn't care.

Now that the die had been cast, Jessie was relaxed and smiling. The guests looked as if they wanted to applaud and were constrained only by the solemn setting. If a marriage's chance of success could be judged by the goodwill of family and friends, Daniel and Jessie should live happily ever after.

Near the door, one of the wedding watchers had risen in the pew and was staring at Jessie. One hand covered her mouth and she looked on the verge of tears.

When Jessie saw, she stopped dead in the aisle, her hand tightening on Daniel's arm like a vise. "That woman," she said in a choked voice. *"There!"*

Daniel caught his breath. The woman was veiled, but even so, she looked like Jessie's older sister, with the same striking bone structure and dark hair. Only her hazel eyes were different. The resemblance was so pronounced that she had to be related.

Her expression changed to horror when she saw that she'd attracted their attention. She spun around and headed toward the church doors with unseemly haste.

Her escape was cut off by Gordon, who had moved quickly around the pews to block her way at the door. "A friend of the family?" he asked genially.

She muttered an oath and tried to slip away to the side, but Gordon caught her wrist. "Surely you want to offer good wishes to the happy couple, madam."

Daniel and Jessie had reached Gordon and the mystery woman, and other guests were following down the aisle. Surrendering, the woman turned to face them. A little shorter and rounder than Jessie and with a few silver hairs among the ebony, she was still strikingly attractive.

Jessie crushed her nosegay in her free hand. Hanging on to Daniel's arm as if it was the only thing keeping her upright, she whispered in a child's anguished voice, "Mama?"

Chapter 20

Wedding guests were beginning to back up behind Daniel and Jessie. This was her *mother*? With his bride looking pale and ready to collapse, Daniel said, "Madam, do join us for the wedding breakfast at Ashton House. You can ride in our carriage." He glanced at Gordon. "I hope you're coming to the breakfast also."

Gordon's eyes glinted with amusement. "I wouldn't miss this for anything." He took the older woman's unresisting arm and escorted her outside to the bridal coach, pulled by four white horses, that would carry Daniel and Jessie to Ashton House.

After handing her into the carriage, Gordon said under his breath, "I don't suppose I could join you on the ride? It promises to be interesting."

"No chance in hell," Daniel said pleasantly as he helped Jessie inside. "We'll see you at Ashton's." He glanced at the coachman. "Make this a slow journey, please."

"Aye, my lord." The coachman smiled indulgently.

As Daniel climbed into the coach he saw Kirkland and Ashton chatting with the other guests with an ease that implied nothing unusual had happened. They were surely as curious as Gordon, but he could count on them to calm the waters.

Now to learn what the devil was going on.

Jessie couldn't stop staring at the woman in the opposite, backward-facing seat. The woman had drawn her veil back and she was staring at Jessie with matching intensity. She was well-dressed in a sober dark blue gown and she looked well-fed and well-kept. There was no denying the resemblance between them, but she didn't look old enough to be Jessie's mother. An unknown cousin or aunt, perhaps?

As the carriage began to move, Daniel said calmly, "I assume you know that I'm Romayne. And your name is . . . ?"

The woman hesitated. "I'm known as Jane Lester," she said. "Mrs. Lester."

Jessie noted that the woman said she was known as Jane Lester, not that that was actually her name. "My mother was named Elizabeth," Jessie said in a brittle voice. "She's dead."

"Is that what that old devil told you?" Jane Lester shook her head. "I was christened Elizabeth Jane Shelby, and as a girl I was called Lizzie Jane. Your father thought that undignified, so he always called me Elizabeth. As you can see, I'm quite alive." She leaned forward, tears in her eyes. "My little Jessie," she breathed, "after all these years!"

Jessie felt rigid as a board. "But my mother is *dead!* You're too young to be she."

"I was only sixteen when you were born, and women in our family keep our looks," Jane explained. "But I'm your mother right enough."

Daniel encircled Jessie's left hand with his large, warm clasp. "I think you'd better tell us the whole story, Mrs. Lester. From the beginning."

"Then I'll have to talk quickly since this is a short ride," Jane said briskly. "How far back do you want me to go?"

"Where are you from?" Jessie asked. "If you really are my mother, who are my people?" Her voice cracked. "You came from nowhere and then you died. I know *nothing* about you!"

Seeing how unnerved Jessie was, Daniel squeezed her hand as he asked, "When telling the story of one's life, it's customary to start with where one was born."

Jane gave them both a straight look. "You're the sort who want the unvarnished truth, aren't you? Very well, though some of it isn't pretty." She brushed an errant lock of dark hair from her eyes as she considered. Beth often made exactly the same gesture.

"I was born in London. My mother was in the chorus of an opera company. Singing, dancing, and entertaining the gentlemen." She smiled ironically. "If she knew who my father was, she never said, so there's a limit to how much of my background I can tell you, Jessie. She did say that he was a gentleman, for what it's worth."

Jessie swallowed hard. Might the theater run in the blood? That's where she'd run when she was desperate. "If that's true, how did you come to meet my father? He despised the theater."

"Indeed, he did. I grew up backstage helping out where I could. Mending costumes, cleaning, whatever else needed doing. I wasn't a good enough dancer to work in the opera chorus. I was only fifteen when my mother died, and I was terrified about what would happen to me."

When she fell silent, Daniel said, "Women with your looks can usually find a way to survive."

She scowled at him. "I'd no desire to become a whore, but it was looking like I'd have to accept an offer to be some rich man's mistress. Then the Reverend Cassius Braxton came along."

Jessie's father. She asked, "What was he doing in an opera house?"

"He wanted confirmation of how evil it was," Jane said dryly. "To be really thorough, he needed to see the girls close up in their skimpy costumes, so he came to the green room. He saw me there acting as maid for the opera singers. Since I was properly dressed, he decided I was an innocent who needed rescuing."

Daniel asked, "Were you?"

"Depends on how you define innocent. A drunk caught me backstage when I was fourteen and I couldn't escape. Braxton never forgave me for not being a virgin." Her mouth twisted. "Claimed he wanted to save my soul, but what he really wanted was to toss up my skirts and roger me. After I said no a few times, he asked me to marry him."

"Why on earth would you accept such a horrible man?" Jessie burst out. "He hated women and pleasure and anything that wasn't miserable!"

Jane sighed. "He wasn't so bad then. Very handsome, for one thing. But also, he wanted *marriage.* Can you imagine how good that sounded to a girl like me? A bastard facing a life of poverty and shame? He was educated and well connected and had money. I'd learned how to speak properly by listening in the green room, so he passed me off as a well-born orphan after we wed and he took me to Pulham."

"Going from London to a village must have been difficult," Daniel observed.

"Yer not half jokin', ducks," Jane said, her accent deliberately Cockney. Reverting to proper English, she continued, "But I was willing to be bored in exchange for enough to eat and a nice home and clothes. Living in Pulham wasn't so bad. I didn't have to dodge drunks in the back corridors. Some biddies criticized me for being too young and too pretty for a vicar's wife, but I acted the part well enough that most of the parishioners were pleasant to me."

Jessie no longer doubted that Jane was her mother. No imposter could know so much of the Braxton household. "I must have been born very soon if you were only sixteen."

Jane nodded, her face softening. "You were, and once I had you, Jessie, it was all worthwhile. Do you remember our walks in the garden? Or when you played dress-up with my clothes?"

Jessie's face tightened. "I remember," she whispered. "And then you were gone and my father said you'd died. He showed me a new dug grave and said it was yours. Not long after, he fired my old nurse and we moved to the parish in Chillingham and he never spoke of you again."

"Since you were so young, he could have shown you any new grave," Daniel said.

Jessie had wept and laid flowers on the raw earth. She hoped whoever occupied it didn't mind flowers under false pretenses. "How did you come to leave my father?"

"I didn't leave Braxton. He threw me out," Jane said bitterly. "He said I was a vile harlot determined to tempt him into mortal sin."

Jessie frowned. "What did he mean by that?"

"He had strange ideas that husband and wife should stay apart on the Sabbath, or church holidays, or when a woman has her courses. But he couldn't keep away from me, and he claimed that was *my* fault!" Jane glared at Daniel. "They say you're a vicar. Do you believe such nonsense?"

"No, but I know men who do. To desire a woman is to admit she has power over him," Daniel replied. "Such men despise women because they fear that power."

Jane nodded vigorously. "That was Braxton. He'd succumb to lust, then bellow and beat me for seducing him. His rages got worse and worse until one night he drove me from the vicarage with a horsewhip and threatened to kill me if he ever saw me again."

Jessie pressed her hand to her mouth. "He had a horrible temper," she said in a raw whisper. "He was terrifying."

"I wanted so much to take you with me, Jessie, but he kept the house locked and guarded. And I was so afraid of him." Jane's voice faltered. "I took refuge with a friend in the village. She gave me some clothes and enough money to get to London. When I got there, I forged references to get a job as a companion to a lady in Richmond."

"I'm surprised you could get such a position," Daniel said. "Many women would consider an attractive young woman in the house to be trouble."

Jane grinned, looking very young. "Usually that's true, but this particular lady, Mrs. Lester, was the widow of a prosperous merchant and she wanted a young woman who would tempt her son to stop working long enough to marry. After she decided I was sufficiently genteel, she put me into her son's path. She's now my mother-in-law and well pleased with the fact that she found her son a wife."

And so Mrs. Braxton had become Mrs. Lester. She was a resilient woman who had done what was necessary to survive. Jessie had done the same. In fact, there were eerie similarities between their lives.

"Do you believe me now, Jessie?" Jane smiled mischievously. "I can tell you about a birthmark you have that no one except your husband should ever see, and maybe not even him. I thought it looked like a little heart. You were my little sweetheart."

Jessie didn't know what Jane was talking about, but there were parts of her body she'd never seen. "Why did you let my father name me Jezebel?"

"I thought it was a pretty name, rather grand," Jane said apologetically. "I hadn't had any Bible study then, so I didn't know Jezebel was a bad woman. That was Braxton's idea of a joke, the swine." For a moment a deeper, tougher side of her was visible. The part that had enabled her to survive cruel circumstances.

Jessie closed her eyes, battered by her past. She

felt an odd blend of relief mixed with regrets for unfinished business. She'd dreamed sometimes of returning to her father's house and confronting him with her anger and his failings. "So my father is dead and my mother is alive."

"I think he must be dead, but I don't know for sure," Jane admitted uneasily.

Daniel's gaze became piercing. "So you contracted a bigamous marriage."

"Braxton screamed that I was no wife of his!" Jane said defiantly. "If I wasn't his wife, he wasn't my husband, eh?"

"Very pragmatic," Daniel murmured.

Jane scowled. "And you think I'm going to burn in hell. Maybe so, but I know I was in hell on earth."

"God decides eternal justice, not me," Daniel said in a quiet voice. "But if Mr. Braxton is alive and learns you've taken another husband, there will be an unholy mess."

"He'll never learn," Jane said firmly. "I told Mrs. Lester I was a widow when she hired me. My George has never known any different."

"How will you explain Jessie to him now that you've found her?" Daniel asked.

Jane shifted uncomfortably in her seat. "George is a good man, but he's used to doing things all right and proper. He wouldn't like knowing about my past, and you'd be a fool to tell him. If he threw me out, I'd have to come live with my oldest daughter, so better he knows nothing about this, eh?"

"It's not my duty to hunt down your husband and tell him that his wife has a complicated past," Daniel said. "You gave Jessie her strength and her resilience, and for that I must give thanks. But what kind of relationship can you have with your daughter if your husband doesn't know about her?"

Jane looked even more uncomfortable. "I can visit now and then when you're in town. He'll never have to know."

Daniel's hand tightened on Jessie's. "That sounds limited and unsatisfying."

Jessie squeezed his hand back, glad he was accepting her sordid family history so well, but she was caught by something else Jane had said. "You said I'm your oldest daughter. You have other children?"

"Oh, yes," Jane said proudly. "Two boys, two girls, the youngest just out of leading strings. Gifts from God, so I think He must have forgiven me."

It was another massive shock to Jessie. Four half brothers and sisters. She was too numb to know how she felt about that. "I'd like to meet them someday."

"No!" Jane shook her head sharply. "George would be angry if he found out I'd kept the existence of a daughter secret. I'm glad you're well, but now that we've talked, I see there's no room for you in my real life."

Jessie stared at her, shocked and furious. "Then why didn't you just leave me alone? How did you find me? Why did you come to my wedding?"

"I saw you shopping in Bond Street with two other women and knew you must be my girl. You're the only one of my children who looks so much like me. I found out who you were. There was a great amount of talk when you accepted Romayne's offer. I wanted to see you and my beautiful granddaughter, so I went to the church. Anyone can go to a church," Jane said defensively. "I would have slipped away after the ceremony if that friend of yours hadn't cornered me! You'd never have known."

Jessie stared at the woman who had given her life. "Perhaps it would have been better if I didn't."

Jane's mouth tightened. "Maybe so, but that horse has left the stable." She glanced out the window. "Stop the carriage. We're just outside Ashton House, so I need to get out here."

Silently Daniel signaled to the driver, and the coach rumbled to a stop. Expression softening, Jane leaned forward and touched Jessie's hand. "Be happy, my little sweetheart." She pulled her veil over her face, opened the door, and jumped to the ground, then started walking away with a brisk step.

Jessie stared after her. "I'm not hallucinating, am I? That really happened?"

Daniel pulled the door shut, then signaled the coachman to go through the Ashton House gates. "Indeed, it did." He put an arm around her shoulders in a comforting embrace. "If you don't want to sit through the wedding breakfast, I can tell our guests that you're not feeling well. Too much excitement."

She buried her face against his shoulder and ordered herself to stop shaking. "It would be very odd to miss my own wedding celebration," she said, her voice muffled. "I'll be fine." She'd learned how to be quite a decent actress, after all.

"We'll leave for Milton Manor fairly quickly," he said. "Everyone will assume they know the reason why."

She laughed a little at that. "I should have recovered from the shock of meeting my mother by then. But now I'm wondering if my father is dead or alive." Her brief levity faded. "I've done my best not to think about him since I ran away from home. I'm sorry, Daniel. My background is even stranger than I realized."

He smiled with deep warmth and brushed his knuckles down her cheek. "Life will never be boring with you, my dear."

She leaned her cheek against his hand, thinking how lucky she was to have found a man like Daniel. Now it was her job to make sure he didn't regret marrying her.

Chapter 21

The wedding breakfast was splendid, as were all functions held at Ashton House. Fine food and drink were followed by toasts and teasing jokes and great goodwill. Beth attended the celebration, carrying her little cat Smoky in a ribbon-trimmed basket. The cat didn't seem best pleased, but he was mollified by regular morsels of food, and the chance to savage the ribbons.

Daniel was impressed by how graciously Jessie occupied the spotlight despite the shock of meeting the mother she'd thought dead. But when he stood and announced that they were leaving, he saw gratitude in her eyes.

Jessie hugged Beth good-bye, saying, "We'll collect you at Ralston Abbey soon, little finch. Be sure to behave for the duchess!"

"I will," Beth said blithely. "Smoky will behave, too!"

Mariah chuckled and stroked Beth's curls. "We'll

have a fine time. No need to be in a hurry to have her back."

Jessie hugged Mariah, Julia, and Laurel while Daniel shook hands with his friends and hugged his sister. "Be happy, Daniel," Laurel whispered. "As happy as we are."

He smiled back, not wanting her to know that this marriage was built on a much shakier foundation. "I'll try, but having seen you and Kirkland together, I'm not sure that's possible."

She grinned mischievously. "Probably not, but do try."

Jessie took Daniel's arm and they left in a shower of good wishes. As she settled into the luxurious coach that would take them to Milton Manor, Jessie said, "You were right. Beth is less upset by our separation than I am!"

Daniel laughed as he sat down on her left. "She's a very adaptable young lady." He'd observed it as a trait that ran in Jessie's family.

The coil of tension inside began to unwind. Finally he was alone with his exquisite bride. Should he tell her that he'd commissioned Gordon to investigate the Reverend Cassius Braxton and find out whether the man was dead or alive?

No, that could wait until there were results. He didn't want Jessie to have any more distractions on her wedding day. Or her wedding night.

As the coach pulled through the gates onto the street with a gentle rocking motion, Jessie relaxed into the deeply upholstered seat with a sigh of relief. "Thank you for extracting us when you did. I'd used up almost all my ability to be gracious."

Daniel smiled. "You were still charming, but you've had an unusually exhausting wedding day. It's time to relax."

"Getting married was easy compared to meeting my dead mother, the bigamist." Jessie tried to make her words light, but suspected that she had failed. "I don't know what to think of her. But if I'd been in her place, I would *never* have abandoned my child." Just the thought of abandoning Beth made her feel ill.

"No, you would have found some way to get your daughter back," Daniel agreed. "Even if you'd had to burn the parsonage down to get to her. But your mother was in a difficult situation, with no re-sources. Her choices were made from desperation."

"You're kinder than I am," Jessie said in a low voice. "My mind doesn't disagree with what you say, but my heart cries that she abandoned me, made an illegal marriage, and had more children so I . . . I no longer matter." Her eyes squeezed shut to con-ceal the pain. "She sought me out only to decide I have no place in her life."

Daniel took her hand, his calm warmth flowing into her. "She's afraid of losing what she has. Which she might, if George Lester discovers that his mar-riage is bigamous and his children are illegitimate. But if Braxton is dead and that fear is removed, she'll want to see you again."

Jessie sighed. "She satisfied her curiosity today, and that's enough."

"If we have children someday, will you love Beth any less?"

Jessie stared at him. "Don't be absurd. Beth has

owned my heart since she was born. Having other children won't change that."

He didn't reply, but his brows arched in question. She smiled wryly. "I take your point. But my mother has managed without me for over twenty years."

"Not because she wanted to. And don't forget Beth. How could any grandmother resist her?" He smiled. "I certainly can't."

The thought of Beth was soothing. "You do know the way to a mother's heart."

"You are equally in your mother's heart. I'll wager any amount you want that she wept for your loss for years. Now that she's found you, she needs time to work out the best way to include you in her life," Daniel said. "Explaining a living husband to the man who thinks they're legally married would be impossible, but if your father is dead, she can surely come up with a story to explain how she misplaced her firstborn child."

Jessie considered that, grateful for the distraction. "That's easy, actually. Her first husband died when she was nearing her time. Distraught, she gave birth early and almost died of childbed fever. By the time she recovered, her child was gone and her mother-in-law sadly told her the baby died because the treacherous woman wanted the baby for herself. So Jane went away, widowed and thinking herself childless, and eventually found work with Mrs. Lester the elder, and George knows the rest of the story."

Daniel blinked. "You're very good at this."

Her mouth twisted. "Lying, you mean? I learned at my father's knee. I was so afraid of him that I always evaded the truth because I didn't know what would make him explode into rage. Truth was too fragile and precious to risk. With Philip, I learned to trust that I could speak the truth and not risk being struck, and now I prefer honesty whenever possible. But the instinct to prevaricate for safety's sake is still there."

"My dear girl!" he said softly. "You've had to endure even more than I realized."

The understanding in his eyes was both moving and unnerving. No one had ever understood so well, even Philip, who had been too gentle a soul to understand darkness.

She dropped her gaze and peeled off her gloves as she collected herself. This was her wedding day, and it wasn't fair to Daniel to moan about her past. "My luck has improved greatly. Thank you for marrying me, Daniel."

"And my thanks to you for marrying *me*." His smile came from deep inside. "Finally we can be together in complete respectability."

She studied her new husband. He was all lean strength and mastery, and his calm had kept the meeting with her mother from being a full-on disaster.

Tonight they would share a bed. The thought was intoxicating, but surprisingly intimidating. Thinking she should admit that, she said, "I'm looking forward to finally sharing a bed, but it might be simpler if I were a nervous seventeen-year-old virgin. Then I'd have an excuse if I fail to please you on our wedding night."

"Jessie." His gaze was steady. "Neither Rome nor a marriage is built in a day. It will take time to learn how to best please each other, but there is undeniable attraction, and we're both sensible adults. We'll manage."

Their gazes locked, and the rest of the world fell away. As of today, Daniel was officially the most important man in her life. And no matter how many private doubts they might have individually, as a couple they were connected by potent mutual desire.

The atmosphere in the coach intensified as they regarded each other. Still holding his gaze, she lifted her hand and drew the curtains across the window on her side of the vehicle. He did the same on his side, darkening the coach to twilight mystery. With his strong features, he looked mythic, like a Greek god.

She hoped he'd kiss her, but instead he carefully unpinned her floral headdress. "When I first saw you, I thought you were the most beautiful woman I'd ever seen." He freed the circlet of flowers from the veil that fell almost to her heels and laid it on the opposite seat. "Now I *know* you're the most beautiful woman in the world. Luminous and entrancing."

His words were ravishing, but she said uncertainly, "It's good to be seen as beautiful, but I hope that's not all, because beauty fades."

Daniel's hands stilled and he studied her face for long moments before he replied. "You are lovely enough to stop men in the streets. I've seen it happen," he said, choosing each word with care. "But I've met other beautiful women. The Duchess of Ashton is like a laughing angel descended to earth, yet she has never affected me as you do. You have strength and vulnerability and the wisdom that comes of hard experience. Without those things, you would be merely beautiful, as a great statue is beautiful. A woman to be admired and forgotten. You, Jezebel Elizabeth Braxton Trevane Kelham Herbert, are unforgettable."

She bit her lip, on the verge of tears. "I asked you for a flower of reassurance, and you've given me a great entrancing bouquet. Thank you, Daniel. I shall never forget your words."

His answering smile was bashful. "That's good, because I'm not so sure I can be as eloquent again. But when better than on our wedding day?" He returned to her hair, removing pins with delicate precision.

He had deft, powerful surgeon's hands, she thought distractedly as he freed her hair from its formal style. Each pin released a heavy coil of dark hair to fall around her shoulders, increasing the sense of intimacy between them.

"I've wanted to see your hair down since we met. It's like wild silk," he murmured as he stroked a handful of locks smoothly over her breast. Even through layers of fabric and corseting, that light touch caused her nipple to tighten.

After he removed the last pin, he began lightly massaging her scalp with his fingertips. She wanted to purr like a cat. "That feels *wonderful*. I didn't know that my head was capable of such enjoyment."

"Most parts of a body enjoy being touched, and we have a whole week to discover each other's favorite places. Lessons in applied anatomy." He demonstrated by tracing the curve of her ear with his fingertip. The sensation was so delicious, her toes curled.

"How splendidly academic that sounds," she said breathily. "I've always enjoyed learning new things."

She leaned into him, stroking under his coat along the length of his solid, powerful torso. Her breath was quickening and she shifted restlessly in her seat. "How long is the drive to Milton Manor?"

"A bit over an hour, I'm told. Sadly, we're less than halfway." He bent his head and licked the sensitive junction between her throat and shoulder.

Hot desire shot straight to her loins. "Time enough for some serious kissing." She lifted her face and found his lips with her own. She craved a kiss, and instead triggered a firestorm.

"Jessie." Daniel responded to her with swift, open-mouthed carnality. "Dear God, *Jessie!*"

Until now, he'd been gentle in his touch and explorations, but no longer. As his control splintered, she recognized that this fierce desire had always been part of him, a powerful current that thrummed beneath his calm surface. She'd always sensed that intensity; it had been part of his appeal. Now he was flame to her tinder, and she shattered into fire.

As one arm held her close, his other hand caressed down her body, kneading and bringing every fiber to heated life. From shoulder to breast, skimming over her ribs, rounding her hip, stroking down her leg to her knee. He tugged up her hem and his warm palm sleeked upward over her silk stocking to her sensitive inner thigh.

She gave a gasp that turned into a choked cry when his exploring fingers first touched her moist, secret folds. The sensations were almost unbearably arousing, and her legs separated to allow him to probe deeper, ever deeper.

She clawed at his back with frantic force. She wanted to meld with him, bury herself in him. Wanted him to bury himself in her. Her right hand moved down to the fierce erection straining to free itself from his formal clothing.

She squeezed and he groaned, the deep sound dissolving her remaining shreds of restraint. Too impatient to unfasten the fall on his trousers, she yanked at the fabric. Threads tore and buttons popped off to rattle across the floor of the coach.

Her eager hand closed over the silken power of heated male flesh. He jerked under her hand and groaned again as if desperate for breath.

Urgent, mindless, she raised herself from the seat and swung her right leg over him, catching his shoulders for balance as she straddled his lap. Then she lowered herself, using one hand to guide them together. They joined in one smooth movement. Lock and key, male and female, perfectly mated.

She whimpered with sensual need as he throbbed inside her. Daniel gasped and crushed her hard against him as he rammed his hips upward. She shuddered out of control, driving against him over and over as she found release. He surged into her one final time, then went still, his breathing ragged.

They were locked so closely together that she couldn't tell his hammering pulse from her own. She felt flayed, so intensely alive and sensitive that she could scarcely bear it.

Her cheek rested against his and she felt his struggle for breath, the movement of his jaw when he murmured ruefully, "I'd planned on waiting for a bed."

Her catch of laughter helped bring her back to

awareness. They were in a coach, their marriage consummated rather sooner than they'd intended. "As least we're legal now. Man and wife, wedded if not precisely bedded."

His embrace eased. "I trust there's a bed waiting at the end of this coach ride. We must be almost at Milton Manor."

"I suppose." She exhaled with boneless contentment as she settled into his embrace. "You said it would take time to learn to please each other, but it didn't take any time at all."

"Do I please you, Jessie?"

To her surprise, there was a note of uncertainty in his voice. Perhaps he was inexperienced with mating in carriages. Well, so was she, but based on what had just happened, she was ready to make it a permanent part of their love life. "Indeed, you did. I might never move again. It's been so long. . . ." She hummed with contentment.

"So long?" he asked.

Some intimacies were too personal to share, but she saw no harm in explaining this. "Philip was almost fifty years older than I. It was a great scandal in some circles when we wed. But we truly cared for each other, and for him, it was a second springtime. He'd had a long and happy marriage, and he knew how to please a wife. There was such sweetness between us."

"A blessing for you both, and one that produced Beth," Daniel said softly.

"The greatest blessing of my life." She sighed a little. "But he was so much older. The sweetness never faded, but the springtime did."

"A lovely thing about the seasons is that they

come round again and again." His hand stroked down her back. "And all seasons are beautiful in their own way."

She smiled to herself as her eyes drifted shut. Soon she'd have to move and they'd have to straighten their clothing and try to look less wanton.

Then they could settle down in Milton Manor for a week, and celebrate a new season of their lives.

Chapter 22

Milton Manor was a serenely proportioned Palladian-style building, and the closer the carriage drew along the tree-lined drive, the more Jessie admired the structure. "What a beautiful house!" she said as their carriage halted under the porte cochere. "The gardens look lovely as well. I'm surprised the Kirklands don't live here full-time."

"Kirkland often needs to be in London, but they both like the peace and quiet of the country. Because his principal estate is in Scotland, he bought this place as a convenient retreat," Daniel explained as he helped her from the carriage. "I've not visited, but my sister says it's a jewel box with all modern conveniences added."

Jessie took his arm as they ascended the steps. "Perfect for a honeymoon. I'm very ready to relax."

Daniel gave her a private smile, and she knew that he was thinking of that bed they'd finally get to share. Which might not be relaxing, but it would certainly be invigorating.

They were admitted by a young but properly dignified butler who bowed them into the house. The two-story foyer was decorated in restful shades of cream and light blue, and a magnificent staircase swept up to the floor above.

"Lord Romayne. Lady Romayne. Welcome to Milton Manor. I'm Martin." He didn't react to their rather disheveled appearances by so much as an eye blink. "The staff and I will be happy to provide whatever you require."

"A bath," Jessie said promptly.

"I'd like one also," Daniel said. "And a light supper after. The food at the wedding breakfast was first-rate, but I ate almost nothing. I was too busy talking to all the guests."

"So was I." Jessie chuckled. "We should have asked the Ashton House butler to pack a hamper for us."

Martin managed to look disapproving without moving a muscle. "I'm sure you'll find the cuisine of Milton Manor acceptable."

"I don't doubt it," Daniel said peaceably. "I'm sure the wine cellar is extraordinary as well."

Mollified, Martin said, "Lord Kirkland has excellent taste in wine and spirits. Let me escort you to your rooms now so you can refresh yourselves."

"I hope I don't fall asleep in the bath," Jessie said as they climbed the grand staircase. "It's been a tiring day."

"And it's not over yet," Daniel murmured provocatively.

Their rooms were as splendid as the rest of the house, with bright bouquets of autumn flowers. In the spacious sitting room, Martin said, "Lady Romayne, your dressing room is to the right. Lord Romayne, yours is to the left. There is a hip bath in each, and hot water will be brought up directly. Ring if you need anything more." With another bow, he was gone.

Jessie peered into her dressing room. "All my luggage has magically appeared here, and what a splendid large hip bath! There's a fire burning in the fireplace to warm the room. Clearly they were ready for us."

"The staff probably gets bored since the Kirklands aren't here full-time, so they welcome the opportunity to be busy." Daniel looked into his dressing room. "Another large hip bath and fire. A drinks table as well. Do you have one?"

Jessie took a second look. "Yes, there's a table with bottles and glasses. I've never been so pampered in my life!"

Daniel laughed. "Laurel apologized for the fact that they haven't yet installed built-in bathing tubs, but this seems quite fine to me. She and I often ate in the kitchen in Bristol. Since most of our servants were training to go into service, the results were sometimes erratic. Milton Manor obviously is up to Kirkland's standards."

"I can't wait to see the bedroom." Jessie crossed the sitting room and threw open the double doors to reveal the adjoining bedroom. "Good heavens! That is the largest bed I've ever seen," she said, awed by the massive four-poster. The canopy and counterpane were richly woven in gold and burgundy brocade. Fit for royalty.

Daniel came up behind her. "Impressive." He ran a warm hand down her arm. "Should we try it out?"

She laughed and looked up over her shoulder. "Tempting, but I do want that bath and supper!"

He patted her bottom appreciatively. "Until later, then."

By the time Jessie returned to her dressing room, servants were filling the tub, having entered by a door leading into the corridor. A cheerful young maid bobbed a curtsy. "I'm Elsa, my lady, and I'll be looking after you during your stay. What scent would you like added to your bath water?" She gestured at a collection of small bottles.

Naturally Jessie had to take a sniff of each. The scents were marvelous. She wondered if they'd been blended by Lady Kiri Mackenzie, the wife of another Westerfield old boy, and a talented perfumer. With difficulty, Jessie settled on a fragrance based on roses, though other subtle scents were present as well.

As Elsa unlaced her gown, the girl said, "A gift was sent to await your arrival. I took the liberty of brushing it out and hanging it in the wardrobe. There was a note included." She handed Jessie a folded piece of paper whose wax seal bore the Ashton coat of arms.

Jessie broke the seal and read the note.

> *Dear Jessie,*
> *Though you said that you would continue to wear half mourning in public, Julia and I thought you might like to have something deliciously decadent to wear for Daniel. We hope you both enjoy it!*
> *—Mariah*

When she glanced up, Elsa ceremoniously opened the door of the large wardrobe. Hanging inside was a sumptuous scarlet satin gown. A richly patterned scarlet and black shawl hung beside it, and neat kidskin slippers with scarlet embroidery were set below.

"Oh, my!" Jessie gasped as she stepped forward for a closer look. The gown was designed for the boudoir, with full skirts and a built-in train. The bodice laced up the front so a woman could put it on without assistance—and a man could take it off with equal ease. A discreet drawstring around the neckline made it possible to adjust the amount of décolletage from prim to falling off the shoulders.

"Is this a new fashion in London?" Elsa asked in a hushed voice. "I've never seen a gown like it!"

"Nor have I. It's designed for seduction, not public display." Jessie stroked the heavy satin, which rippled sensuously under her palm. "I'm not sure I dare wear it!"

"That red will look splendid with your dark hair, my lady." Elsa smiled mischievously. "And what new husband wouldn't like to see his bride in this?"

Elsa was right. The marriage had already been consummated in the carriage, so why not wear something magnificently wicked for the actual wedding night? "I'll wear it to dinner, then."

Elsa nodded approval and poured the rose bath oil into the hip bath. Jessie took off her cotton robe and sank into the fragrant bath water with a glass of sherry in hand. She felt marvelously decadent. If her father could see her now, he'd die of a heart spasm.

She grimaced into her sherry. Her mother's shocking visit had made her think of her father, and she didn't want to think of either of them. Tonight was for Daniel and her and no one else.

Daniel. She closed her eyes and leaned against the back of the hip bath and remembered their mad, magnificent coupling in the carriage. What had she been thinking? She laughed softly to herself. It was obvious what she'd been thinking.

Tonight they could take all the time they wanted, then sleep in each other's arms and wake to do it again. No wonder a wedding trip was known as the moon of honey.

Rosy from her bath and with her hair swooped up in an elegant mass that would tumble easily around her shoulders, Jessie donned her amazing new gown. The laces were black silk cords with oval pearls fastened on the ends. She tightened the lacing enough to give her an hourglass figure, which was easy since the billowing skirt and flowing bodice lent themselves to that shape. But she didn't tighten the cords so much as to interfere with her eating. It had been a long day, and she was hungry and not in the mood to nibble daintily. Except, perhaps, on Daniel.

She kept the décolletage relatively modest since she should leave a few surprises for her new husband to uncover. Turning, she checked her appearance in the long mirror. She looked like a pirate wench or a really expensive courtesan.

Behind her, Elsa said in a hushed voice, "You're beautiful, my lady! Would you like the shawl? The corridors will be chilly as it gets dark."

The shawl would also spare male servants from having a heart attack if they saw her. "Yes, please."

She draped the wrap around her shoulders. Except for the bright gleam of gold earrings, she was all scarlet and black. Perfect for a wicked woman.

"Has Lord Romayne gone down yet?" When Elsa nodded, Jessie said, "Then I have a once-in-a-lifetime opportunity to make a grand entrance. Thank you, Elsa."

The skirt was perfectly proportioned, short enough in front to show her black slippers and black silk stockings, and allow her to walk easily as the longer length in back whispered silently behind her. Buoyant with anticipation, she walked to the top of the grand staircase, and called, "Daniel?"

He stepped from the dining room and looked up. Smiling mischievously, she began descending the steps, one hand gliding down the banister so she wouldn't trip and fall unromantically at her new husband's feet.

She'd almost reached the bottom when she realized that Daniel seemed stunned, not dazzled. She stopped, clenching the railing, and feeling like an idiot.

He was a vicar, for heaven's sake! How could she have forgotten that? *"Harlot!"* Her father's raging voice echoed through her mind. *"You're a wicked slut like your mother! A filthy disgrace! You'll burn forever in hell!"*

"I look like the Whore of Babylon," she whispered in humiliation. "I-I'm so sorry. I'll change into something more respectable." She spun around to escape, and tripped on the long trailing hem. For a panicked moment she was falling.

Then Daniel was there, one arm around her waist and his other hand anchoring them to the banister. "Good God, never think such a thing!" he exclaimed. "I was just stunned. Whenever I think no woman could ever be lovelier, you turn around and are even more beautiful, and my brain becomes numb."

Her voice was unsteady. "I thought you looked horrified."

"Stunned, but in a good way." He kissed her temple. "I do hope I become somewhat accustomed to how lovely you are, or I'll be useless for the rest of my life." He descended to the bottom and offered his hand to assist her down the last steps as if she were made of spun glass.

It was impossible to doubt the sincerity in his voice, but her nerves were still twanging violently. "The gown was a gift from Mariah and Julia, and it's quite clear what it was designed for," she explained apologetically. "I should have saved it until you become a little bored with me."

"I can't imagine that happening ever." Side by side, they entered the dining room, where the staff had done their considerable best to create a perfect romantic dinner. A fire crackled quietly, candles glowed with flattering gentleness, and flower arrangements filled the air with subtle fragrances. The two place settings on the table were at right angles and close enough for the two of them to touch.

"I can already see normal life will seem sadly slow once we return to it," Jessie said as Daniel pulled out her chair.

"We haven't even worked out what and where normal life will be," Daniel said as he seated himself. "But I'm not designed for a life of leisure. I'll have to build a few hospitals to keep me busy."

"Is that a joke? I suspect not," she said curiously.

Conversation was suspended as Martin and the footman entered with trays of food. A variety of dishes were set on the table within easy reach, along with bottles of red and white wines. The butler said, "We can give you traditional service, but Lady Kirkland thought you might enjoy serving yourselves in privacy."

"My sister knows me well." Daniel poured a bit of white wine into his glass and tasted it. His eyebrows lifted. "So does my brother-in-law. I think we'll do fine on our own." He poured wine for Jessie.

"Ring if you wish anything more, my lady, my lord." The servants withdrew, leaving them blessedly alone.

Replying to Jessie's earlier question, Daniel said, "Starting new hospitals is no joke. The previous Lord Romayne was a keen and talented financial speculator, and he left a very substantial fortune. I now have the pleasant task of deciding how to spend it. I started a Zion House infirmary and dispensary in London, and I'd like to establish cottage hospitals in rural areas where I've worked and seen the need. The rich can get medical care in their own homes, but so many haven't the resources they need. Can you imagine trying to get a man with a broken leg up a ladder in a damp, tiny hovel?"

Jessie winced. "Unfortunately, I can. Actually, we could use a cottage hospital in the village of Kelham. I thought about it, but I wasn't sure where to start. How would you go about this?"

"I'd start with a good-sized house with several ground-floor rooms for patients, and quarters above for trained nurses and servants to care for the patients," he explained, his eyes bright with enthusiasm. "Many women already have basic nursing skills. Lady Julia and I have discussed establishing training programs where women can apprentice with more experienced nurses to learn what is needed."

"This sounds wonderful and feasible, but we do need to eat." Jessie stabbed a buttered prawn and held the fork to his lips.

He smiled and ate the prawn. "You are a splendidly practical woman, Lady Romayne." He speared another prawn and offered it to Jessie. Discussion died until all the prawns were gone.

After finishing the last one, Jessie licked butter from her lips, pleased to see Daniel's gaze riveted on the gesture. When she sipped her wine, he gave a small shake of the head, and asked, "How will you wish to spend your time, Jessie?"

She swallowed a bite of deliciously light cheese soufflé as she considered. "I'll probably have three or four households to manage, not to mention supervising estate work, and of course time with Beth and occasional work with the Sisters Foundation." And possible future children, a delicious prospect she hugged to herself. She swallowed the last of her wine and held out her glass for more. "I foresee much enjoyable problem solving in the future."

Daniel poured more wine for them both. "I don't think either of us will lack for occupation." Rubbing his foot gently against hers, he lifted a platter with small collops of chicken in a wine and mushroom sauce and served them each a piece.

Feeling very domestic, Jessie added a spoonful of an egg and onion mixture that was pleasantly flavored with mustard. As she leaned forward to put some on Daniel's plate, her loose bodice fell forward.

Daniel swallowed hard. "Perhaps it's time to feed other appetites."

She drank from her wineglass, then deliberately turned it and handed it to him so he could drink from the same place she had. "We have a few more dishes to sample."

He sipped from her glass, his gaze holding hers. After he returned it, his hand not so accidentally brushed her breast. Her nipple tightened instantly and she mentally moved the end of dinner closer.

Flirting outrageously, they tasted the other dishes, all of which were excellent and rather light, so as not to weigh them down with too much food on their wedding night.

Suddenly impatient, Jessie rose. "I've been yearning to see if that bed upstairs is as comfortable as it looks. Catch me if you can!"

Laughing, she pivoted and headed out the door, across the foyer, and up the stairs. What woman wouldn't like to be chased by an irresistibly handsome new husband?

Chapter 23

Grinning, Daniel pursued his beautiful bride up the sweeping stairs, her brilliant skirts billowing behind her. She was *fast*. Not that he wanted to catch her too soon.

She grabbed the newel post at the top of the staircase and used it to swing swiftly to the right. As she raced down the corridor to their rooms, he followed, slamming the door shut behind him.

The Milton Manor staff had built up the fires and lit the lamps, turning the illumination down enough to create a perfect seduction chamber. Jessie darted behind one of the sitting room sofas, which was part of a conversational grouping in the middle of the room but made a good barricade.

"Stalking the wild bride!" she called gaily. Her face was flushed with exertion and her breasts rose and fell tantalizingly under her scarlet silk bodice.

Distracted, he wondered what she was wearing under that wonderfully shocking gown. Not much, he suspected. "Is this where I prove that the male of the species is bigger and stronger than the female and resistance is futile?"

"Not futile at all," she purred, her striking eyes bright with pleasure. "Because the chase is part of the fun, my sober vicar husband!"

"Considering the amount of wine we drank, I don't think either of us is very sober just now." He edged around the sofa like a prowling lion.

"It's important in these matters to find just the right balance between sobriety and recklessness," she said in a firm, academic tone as she retreated step by step.

"And I am just reckless enough." He put one hand on the back of the sofa and vaulted over, landing right in front of Jessie.

She skittered backward. "So am I, my lad!"

When she was out of his reach, she clasped her hands with exaggerated terror, her lithe body enhanced by the cascading silk. "I risk your wrath when you finally capture me! What dreadful things might you do to a poor innocent bride?"

He laughed. "I believe you as a wild bride. As an innocent bride, you're less convincing."

"Oh?" She tried a little-girl pout while rolling her hips in blatant invitation.

"Try for Aphrodite, goddess of love." He closed the distance between them again.

She whirled to escape, but this time he wasn't letting her go. He caught her around the waist and pulled her back against him. He gasped as she wriggled her lush, entrancing backside against his groin. Was it softly firm or firmly soft? No matter, it was definitely entrancing. He cupped her amazing breasts, thinking he'd never be able to let them go. "Surely we're ready for that bed?"

She arched back against him, voice choked as she said, "Perhaps . . . we are."

He nuzzled his face into her hair and must have dislodged the only pins, because heavy dark coils tumbled free to fall silkily past his face and over her lovely shoulders. He closed his eyes, shaking with the force of the passion blazing through him. Through her. Binding them in a primal mating dance of seduction, possession, and delight.

He slid one arm under her knees, the other behind her back, and lifted her in his arms. "Now you can't run away," he said as he moved into the bedroom.

"I shall kiss you senseless and then make my escape." She wrapped her arms around his neck and proceeded to make good her threat.

She tasted of wine and warmth and infinite promise. He almost crashed into the door frame and barely managed to swerve away. Bruising his bride would dim the mood.

He ricocheted into the bed. He hadn't planned to drop her onto the broad mattress, but when he did, she bounced nicely. "Come here, big strong male of the species," she said as she opened her arms. "I surrender to your masterful superiority!"

"You definitely have had enough wine if you're going to pretend males are superior." He dragged off his coat and tossed it toward a chair, not caring where it landed. Knowing he'd not want to wrestle with boots on his wedding night, he'd worn light indoor shoes. He kicked them off, never taking his eyes from Jessie.

A maid had turned back the bedcovers during their meal and Jessie lay in a swirl of scarlet silk and shining dark hair, a blazing hot beauty framed by cool white linen. One of her black kid slippers had fallen off when he carried her, so he caught her other foot and freed it, sending the slipper in the general direction of his coat.

Having freed her foot, he decided to pay it due attention, massaging over toes and arch and up her ankle, his hand sliding over her black silk stocking. As he reached for the other foot, he said, "Your feet are as lovely as the rest of you."

"That feels wonderful." She wiggled her toes. "But my feet aren't small and dainty as a proper lady's feet should be."

"Nonsense. They're shapely and strong. And ticklish," he added when he ran a light finger under her left arch. She squeaked endearingly and pulled her foot back. "As a physician, I value strength and health. And you are a very healthy woman."

She wiggled her toes again. "In the long run, health is more useful than beauty. I shall be an ugly but healthy old crone."

"Never." He ran his hand up her stockinged calf to the knee. "You have beauty in the bones and in the heart." He pulled up her hem and undid the provocative garter tied just above her knee. "Black and red even here. Your friends are nothing if not thorough." He was unable to resist stroking her inner thigh. The road to paradise.

With difficulty, he managed to say, "Being women

of the world, surely they know that a man finds bare skin more beautiful than any gown."

He peeled off the other garter and stocking and was about to join her on the bed, when she said, "The same is true of both sexes, Daniel. I want to see all of you." She sat up, gazing at him with glowing eyes. "Please. Or I shall have to tear your clothing off. You are wearing far too much and I'm rather desperate to see your beautiful body."

He suspected he was blushing. "Not beautiful like yours, but healthy."

"*Very* healthy!" She gestured meaningfully at his straining trousers.

He was definitely blushing. "As you will, my lady, but I'm not all that interesting."

"I'll be the judge of that." She sat up and swung her legs over the side of the bed so that she was within touching distance.

His coat was already gone, and his cravat quickly followed. He unbuttoned his shirt and removed it more slowly, feeling self-conscious.

"You look very healthy, too, Dr. Daniel. Such lovely wide shoulders." Jessie leaned forward to touch, running her palm from his shoulder through the dusting of fair hair down his chest until she reached the trouser edge. "Lots of lovely lean muscle."

He sucked in his breath, feeling as if her palm had burned a path down his torso. "I'm glad you approve."

"I do." She grinned. "And you will become even more interesting as more of that fine hide of yours is revealed."

Fair was fair, but he was finding an unexpected strain of modesty in himself. As he undid his fall, he said, "Usually I'm the one dealing with bare skin while doing surgery. This is different."

"The change in roles will be good for you," she said callously.

Her interested gaze wasn't enough to reduce his state of arousal, but it was somewhat daunting, particularly when she frowned. Before he could dive for cover, she said, "What's this scar? It looks like it might have been made by a knife." She traced the curving line across his left hip.

"I was slashed by a drunken patient who thought I was a Barbary pirate or some such," he explained. "It wasn't serious."

She frowned. "I hope you'll check for weapons in the future. I have a vested interest in seeing that you maintain your present state of health."

"I'm in favor of that also," he assured her.

He stepped back to remove trousers and drawers, thinking it was a good thing the fires were lit to keep the room warm. "Now your turn, my lady! I've been entranced by the front lacing on your gown since you swept down the stairs."

She gave him a long, slow smile. "Then it's time you did something about it."

"The pearls on the ends of the laces are a particularly nice touch." He stepped in front of her where she perched on the edge of the bed and tugged at the black silk cords. "An invitation to pull."

When he loosened the laces, her bodice opened up in a long V all the way to her waist. "Good heavens, you really don't have anything underneath!" Except warm, silky skin that begged to be licked, and the most perfect full breasts he'd ever imagined.

"The stockings and garters are all I have in the way of undergarments," she said breathlessly as he bent his head to her left breast.

As his mouth closed over her nipple, he skimmed his right hand up her left leg under the layers of scarlet satin and found nothing but soft, smooth skin. He thought that his heart would stop, except that like Jessie, he had rude health on his side.

"My heart is going to give out before this night is over," he gasped as he forced himself away from her. "But what a wonderful way to go!"

"Please don't die on me, Daniel," she said, her great eyes suddenly serious. "I need you alive and well."

She did need him alive and well—the protection he offered was the basis of her accepting him. The thought was the smallest of shadows, of no importance on this night. Now was not the time to share his doctor's knowledge that life was uncertain and ultimately fatal. Better to draw on the minister's faith. "I shall do my best to maintain the good health of both of us. In fact, it's time I gave you a thorough physical exam."

He put his hands around her waist and pulled her to her feet. She came laughing, her gown half off of her. It wasn't much effort to loosen the bodice enough to slide it over her shoulders and hips. The gown fell to the floor in a whisper of silk to pool around her ankles.

"You look extremely healthy," he whispered as he followed the fabric down with his lips.

She swayed and clutched his shoulders. "Now. *Now* it's time for the bed!"

Agreeing, he wordlessly lifted her in his arms

and laid her on the mattress, then stretched out beside her. Though he intended to take his time, she pulled him to her with harsh urgency. "I want you so much, Daniel," she whispered as she grasped him with ultimate intimacy and urged him between her legs.

"Soon, my lady. Soon." He wanted something more than swift, mindless coupling this time, so he took exquisite moments to explore the moist, heated secrets of her hidden places. She moaned softly, her fingers curling into his back, taking him higher and higher.

When he could bear it no longer, he sank into her with a long, ragged exhalation. He'd thought nothing could match the mad rapture on the coach ride earlier, but he'd been wrong. Joining now was all that and more as they lay skin-to-skin, finding a rhythm together with accelerating need.

He wanted to make this mating last forever, or at least longer, but that goal splintered under the hammer of urgency. "Daniel," she said hoarsely. *"Daniel!"*

Her nails bit into him as she raged to culmination, taking him with her. He closed his eyes and surrendered to rapture. When he'd first seen Jessie, he'd thought reality could never match his mad yearning.

He'd been wrong.

As they lay exhausted in each other's arms, Jessie gave a small, silent thanks to the servants who'd built the fires that warmed these rooms. Even so simple an effort as pulling up a blanket seemed too great. The combination of wine, food, warmth, and incredible sensual satisfaction had left her drifting in hazy contentment.

Daniel stirred a little to pull her closer, his hand stroking tenderly down her back. "That was worth waiting for."

She breathed laughter on his shoulder. "Indeed." She felt very, very close to her new husband, and that was even more valuable than the incredible pleasure of their coupling. Even more than passion, emotional closeness could bind two very different people together into a real marriage.

"You're not like any vicar I've ever known," she mused as she admired his strong, regular profile. "I probably should have asked this earlier, but what part does your faith play in your life? Do you have any ambitions to someday work full-time for the Church, perhaps take on a parish? I don't think I'd make a good vicar's wife."

"That's not for me," he said. "Faith is a strange thing. I was born with it, like having blue eyes and fair hair. I've not always been on good terms with God, but I've never stopped believing. What I didn't inherit was a need to make others believe exactly as I do."

She smiled crookedly. "Which is why you're so very different from my father. He required absolute adherence to his beliefs from everyone around him."

"That's an excellent way to drive people from the Church," Daniel said dryly. "My faith would have stayed a quiet, private part of me, but since my parents were horrified with the idea of my becoming a surgeon, studying for the Church was a good compromise. Either way, I'd be helping people."

"In very different ways," she observed.

"True, but there are similarities." His hand came to rest warmly on her breast. "Both medicine and ministering require the ability to listen. To hear both what is said and what isn't said. When I chose to study medicine full-time, I was near enough being ordained that it seemed worth going all the way. Several times a year, I'll travel to some remote area that lacks doctors to perform surgery and provide other treatments. Sometimes it proves useful to be able to marry people."

She hadn't known of his medical journeys, but they didn't surprise her. He was, after all, a saint. She suspected that he would marry couples who might be rejected by people like her father, and that was a valuable service since a marriage wasn't legal unless performed by a cleric of the Church of England. The only exceptions to that were Quakers and Jews, who were allowed to marry with their own rites. "Is the listening different for doctors and pastors?"

"As a doctor, I must listen to discover what the real problem is, which isn't always obvious. As a minister, often I just let people talk until they work out for themselves what they must do. They usually know, but they have to say the words out loud to accept them." He shrugged. "If they need specific help, like food or work, I do what I can."

His ability to listen was one of the most restful things about him, she realized. "You've listened to me very well, and for that I'm deeply grateful."

"Listening to you is a pleasure, not a duty." Daniel pushed himself up on one hand to study her.

She would have felt shy, except for the warm admiration in his eyes.

"What a marvelous creation is a woman," he mused. He stroked down her body from ear to knee, not with lust but deep appreciation. "I just remembered that your mother said you had a heart-shaped birthmark on a place where it would not be seen, except perhaps by a husband. Probably that would mean on your back."

Before she could object, he deftly rolled her over so that she was lying on her stomach. "You have a lovely back. Such subtle, elegant curves. Now where's that birthmark? Ah, this might be it." He touched a finger to the upper part of her right buttock.

Intrigued, she said, "No wonder I've never seen it. Is it really shaped like a heart?"

"More like a set of lungs," he remarked. "Or possibly a pair of kidneys."

She laughed. "So unromantic, Doctor!"

"I haven't a poet's imagination, but I do feel quite romantic." He bent and pressed his warm lips to the birthmark.

She smiled, feeling deliciously relaxed, but ready to be reawakened for a sufficiently good reason. Then Daniel inhaled sharply.

Her lazy contentment knotted into fear. She'd been so enchanted by passion that she'd forgotten how much she had to conceal. She was such a *fool*!

"I recognize this scar," he said slowly, tracing a finger from her left shoulder blade down to her ribs. A jog to one side, then down to her waist. "From my Bristol infirmary. No wonder I thought you seemed familiar. But I didn't recognize your face because it was so badly bruised your own mother wouldn't have recognized you. You said your name was Jane. Why, Jessie?"

With a horror that threatened to stop her heart, she realized that the secret she'd desperately wanted to conceal had been exposed.

It would be better if she were dead.

Chapter 24

Daniel was still frowning with surprise when Jessie made a low, anguished sound and rolled away from him. She was off the bed and bolting toward the door before he collected his wits and went after her. He caught her from behind and pulled her close, wrapping his arms around her and wondering how his happy, self-confident bride could break down so quickly.

"It's all right, Jessie," he said in his most soothing voice. "You're safe now."

She stilled, but her breathing was harsh and she was shaking in his arms, her body chilled. Shock.

A knee robe was folded on the sofa, so he pulled it over and wrapped it around Jessie. Passive as a doll, she let him lead her to the bed. He laid her on the mattress and pulled the covers over her, then tossed more coal on the fire before he joined her.

Jessie rolled away and knotted herself up in a ball, so he enfolded her in his arms, her back against his front. Even with the robe, the blankets, and his body heat, she was shivering and her skin was clammy. "What happened to you was a crime, but not your fault," he said firmly. "You were the victim. There is nothing to be ashamed of."

When she didn't respond, he thought back to her infirmary visit. It had been seven or so years, and he'd seen many patients before and since. But even after all this time, he remembered the masses of bruises that rendered her unrecognizable, and his appalled shock when he discovered the long, bloody slash down her back. She was lucky to be alive.

What else did he remember? After a moment of thought, he said, "It was your husband who beat you, wasn't it? That's what you said." A memory of her dragging off her wedding ring and throwing it across the room seared his mind.

"Yes," she said in a barely audible whisper. "My first husband."

Glad to get some response, he said conversationally, "I suppose you became Jane because you started to say Jessie, then didn't want to reveal your real name. Jane is safely anonymous while Jessie is memorable."

"*Jezebel.*" Her voice broke. "My name is Jezebel. My father said it suited me."

"Your friends all know you as Jessie, which suits you much better." He was fully alert, trying to read her reactions, not easy when she was still turned away and knotted with misery.

"Ivo called me Jezebel," she said dully. "He said I was a slut and he should never have married a woman named Jezebel."

"Is that why he was so angry that he beat you? Because he was jealous?"

"I never gave him any reason to doubt my fidelity, but whenever he drank, he started accusing me of being a whore." Her voice broke. "He was drunk a lot."

"And his violence got worse over time." Daniel had seen that with other patients who had been battered by their menfolk.

She swallowed. "Yes, he said I was too beautiful to be faithful. That last night . . . he came at me with a knife, saying that when he got through cutting my face, my beauty would be gone and people would turn away from my ugliness." She began to cry, great shuddering sobs that threatened to rip her in half.

Daniel held her tighter and cursed the brutality of his sex. "He should have thanked God to have you for a wife." As Daniel thanked God. When her tears began to diminish, he asked, "How did you meet him? I would have thought your father kept a tight control on you."

She swallowed hard and managed to reply in a steady voice. "He usually did. I was never allowed out without a servant to watch me even in our small town where everyone knew everyone else. But one day when my father was out, the scullery maid was ill and the cook needed some chops for our dinner. She was busy and there was no one else available, so she sent me. There seemed no harm in it. Market day in Chillingham was very public."

"I imagine you were pleased to get outside and have a bit of freedom," Daniel remarked, hoping to encourage the flow of words.

"For me, going to the town square on market day was a grand adventure." Her voice turned ironic. "It turned out to be much more of an adventure than I could ever have imagined."

"You met Ivo Trevane there? Trevane was the name for the marriage license, wasn't it? A good West Country name."

She nodded, which he could feel even though her face was still turned away. "Ivo was passing through the village and decided to stop at the market so he could be entertained by the rustics."

"And then he saw you."

"And I saw him." She sighed. "I was young in years and younger in experience because I'd been allowed to see little of the world. Ivo was every girl's dream. Dark and dashing and terribly handsome. He was only a little older than I, and wonderfully romantic. He quoted poetry and claimed to adore me. I was dazzled by him." Her voice turned bitter. "I was sure it must be love everlasting."

"So you began a clandestine courtship."

Jessie nodded again. "I was a foolish girl ripe for the plucking, but since I was a vicar's daughter, he knew he'd better offer marriage, not just seduction."

Remembering the madness of young love, Daniel said gently, "He was probably just as smitten as you. You're enough to knock even a sober doctor off his feet." He hoped that would make her smile, and perhaps it did, but she was still turned away.

"Shakespeare was right about young love when he wrote *Romeo and Juliet*," she said flatly. "Mindless lust led to disaster."

"I always thought that it was politics and feuding

that led them to disaster. More tolerance and forgiveness would have meant no tragic ending. Of
course, then there would be no great play either."

"Tragedy is in greater supply than tolerance and
forgiveness."

Unfortunately, Jessie was right about that. "Ivo
lived in Bristol?"

"Yes, he had an estate in Dorset, but I never saw it
because he preferred his Bristol house. To me, the
city was magical. Plays and music and lending li-
braries. I couldn't believe how lucky I was to have
all that plus a passionate, adoring husband."

Daniel's mouth tightened and he had to remind
himself that he needed to know about her past, no
matter how much that knowledge might sting.
"How did you go from heaven to hell to the Herbert infirmary?"

"I hadn't realized how much Ivo drank before we
eloped and married. That was worrisome from the
beginning, but it became much worse after he
started inviting his friends to the house. They were
a rackety lot of young men, no real harm in them,
but they were madly flirtatious."

Daniel frowned. "And naturally your husband
blamed their behavior on you, which stoked his
jealousy."

"Exactly." Jessie rolled onto her back, wrapping
the blankets tightly around her and staring up at
the bed's canopy. Her words began to tumble over
each other, as if she was desperate to release long-
buried pain. "His jealousy became worse and worse.
His drunken rages started with screaming and soon
became violent. I learned to lock myself in a small
bedroom when his friends came over. I'd hide

there until the next day. He'd always be so apologetic the morning after. He'd swear never to do it again, and I wanted so much to believe him."

"Did you consider leaving?"

"Sometimes, but I had nowhere to go. I could never return to my father or Chillingham. I had no friends or family who would take me in." She bit her lip. "Worse, most of the time I didn't want to leave. When he was sober, life was wonderful. He'd be so charming, an ideal companion. Until he got drunk again."

"How long until the night you showed up at the infirmary?"

"Not quite a year." She closed her eyes and her voice fell to a whisper. "He came home from some stupid prize fight where he and his friends all drank till they could barely stand. I was reading in the library when he came in. Seeing how drunk he was, I excused myself. He became furious and started chasing me. When I ran upstairs, he tripped on the steps, which made him even more furious with me."

Daniel winced at the rising panic in her voice, but he owed it to Jessie to bear witness to the full terror of that night. Softly, he said, "Such men always blame others."

"I managed to get into my little safe room and lock the door, but he battered it down with a chair." She took a shuddering breath. "He began beating me much more badly than anything he'd done before. Then he choked me until I was unconscious."

Daniel took her hand, holding it tight. "What then?"

She drew a rasping breath. "When I regained my wits, he was slumped in a chair finishing off a flask of gin, ignoring the fact that I was in a bleeding heap in the middle of the floor. I managed to struggle to my feet and said I was leaving him. That I'd become a whore on the streets rather than live with him a day longer. I had almost reached the door when he caught me again. He pulled a knife from his boot and that's when he threatened to slash my face so no man would ever want me." Her mouth twisted. "I thought it more likely he'd kill me, given how out of control he was."

"If he'd been a little closer, that slash down your back could have been fatal. But you did get away." He squeezed her hand again. "Then you used a false name at the infirmary and left Bristol so he couldn't follow you. Brave girl."

Her eyes opened, pale and half-mad. "Oh, I knew he wouldn't follow me."

Icy dread warned him of what was coming. "Why not?"

"Because I killed him." Her voice broke. *"I murdered my husband with his own knife!"*

Chapter 25

Jessie had spent years suppressing memories of that ghastly night, but now they scalded through her like boiling blood. The terror and agony of Ivo's fists slamming into her. The ghastly experience of his large hands choking her until she was almost unconscious. The razor edge of his blade hovering by her face as he threatened to mutilate her. When he'd paused to shove his dark hair from his sweaty, raging face, she'd jerked away and made a panicky dash for the shattered door.

That was when he stabbed her. The knife point hit her shoulder blade, then sliced down her back with a jog to the left when it hit her stays before cutting down to her waist. She screamed and collapsed onto her knees, paralyzed by the pain and convinced she was dying. Ivo yanked her to her feet, screaming filthy threats as he brandished the knife, his handsome face distorted like one of hell's own demons.

She'd struggled frantically to escape, grabbing his wrist as the bloody blade slashed inexorably down at her. With the strength of desperation, she managed to force the knife away from her—and it plunged lethally into the base of Ivo's throat.

"Are you sure he was dead?" Daniel's voice was calm, as if he heard such tales every day. Perhaps he did.

"Oh, yes." She shuddered. "I managed to check for a pulse, but there was none." She pressed a hand to her stomach, feeling like she wanted to vomit. "No one could survive losing so much blood."

"What kind of wound did you inflict?"

For a moment she hated his calm, doctorly questions about the horror she'd experienced, but it was better than if he threw her from their bed and cursed her very existence. Trying to match his calm, she drew a line just above the collarbone. "I cut his throat."

"A man could bleed to death very quickly from such a wound," he said dispassionately. "No wonder you were in shock when you arrived at the infirmary. You were very strong and very brave that day."

Her lip curled at his words. "I was a terrified murderer running for my life! Though my father would probably have been pleased to see me hang. That would have confirmed all his worst beliefs about me."

"It was self-defense!" Daniel said sharply. "You'd never have been convicted."

"I wasn't so optimistic. So I ran as far and fast as I

could." She drew a deep, shaky breath. "I've never forgotten the kindness you and your sister showed me that night. I might have gone mad if not for you. If you hadn't given me that money, I never would have made it to safety. You also reminded me that not all men are evil."

"Most men aren't," he said thoughtfully. "Even Ivo probably wasn't, but he was a drunk, which can bring out the worst in anyone. He was responsible for his own death."

"I'm glad you think so," she said wearily. But she would never forget that the husband she'd once loved passionately had died in front of her, by her hand.

"If it's any comfort," he said, "your visit to the infirmary that night convinced Laurel that we must establish a refuge for women and children. That was the beginning of Zion House, and many, many people have benefited from her work."

"If I hadn't been the inspiration, some other woman would have been," she said, her voice dull. "Helping women and children is your sister's calling. A saint, like you."

A trace of exasperation showing, Daniel said, "I wish you'd stop thinking I'm a saint. I'm not. Neither is Laurel, though she comes closer."

Jessie shrugged. They were too far apart on the moral scale for him to understand. She'd tried so hard to resist her attraction to him because she hadn't wanted him to know who and what she was, or how they'd first met.

Now he knew the worst of her, and even a polite saint would be affected by that knowledge. Affected and eventually repulsed. For a few brief hours, she'd manage to bury all thoughts of her past and just enjoy her new husband. Now that golden moment had been shattered, and such moments did not come again.

Wearily, she asked, "Will you report my murder to the Bristol magistrates? I imagine there was quite a furor when Ivo died, since he was a gentleman of means."

"He may have had means," Daniel said dryly, "but he was no gentleman. No, of course I won't turn my own wife in. A painful trial with you acquitted on the grounds of self-defense would benefit no one and would cause great damage. It would haunt Beth forever, and she certainly is an innocent."

So protecting Beth would also mean protecting herself. Jessie realized that in some deep, irrational part of her, she believed she deserved to be punished for killing Ivo. Though God knew she'd suffered plenty of punishment while he was still alive. "So you believe me when I say it was self-defense? I have no evidence to support my word."

"When we negotiated our marriage, you told me you wouldn't tell me everything, but what you did say would be the truth," he said thoughtfully. "I imagine this is what you never wanted to reveal, isn't it? You don't have any more dreadful secrets?"

She almost smiled. "Today you met my bigamous mother and found out that you married a murderer. I think that's about it."

"All in all, it's been a momentous day for all sorts of reasons." His voice softened. "Go to sleep, Jessie. Tomorrow will be a better day."

She certainly hoped so. But something inside her had been broken, and she doubted it could ever be repaired.

At least she wouldn't be going to jail. "Thank you, Daniel," she said softly. Then she rolled away from him and prayed that she would sleep and not dream.

Daniel slept badly. It wasn't easy sharing a bed with an unhappy bride even if he wasn't at fault. Jessie lay on the edge of the mattress, her back turned to him. He suspected she wasn't getting much sleep either, and her body language made it clear that she wanted to be left alone.

As dawn lightened the windows, he finally rolled over and spooned her, lying along her back and tucking his arm around her waist. "A difficult night?"

Jessie sighed. "I'd done a fairly good job of burying my time in Bristol. Not that I ever forgot, but the memories were hidden away where I didn't have to think of them. Last night, they all flew out like the evils released from Pandora's box. There's no burying them again."

He grimaced. "I'm sorry I mentioned the knife scar. But once I recognized it, I couldn't ignore it. I'd wondered sometimes if Jane got away from Bristol safely, and what happened to her after."

"As harrowing as last night proved to be, I'm not entirely sorry you recognized me," she said slowly, surprised by the insight. "I didn't want you to ever learn what I'd done, or recognize me from the infirmary, so I tried to keep you at a distance. Yet it was such a huge secret to keep from my husband. Given a choice, I much prefer honesty."

"So do I." Cuddling the most desirable woman in England was having the predictable effect on his male parts. "Would doing something pleasurable drive away some of the demons of memory?" He accompanied his words with a gentle caress that ended with cupping her breast, his thumb teasing her nipple.

The nipple stiffened and so did she, but not in a good way. She was still as a rabbit hoping a wolf will pass it by. As a doctor, Daniel knew a great deal about physical reactions and it was clear what hers was.

Doing his best to sound conversational, he said, "Not in the mood?"

Strain in her voice, she said, "You are my husband. I will not deny you."

In other words, she'd do her marital duty no matter how much she'd rather not. For a long, tense moment, he was tempted to take her at her word. The joyful passion of the day before was vivid in his mind and in his loins, and he had enough male arrogance to think that he might be able to put her in the mood.

But this was a woman who had been abused by her father, nearly murdered by her first husband, and raped and ill-used by her fiancé. She did not need more evidence that men were selfish pigs. Nor did he want to put himself in the same category as the men who'd used her so badly.

He forced himself to remove his hand from the

soft delight of her breast. "Better to wait until you're not drowning in demons."

Unable to conceal her relief, she said, "I'm sorry. It was like this after . . . after Ivo. Every shred of desire in my nature vanished for months."

Months. Suppressing a sigh, he rolled away from her onto his back, thinking he deserved a damned gold medal for restraint. A honeymoon was supposed to be full of mad, passionate exploration, enough to bind a couple together until death did them part. But he'd never done things the rational way—and Jessie was the woman he wanted. "I presume you don't wish to be touched at all."

"No!" She also rolled onto her back and took his hand. "Touch for comfort would be lovely, but . . . I don't want anything more." Her voice turned rueful. "Which would be so unfair to you that I'm sure you'd prefer not to touch me at all."

Relieved, he slid an arm under her shoulders and pulled her close to his side. "Wrong. Touching from affection is even more vital than touch from desire."

She exhaled softly and the tension eased from her taut body as she rested her head on his shoulder. "This won't last forever. I'll return to normal in time."

"Was yesterday's passion what you would consider normal?"

She ducked her head as if blushing. "Yes."

"That's worth waiting for." Concealing his regrets, he pulled the covers over them. It hardly seemed fair to be lying naked in bed with his beautiful and charming bride, and be constrained to do nothing more than merely hold her. He wondered if he'd ever see Jessie's amazing scarlet seduction gown again.

Sometimes God had an extremely strange sense of humor.

Chapter 26

The next few days made an odd sort of honeymoon, but it wasn't unpleasant. Jessie and her very patient new husband walked in the gardens, rode on the estate, and ate marvelous meals. And they talked. Now that she had no secrets left, conversation flowed easily. Daniel had an impressive range of knowledge.

She also came to enjoy his wry, subtle sense of humor. The good doctor was not always as serious as she'd first thought.

Occasionally some touch or scent or image would remind her sharply of the passion they'd shared on their wedding day. She remembered clearly how joyful and satisfied they'd both been, yet the thought of lying with him now made her want to curl in a ball like a hedgehog.

She wondered how many men would have exercised Daniel's restraint. Very few, she suspected. If he'd insisted on claiming his marital rights, she would have cooperated in her wifely duty. But she would have felt invaded and despairing.

Surely this would pass, and she hoped that would happen more quickly than after her marriage to Ivo ended. But for now, she was deeply grateful to Daniel, a man who had seen everything and accepted life's strangeness with tranquility.

He also had a quiet confidence that was immensely appealing. She'd done well when she'd chosen him. She just hoped that his tolerance would enable him to accept all the problems that came with her.

Jessie was a splendid companion, which was some compensation for the fact that they weren't sharing a bed. Daniel had excellent self-discipline, but he had no desire to torment himself any more than necessary, so on their second night at Milton Manor, Daniel had silently piled spare blankets in front of the fireplace to make up a pallet.

Jessie accepted his action with equally silent gratitude. In the morning, they wordlessly folded the blankets and put them away again. Cooperation without conversation. If the servants knew that they weren't sleeping together, Laurel and Kirkland would know very shortly thereafter, and this was a situation Daniel had no desire to discuss.

The fifth morning dawned to a steady rain, so they retreated to the small library, where they cozily settled down to read in wing chairs set on opposite sides of the fireplace. A small coal fire drove off the autumn chill and damp.

After a couple of hours, Daniel rose to stretch his

legs. It was time to visit the adjacent music room, which he'd not seen yet. Pride of place was held by a fine piano, as would be expected in any Kirkland residence.

He sat down and ran some scales. The instrument had a beautiful tone and it was well-tuned, so his fingers slid into a favorite piece by Bach.

Even turned away from the connecting door, he knew when Jessie joined him. She was a warm presence at his back as he finished the piece. When he was done, Jessie clapped her hands. "Lovely! I didn't know you were a musician."

He glanced up and briefly lost himself in her marvelous eyes. Clear as fine diamonds, yet with depths to drown in. . . .

Shaking off his momentary distraction, he said, "I'm a journeyman pianist, not a real musician like Laurel and Kirkland. I play for pleasure and well enough to accompany dancers or informal singers." He began to play and sing the wistful, minor key old favorite, " 'Are you going to Scarborough Fair? Parsley, sage, rosemary, and thyme. Remember me to a lass that lives there, For once she was a true love of mine. . . .' "

His hands stilled as the poignant sadness of the song struck him. Parsley, sage, and Rose, his lovely Rose, lost for all time. Jessie laid a quiet hand on his shoulder, understanding.

Shaking off the sadness, he said, "You must be missing Beth madly. Should we leave tomorrow so we can collect her early?"

"Madly," Jessie agreed, but to his surprise, she continued. "But the note I got from Mariah this morning said Beth is flourishing, and I'm really enjoying this quiet time with you. Life will become very busy once we leave here."

Pleased, he said, "As you wish." He played a series of ringing chords. "I play a lot of hymns, too. There's nothing like music for rousing the spirits."

He blasted into a thundering rendition of "A Mighty Fortress Is My God" and sang along, his spirits lifting. " 'A mighty fortress is our God, a bulwark never failing. . . .' " Jessie joined in, her alto blending well with his baritone.

When he finished the hymn, Jessie said admiringly, "You're a good pianist, but your singing is outstanding. You have a wonderful deep voice."

"Useful for dragging a congregation into song," he said with a smile. "I can play hymns all day long. Raised in a vicar's house, you must know your share."

"Fewer than you might think. My father considered singing frivolous and too likely to lead to frolicking, and he did *not* approve of frolicking! So he kept the music to a minimum in his services."

"He still does." The comment came from behind them, and Daniel rose and turned in one swift motion. Standing in the doorway was his old classmate, Gordon, mud spattered and travel worn.

"Sorry," Gordon said. "I didn't mean to startle you. When I said I needed to speak to you, your butler sent me to the library, and from there I followed the music."

"You made good time," Daniel said. "Jessie, this is Gordon, another old schoolmate of mine. He was at the wedding."

"Ah, the man who kept my mother from escaping." Jessie smiled warmly. "I'm glad to meet you properly. Were you traveling nearby and decided to pay a call?"

"Actually, I asked him to do a bit of investigation for me," Daniel said. "Have you had any success?"

When Gordon glanced at Jessie, Daniel said, "It's all right to speak in front of my wife since this concerns her. Jessie, Gordon does discreet investigations, so I asked him to find your father, dead or alive."

As Jessie inhaled sharply, Gordon said, "It was easy enough. Mr. Braxton is still vicar of the parish church of St. George in Chillingham."

Jessie sank onto the piano bench, looking pale. "So my father is still among the living."

"He appears to be in rude good health," Gordon replied.

"Certainly rude, I'm sure," she said dryly. "Has he alienated all his parishioners?"

Gordon hesitated. "He inspires some respect, but little affection."

Jessie's gaze moved to Daniel. "Why did you ask Mr. Gordon to seek him out?"

"Because it's better to know than not," Daniel replied.

"I suppose you're right," she said without enthusiasm.

From Jessie's expression, she had the same thought Daniel did: that her mother was a bigamist. Luckily, the Reverend Braxton was unlikely to ever find out.

"Is there anything remarkable about my father's life that I should know about?" Jessie asked. "Has he acquired a mistress or adopted orphans or started to wear a color other than black?"

"If so, he's been very discreet about it," Gordon said dryly. "But I believe he's published a theological article or two."

"He was never a very interesting man." She rose. "I'm not much of a hostess. Would you care for some refreshment? Or given the weather, would you like to spend the night?"

Gordon chuckled. "I'm not such a fool as to stay with honeymooners. An hour's ride and I'll be home." He bowed. "A pleasure to meet you properly, Lady Romayne."

"I'll walk you out," Daniel said as a thought struck him. After they were away from the music room, he asked, "Do you have time to take on another investigation?"

"I've some time." Gordon cocked a brow. "What would you like to know?"

What had been the date when "Jane" showed up at the infirmary? Daniel couldn't remember exactly, but it had been early autumn. "About seven years ago at this time of year, a young man called Ivo Trevane was murdered in Bristol. He was a gentleman of some means with a house in the city and an estate in Dorset."

Gordon pulled a small notebook from inside his coat and jotted down the details with a short pencil. "What in particular would you like to know?"

"Was there a furor when he died? Was his murderer ever found? Did he have family? Anything that might be interesting."

Gordon tucked the notebook away. "The fellow

has to be more interesting than Braxton. I'll see what I can find. Where should I send the information?"

"After we leave here and collect Jessie's daughter, we'll head down to Castle Romayne in Dorset. I have no idea what we'll find."

"Responsibilities," Gordon said tersely as they entered the front foyer.

Daniel laughed. "I'm sure you're right. Thanks for finding Mr. Braxton." He offered his hand. Gordon gave it a firm shake and headed out into the damp day. At least it was no longer raining.

Daniel returned to the library, where Jessie was sitting by the fire and gazing at the flames rather than reading the book in her lap. When he entered, Daniel said, "I hope you don't mind my sending Gordon to look for your father."

"It's just as well you didn't mention it. The less I think about him, the better." She smiled ruefully. "The big question now is whether to tell my mother."

"Don't." Daniel reclaimed the opposite chair. "She would not want to know."

Jessie's brows arched. "You have no vicarly qualms about the immorality of my mother's behavior?"

"I was put on this earth to heal, not to judge," he said dryly. "A good rule of thumb is to consider the benefits of revealing such a truth. In this case, no one would benefit, other than eager gossips who enjoy chewing over the misery of others. Exposing your mother's bigamy would badly damage her family, perhaps shatter it altogether. And for what purpose? She'll never go back to her legal husband, and it's unlikely he'd be willing to take her back. She seems to be a loving wife, mother, and daughter-in-law. Though she's breaking the law of the land, she may not be breaking higher law."

Jessie nodded slowly. "I like your rule of thumb. I, more than anyone, know why my mother behaved as she has because I also ran away from Cassius Braxton and did what I needed to survive."

"Would you have committed bigamy like your mother?" Daniel asked.

She frowned, then shook her head. "No, no matter how much I wanted to be with a new man, I could never stand at the altar and live such a great lie. It would be an unforgivable crime against the man standing beside me."

"I find that reassuring," he commented.

Her rueful smile returned. "As I said, I haven't left any abandoned husbands along the way. What I'm really wondering is whether I should visit my father."

It was Daniel's turn to arch his brows. "Are you sure you want to do that?"

"I don't want to, but I think I should." Her mouth twisted. "I'm my father's daughter after all. 'Ought' and 'should' were two of his favorite words. I can't imagine that such a meeting would be pleasant or productive, but now that I've confessed the truth about my first husband, I'm feeling some desire to face the great fears of my past. To be free as I enter this new phase of my life. What do you think?"

"I think meeting him would be wise as a way of clarifying to yourself how far you've come," Daniel said slowly. "Would you want me to go with you?"

"Oh, please, yes! I don't think I could face him

on my own." She cocked her head to one side. "Can you bear it?"

"He's not my father, so it shouldn't be a great strain. I've dealt with my share of abusive bullies." He considered. "Shall we go to Ralston Abbey for Beth, then to Chillingham and on to Castle Romayne later? That would be the most efficient route."

"I don't want Beth anywhere near my father!" Jessie said vehemently. "It will mean more time rattling around in a coach, but I'd rather go to Chillingham first. I can retrieve her on my own if you can't get away."

"We can go together. We'll go to Chillingham, and since that's close to Romayne, we can visit the castle for a couple of days to get a sense of the place and what is needed there," Daniel said. "Then we can collect Beth. Luckily, all these places are in the southwest so the travel won't be too bad."

"That's a good plan. I'll write a note to Mariah to let her know she'll have Beth for a few more days, along with a note to Beth."

"Can she read?" he asked with interest.

"Only a little, but I draw quick little sketches of things to amuse her." Jessie's face lit up. "Beth loves to draw and often we'll send sketches back and forth. Today, I'll do the swans we saw in the lake when we took our walk yesterday."

What a lucky little girl Beth was. Any children Daniel and Jessie might have together would be equally lucky, and have the bonus of Beth as a big sister. "After you write your notes, I'll take them to Martin and ask him to have the carriage ready to go tomorrow morning."

There was a writing desk in the corner of the library, so Jessie moved to it and used the paper, pen, and ink for her note to Mariah, and a pencil for the note to Beth. After sealing both with wax, she said, "Will you address and frank these for me?"

"This is one part of being a lord I keep forgetting about," he mused. "I need to examine my conscience on the subject since peers and members of Parliament are supposed to use franking only for official business, though that's constantly abused."

Jessie looked disappointed. "No franking? I dislike my friends having to pay when they receive letters from me."

"I was thinking more along the lines of general postal reform. Why should those who are best off have free postage when those who can least afford it must pay? Britain needs some kind of national penny post." He joined her at the desk and wrote the address in his own hand, which was a requirement for franking, then scrawled ROMAYNE on the upper right corner of the sealed letter.

As he wrote, Jessie said, "As a member of the House of Lords, you can work on such reforms."

"Indeed, I can. I'm beginning to appreciate the advantages of this lord business." He stood, saying, "I'll take these to Martin now."

The house wasn't large enough to make the butler difficult to find. Daniel arranged for Jessie's notes to be sent and their carriage to be prepared for the morning, but before he left, he asked, "Are you the Martin who was instrumental in saving my sister's life several months ago?"

Martin's professional polish vanished as he said

gravely, "Yes, and I was very glad I was able to assist, my lord."

In fact, this young man's assistance had been critical, and he'd been seriously injured in his service. "You have my profoundest thanks," Daniel said quietly. "If there is ever anything I might do for you, you have only to ask."

"I would do anything for Lady Kirkland, so no reward is required," Martin said simply. "Lord Kirkland was very generous even though I asked for nothing."

"Was his reward this position of butler?" Daniel asked.

"I always wanted to become a butler, but I also wanted to continue working for the Kirklands, so his lordship gave me this position." Martin's smile showed his youth. "And her ladyship gave me and my Molly a grand wedding just last month."

"So you're also a newlywed!" Daniel said warmly. "Congratulations to you both."

Forgetting even more of his professional detachment, Martin said, "Marriage is the grandest thing imaginable, isn't it, my lord?"

"One of God's best inventions," Daniel agreed with a laugh. "Milton Manor would be a fine place to raise a family, I'm sure."

Martin gave a smile that lit up his whole face, and his ears turned pink. Clearly he and his Molly were working hard to start that family.

As he left Martin, Daniel realized that if Rose had survived, they would have had a marriage that was as straightforward and happy as that of Martin and his Molly. Instead, he had Jessie, with her beauty and her complexities and her responsibilities.

Life would have been simpler with that youthful marriage. Yet he could no longer imagine anyone but Jessie as his wife.

Chapter 27

Daniel gazed out the carriage window at the stark Dorset heath. "We'll arrive at Chillingham soon. Does the countryside look familiar?"

She shook her head. "Not really. I recognize some of the village names, but I very seldom left Chillingham, so I don't know much beyond the town itself."

"Does the town have an inn? The day is well advanced, and even if your visit with your father is very brief, there might not be time to find lodgings in another town."

Jessie's hands were clenched into fists as she tried to control her tension. She suspected Daniel was making casual conversation to distract her. "The George is the closest thing to an inn that Chillingham has. There are only a few rooms, but it was clean and the food was good. The owners, Mr. and Mrs. Brown, were always kind to me."

"The George sounds as if it will do nicely. Shall we book a room and freshen up a bit, then go and call on your father?"

Jessie nodded. "The sooner I get this over, the better."

Daniel said seriously, "You don't have to see him."

"I rather think I do." She stared at her knotted hands and remembered her childhood in too vivid detail. After her mother had disappeared, she'd lived in constant fear of her father. Even now, his cruel hand shaped her life. She wanted to be free of that. Not that she'd ever be free of the memories, but perhaps she could banish the fear.

The road descended from the heath into a green and fertile valley. As the carriage entered the town, Jessie stared out the window and was startled by how little had changed. Her breathing tightened as she had a swift, horrible feeling that she'd fallen back into her childhood, and her escape and multiple husbands were just a dream.

Sharply she reminded herself that Ivo had been more of a nightmare, and that she had indeed escaped. And this time, she would not face her father alone and vulnerable.

"The George is ahead on the right," she said. "That's the market square ahead, and today is market day. You can see the tower of the church on the far side of the square, and the parsonage is beside it. Chillingham is a compact little town."

She noticed people peering from windows at their shiny black coach, which was on loan from Kirkland. They would be stirring up speculation even before she was recognized as the returning prodigal daughter. The prodigal son had needed forgiveness and healing. Jessie doubted that she

would receive either of those, but she needed—
something.

Their driver slowed and swung the carriage
under the archway that led into the George's courtyard. Nothing had changed except perhaps the
color of the geraniums in tubs that framed the door
to the small office.

Though Chillingham was not on a major coach-
ing route, the inn did a steady business. It had seemed
an exotic place to Jessie when she was a child because
the coaches were a connection to distant, fascinating places. She'd watch carriages and wonder wistfully where the passengers came from and where
they were going.

As Daniel helped Jessie from the vehicle, he remarked, "We've been living off the generosity of
the Ashtons and Kirklands, but as soon as we stop
moving, we'll need to acquire servants and carriages and all the other paraphernalia to support
our lordly lifestyle. I have every intention of leaving
that to you, since you've been a baroness much
longer than I've been a baron."

She smiled as she alighted and scanned the neatly
kept courtyard. "I shall greatly enjoy spending money
and giving jobs to people who want them. I'll start
with a lady's maid. I didn't need a full-time maid at
Kelham, so Lily took care of me as well as Beth, but
that won't work anymore. Elsa, the maid who
helped me at Milton Manor would do very well,
and she seemed eager to see more of the world.
Would Kirkland and your sister mind if I try to hire
her away?"

"If you ask politely, I'm sure they'll be reasonable." He made a face. "I expect I'll need to acquire a valet as well."

"The right man will make your life easier," she promised as she took his arm and guided him toward the office.

They stepped into the office and the rosy, middle-aged woman working at a battered desk looked up, then gasped. "Miss Lisbet! Is that really you?" She scrambled to her feet, her face alight with excitement.

Jessie caught the older woman's hands. "Mrs. Brown, you haven't aged a day!"

"What a sweet liar you are, my dear. I'm a gray-haired granny now, and happy to be!" Mrs. Brown glanced at Daniel. "I imagine you're not Miss Braxton anymore?"

"Indeed, I'm not. This is my husband, Lord Romayne."

Daniel bowed to the innkeeper. "It's a pleasure to meet an old friend of my wife, Mrs. Brown. I hope you can accommodate us tonight?"

"I have only one room available," the innkeeper said apologetically. "It's our largest, but maybe you'd rather stay at the parsonage? Your father has much more space."

Jessie arched her brows, and Mrs. Brown said hastily, "I suppose not. Well, the blue chamber is the best in our house."

"I'm sure it will be splendid," Daniel assured her.

Mrs. Brown shook her head in amazement as she studied Jessie. "My, you look fine. So you're Lady Romayne now and will be mistress of that great castle down on the coast!" Her gaze was admiring when she studied Daniel. Dropping her voice to a stage whisper, she said, "Such a handsome gentleman! No wonder you eloped with him! Though I'd thought it was that dark boy you ran off with?"

Jessie hesitated, wondering how much to say. Certainly not everything. "Sadly, my first husband died, but I am twice blessed, for I found Lord Romayne. He's only recently inherited, so this will be our first visit to the castle."

But before the castle, she must confront the dragon. Drawing a deep breath, she said, "If you'll show us to our room, we'll freshen up a bit, then call on my father."

"Right this way, then. Do you wish to order dinner here tonight?"

Jessie glanced at Daniel. When he nodded, she ordered the meal and they followed Mrs. Brown upstairs. The room was spacious, with a small sitting area and a comfortable-looking bed. There wasn't much space for Daniel to sleep on the floor, but they'd manage. Sharing a bed was a minor issue at the moment.

After the innkeeper left, Daniel said, "At least one person is happy to see you."

"There will be a few. Women and children who I met in church since I wasn't allowed to go much of anywhere else." Jessie removed her bonnet and inspected her appearance. She was wearing a lavender gown, which was the most cheerful of the colors considered acceptable for half mourning, and it was a shade that suited her very well. Defiantly she added a shawl richly woven in shades of purple, green, and gold.

Daniel stepped behind her and rested his hands on her shoulders as she gazed at her image in the mirror. "You look like a woman of consequence," he said. "Formidable."

"I'm not sure that's true, but it's what I need to hear," she said ruefully. "Now I must beard the beast in his den."

"It's walking distance," Daniel said. "But would you prefer the carriage take us through the market so you won't be recognized?"

Anonymity was tempting, but she shook her head. "That would be pretentious for such a short distance. Plus, all of the town and its inhabitants are part of the fabric of my past. I should face it all."

"What role do you want me to play?" he asked. "Lurk quietly in the background and say little?"

His calm gaze steadied her nerves. On impulse, she brushed a light kiss on his cheek before stepping back and pulling on her gloves. "Yes, and be prepared to rescue me if I fall apart and need it!"

"You will manage this as you've managed everything else that has come up in your life." He opened the door, adding, "For better or worse, this will soon be over."

Jessie hoped he was right. They descended the stairs and stepped out onto the High Street. She took his arm as they turned left and walked toward the crowded town square. As they neared the market, they began to attract attention.

First there was interest in their fashionable appearance. Then a woman said, "Why, it's Miss Braxton, sure enough! Look at those eyes!"

A wizened old woman swung from behind a

table of fruit and vegetables for a closer look. "Sure enough, little Lisbet, all grown up!" She offered a crooked-toothed smile. "You're looking very well, girl! And who's this fine gentleman?"

Mrs. Potts, that was the woman's name. She was a farm woman who came into the market with her produce, and who'd always been generous with the leftover apples at the end of a market day. "Mrs. Potts," Jessie said. "It's so good to see you! This is my husband, Lord Romayne. May I buy an apple for old times' sake?"

The old lady cackled. "Have a couple for free, for old times' sake!" She picked two firm red apples from her table and tossed one at Daniel and one at Jessie.

Jessie would have fumbled and dropped hers, but Daniel caught both, then bowed deeply. "Many thanks, Mrs. Potts!" He straightened and tossed her a bright, shiny sixpence that he'd produced. "Now you have a mug of cider for old times' sake!"

Mrs. Potts caught the coin deftly with another cackle of laughter. "You got yourself a good 'un, Miss Lisbet!"

There was a murmur of general approval from the onlookers, but a furious woman's voice hissed, "Whore!"

Jessie ignored the comment, but Daniel looked in the direction of the anonymous voice, his expression suddenly cold. No more insults were heard from that quarter.

Jessie tucked both apples in her reticule, where they made a rather suggestive double bulge, then took Daniel's arm and they continued through the market square. She returned the greetings of those she recognized, but maintained a pace that discouraged conversation.

The only exception was a bright-eyed blond girl of thirteen or fourteen who cut through the crowd, wild with excitement. "Miss Lisbet, you've come back!"

Jessie stared, trying to imagine the bright hair and blue eyes eight years earlier. "Emily Tipton, all grown up!"

She spontaneously hugged the girl. As a small child, Emily had followed Jessie around, her eyes adoring. The daughter of the local apothecary, she'd had a quick mind and lively curiosity. Jessie had loved helping the child with her reading and telling her interesting new facts as Jessie learned them.

Emily laughed and hugged her back. "I was so afraid I'd never see you again! How long will you be in Chillingham? Mama and Papa would love to see you! Papa has been teaching me how to compound medicines."

Jessie had sometimes been sent to pick up medicines and potions, so she knew the Tiptons better than she knew most of the residents of the town. They'd always been kind to her, too. With real regret, she said, "We're just spending a single night. But I'm glad I've had the chance to see you."

Emily was crestfallen, but she said bravely, "At least I have a chance to say hello. Perhaps you'll come this way again?"

"Perhaps." Jessie pulled Daniel forward for an introduction. Since Castle Romayne was less than a day away, they might come this way in the future. If they wished.

Excusing herself from Emily, Jessie took Daniel's arm again and they continued through the market until the square narrowed down to the east end of the High Street. The church was only a block away, its square Norman tower as sturdy as ever. Jessie's fingers tightened on Daniel's arm. "The vicarage is the large house on the far side of the church."

He patted her hand. "How are you doing? Most of the Chillingham populace seems glad to see you alive and well."

"I never had much opportunity to make enemies," she explained. "It was strange. As the daughter of the vicar, my status was high, but I think most people were sorry for me. No mother and Cassius Braxton for a father."

They passed the church, and she thought of all the hours she'd spent kneeling on the cold stone floor under orders to pray for her miserable soul. The only effect was to reinforce her desire to run away.

The church was behind them and the parsonage now loomed on the left. The warm gray local stone used for the houses of Chillingham was usually appealing, but the sprawling stone vicarage looked cold and threatening. In truth, it was both.

A tall iron fence surrounded the property, and the gate squealed ominously when Daniel swung it open. After they passed through and walked to the front door, Jessie paused, chilled to the bone.

"It's going to be a terrible anticlimax if your father isn't home," Daniel said as he stepped up and wielded the knocker.

She knew he was trying to ease her tension, but all she could do was shake her head wordlessly. If her father wasn't in, she might not have the courage to go through this again.

The door swung open, and standing there was Miss Ludley, the meanest woman in Chillingham. A flamboyantly righteous spinster, she'd been devoted to both the church and its vicar.

When Miss Ludley saw who was on the doorstep, she looked as if she wanted to spit. *"You!"*

Jessie's paralysis dissolved and she offered an insincere smile. "The prodigal returns, Miss Ludley. Are you now the vicarage housekeeper?"

Miss Ludley's chin jerked up. "I have that privilege. Someone must ensure that Mr. Braxton's household is run properly!"

"And I'm sure you do that very well," Jessie said. "Is my father home?"

Miss Ludley scowled. "He's writing his sermon and must not be disturbed."

"Surely an exception can be made for his long-lost daughter," Jessie said breezily. Daniel in tow, she swept into the house with a confidence that made the housekeeper retreat. "If he's working on his sermon, he must be in his study. No need to show us the way. Perhaps you can bring us a tea tray?"

Not bothering to check how Miss Ludley was reacting, she led Daniel down the central hall and to the room in the back left corner of the house that her father used as a study. The door was closed and when she raised her hand to knock, she had another moment of paralysis. She was beset by vivid memories of the countless times she'd stood shaking in this very place as she obeyed her father's summons.

Her mouth thinned and she gave a brisk knock, then opened the door and swept into the study. Her father sat at his desk looking thin and crabbed. He glanced up with a scowl, then froze, his jaw dropping. He surged to his feet. *"Jezebel!"*

Chapter 28

The Reverend Cassius Braxton had always been
tall and thin, but now he looked skeletal, and
the deep lines in his face delineated a lifetime of
anger. His hair had thinned and was now pure
white. The jarring part was that she'd half forgotten
that his eyes were exactly the same as hers: a pale
Arctic blue edged with charcoal. People found
them unnerving even on her. On her father, those
icy eyes made him look like a hanging judge.

Reminding herself that he no longer had power
over her, she said coolly, "Hello, Father. I do not answer to Jezebel, but you may call me Lady Romayne."

He sputtered, unable at first to find words strong
enough to express his fury. "There is no Lady Romayne! That worldly reprobate died without wife or
child. You're a whore and this must be your pimp."
His glare at Daniel was lacerating.

"Sorry to disappoint you, Mr. Braxton," Daniel

said imperturbably. "but I am indeed the new Lord Romayne, and to our mutual regret, your son-in-law."

Her father's gaze swung back to Jessie. "Why the devil are you even here? You abandoned all claim to decency when you ran away with that filthy seducer. You are no longer welcome in my home!"

"Father dearest," Jessie said in her sweetest tone, even though she was shaking inside, "I was *never* welcome in this house. You locked me in closets for taking too large a slice of cheese at the table and let me shiver in a freezing cold bedroom with only a paper-thin blanket because warmth would corrupt my character. Not to mention beating me with a leather strap because sparing the rod would spoil the child. If that was true, I'd have been the most unspoiled child in Christendom!"

Daniel looked appalled, but her father just spat, "You were a vessel of iniquity, just like your whore of a mother! It was my duty to beat the sin out of you!"

"If you had assaulted a neighbor as you assaulted me, you would have been brought up before a magistrate!" Jessie made herself take a deep, slow breath as she struggled to keep her fury under control. "I came here to prove to myself that I am no longer afraid of you."

"You *should* be!" Her father's hand flashed out in a vicious slap.

Jessie hadn't expected a physical assault, not in front of a witness, and she was critically slow at dodging.

But the blow never connected. Daniel's hand shot out and he caught her father's wrist, immobilizing the older man. "You will *not* raise a hand to my wife," he said in a steely voice. "You are a disgrace to the cloth you wear!"

Her father struggled to free his wrist, snarling. "I have a father's right to chastise my daughter in hopes of saving her soul from eternal damnation!"

"You have no such right!" Daniel said flatly. "The Bible says in multiple places that 'a man shall leave his father and his mother, and shall cleave unto his wife: and they shall be one flesh.' That is equally true of a woman. Jessie is now mine as I am hers."

"And the cleaving together part is really lovely," Jessie said helpfully.

Her father's face turned red with fury and veins bulged in his forehead. "You vile, filthy creature! You'll both rot in hell!"

"Why do I have the feeling that you spent all your time studying the Old Testament God of vengeance and totally ignored the New Testament's message of joy and forgiveness?" Daniel said thoughtfully.

"There must be repentance before there can be forgiveness!" Her father jerked his wrist again, and this time Daniel let him go. "But what would a lying, cheating rake like you know about the Church?"

"Rather a lot, actually," Daniel said, cool in contrast to her father's fire. "I'm an ordained clergyman of the Church of England."

"You're lying!" her father exclaimed, horrified. "The Church would never ordain a man like you!"

"Indeed it did. Mind you, I have an unfashionable fondness for Methodism, but my ordination is very real." This time, Daniel's smile had a distinct edge. "I earned double firsts at Oxford."

Jessie would have laughed if she wasn't shaking inside. Her father was glaring at Daniel with loathing, more repulsed by the idea that his son-in-law was a pastor than he would be if Daniel really was a pimp.

"I give you full marks for consistency, Father. You were an angry, hate-filled man when I was a child, and you are still." She drew a deep breath. "I came to pay my respects and to tell you that you have a beautiful granddaughter."

His face twisted as if he'd bitten into something rotten. "Another generation of female wickedness! I wash my hands of you!"

"As Pontius Pilate washed his hands in a futile attempt to reject responsibility for the crucifixion of Jesus," Jessie pointed out. "Or Lady Macbeth tried to wash the stain of murder from her hands. You choose poor company for yourself."

"Leave my house," her father said, his voice shaking. "I will never forgive you for these insults."

"If anyone needs forgiveness, it's you. But being a wicked woman, I have no desire to offer it. Goodbye, Father." Exhausted by emotion, she turned and took Daniel's arm and they left the study.

As they walked toward the front door of the parsonage, Miss Ludley appeared to glare at them. "How dare you come here to disturb the peace of a godly man like the Reverend Braxton!" she said viciously.

Jessie fought to keep her expression calm when she was too drained to respond, but Daniel said courteously, "I don't think that peace is the vicar's strong point, Miss Ludley, but never fear. We shall not trouble you again."

He opened the door and escorted Jessie down

the steps. She clung to Daniel's arm and tried to conceal her bleak knowledge that she would not see her father again.

As they passed the church, Daniel asked, "Is there a different route than the High Street? You don't look up to dealing with friendly folk in the market square."

So very true. Jessie rubbed her temple, trying to clear the numbness. "That alley there. If we cut through, we'll come to a lane that parallels the High. Dovecote Lane."

He followed her instructions and steered her to the lane, which was mercifully empty of people. She guessed he'd also found the meeting difficult, but he maintained his calm demeanor until they were safely in their room at the George. As he peeled off coat, cravat, and boots, he asked, "Did you achieve what you wished by seeing your father?"

"I . . . I don't know." Numbly she removed her shawl and bonnet and gloves, her gaze unfocused. "I'm not sure what I wanted."

Quietly, Daniel asked, "To remind yourself why you ran away from your home?"

Her mouth twisted bitterly. "I was certainly reminded why today. Now and then, not very often, I'd wonder if my father was really as bad as I thought. Perhaps I rebelled because I was young and headstrong and emotional. But no. He really was that bad."

"When he tried to strike you, I was tempted to break his wrist myself, and I'm not even related to him," Daniel said dryly. "I had to remind myself that it would be very bad form to injure a frail, warped old man. But even now, when his end is near, your father is a cruel bully. I'm even more impressed by you than I was before. You endured and became strong and compassionate rather than embracing cruelty yourself."

Jessie shrugged off the compliment. She had learned how to survive, but that wasn't strength, merely desperation. She poured water into the washbasin and splashed her face, trying to clear her mind. After drying her face, she said, "Is his health that bad? He's very thin, but he didn't lack the energy to be angry."

"He shows significant signs of heart disease," Daniel said, his gaze steady on her. "He might last another ten years, or he could have dropped dead while raging at you. Luckily, he didn't."

She shuddered at the thought. "That would have been *ghastly*."

"Is his behavior any different from when you were a child? Sometimes people's temper changes for the worse as they age."

"No, he was always much like this, particularly if I was less than perfectly obedient and well behaved. Today, I stood up to him. I'm grateful that my behavior didn't kill him on the spot." Exhausted and chilled, she kicked off her shoes and stretched out on the bed, pulling the neatly folded blanket at the bottom up over her.

Brow furrowed, Daniel asked, "You were hoping for more from him? Some sign of affection or respect?"

The chaotic emotions that had been churning inside her coalesced into shattering grief. "That's it. I wanted *something* from him. The smallest kind word or sign that he was glad I was alive. Some indication that he cared that he had a daughter." Silent tears began sliding down her cheeks. "I should have been more conciliatory instead of aggressive. I should have apologized for giving him grief. . . ."

"No!" Daniel said sharply. "You were not in the wrong, and there is nothing you could have said or done to get the response you wanted. We can't always have the relationship we want with another person because we can't control how they feel. I don't think your father is capable of love. This is sad for you, and even sadder for him."

Her tears fell faster. "So it was a mistake to come here."

"Only you can judge that." He sat on the edge of the bed and took her hand, his grasp warming her chilled fingers. "But since you confirmed that he really is as difficult as you remembered, did seeing him again at least banish some of your regrets?"

"Yes," she whispered. "But . . . it's hard to lose the last hope that there might be more." She rolled away from him onto her side in a vain attempt to hide the gut-wrenching sobs of a brokenhearted child.

Daniel lay down and spooned himself behind her, warming the back of her from her head to her heels as he wrapped a secure arm around her waist. He didn't speak, simply holding her as she wept for the child who'd yearned for love and received only anger and disapproval. It was time for her to accept what Daniel had said: that she could never have the father she wanted. But after running away from her father, she'd eventually learned how to choose good men. For that, she was profoundly grateful.

As her tears gradually ran dry, Daniel began

singing softly, his deep voice soothing her down to her bones. " 'Flow gently, sweet Afton, among thy green braes . . .' " The song was sweet and slow as a lullaby, and he tweaked the words to fit her. "My Jessie's asleep by their murmuring stream, flow gently, sweet Afton, disturb not her dream. . . ."

She dozed, not coming awake until a knock sounded on their door. "Our dinner has arrived," Daniel said quietly in her ear, his breath as warm and soft as his lullaby. "I'll have to get up."

As he slid from the bed, she sat up, wiped the last tears from her eyes, and smiled at her kind, wise, and wickedly handsome husband. "Good, I'm hungry." As new life surged through her, she said on impulse, "If you're interested, later we might practice cleaving unto one another."

He lit up like the rising sun. "I hope that means what I think it does!"

"Oh, yes," she whispered, her voice sultry. "It most certainly does."

Chapter 29

Gordon knew Bristol from his traveling days, and he was glad to have an excuse to visit. From sheer curiosity, before starting to investigate the death of Ivo Trevane he made a few inquiries about Daniel Herbert.

The damned man was revered for his medical skills and his charitable works. The wealthy consulted him when they needed the very best medical treatment, but more of his time was devoted to running an infirmary for those in need. The infirmary was going strong even with him away. Apparently Herbert had the gift of hiring capable people.

All those good works came at a price, of course. In Gordon's experience, everything had a price. In Herbert's case, he didn't seem to have had much of a private life. There were no rumors of mistresses or flirtations with marriageable young females. That lively piece he'd married would surely be an education. It would be interesting to see how that marriage worked out. Herbert was tremendously easygoing, but any man has his limits.

Still, Gordon wished Herbert well. He might be a boring stick, but he was one of the most genuinely decent human beings Gordon had ever met, and he deserved some good fortune. Of course there was that bloody great title and fortune that had dropped on Herbert's head, but a willing woman to warm a man's bed was a lot more fun.

Curiosity satisfied about Daniel Herbert's blameless past, Gordon turned to the real purpose of his visit. It wasn't hard to find information about what had happened to the dashing young Mr. Trevane seven years earlier. The affair had been quite the scandal, and very interesting the story was.

With the general outlines of the case in mind, Gordon visited Trevane House, which was still owned by the family. And he was in luck—the same butler still worked there. Sometimes investigations were just too easy.

The owner of the house wasn't in residence, so there were few servants, and the butler, Tuttle, was in charge. He looked wary when Gordon called on him in the servants' quarters. Gordon dressed like a prosperous solicitor for the occasion.

After introducing himself with an expensive engraved calling card, one of several Gordon carried, he said, "I'm sorry to disturb you with questions about such a painful matter, but I'm seeking information about your former master, Mr. Trevane. It's a matter of an inheritance."

"Oh?" Tuttle looked more interested. "What do you wish to know?"

"What sort of man was Trevane? He was quite young when he lived here, wasn't he?"

"Only twenty-two. A very charming chap." Tuttle shook his head mournfully. "I could have told him that wench he married was trouble, but young men don't listen to old ones about such matters. Mr. Trevane was besotted."

Gordon permitted himself a slightly salacious leer. "Was she as beautiful as everyone says?"

"All that and more," Tuttle said. "Dark hair, great light eyes, and a figure to keep a man awake at night, yet the doxy acted like butter wouldn't melt in her mouth. Even claimed her father was a vicar!"

"Shocking!" Gordon said, increasingly interested since it seemed pretty clear who the wife was. How much did Herbert know? "I assume her innocence was an act?"

"That Lisbet was a cat in heat," Tuttle said baldly. "Even waggled her tail at me a time or two, though of course I ignored her lures. I can't say I was surprised when she cut loose with a knife and ran off with a new lover. She planned it well. No trace of her was ever found."

"No doubt her wicked ways have since caught up with her," Gordon said piously. Instinct prodding him to ask more questions, he took out his wallet and pulled out a substantial bribe, holding it visible while he asked, "Can you tell me more about Ivo Trevane? What about his family? As I said, there's an inheritance involved."

"Well, that's an interesting tale." Expression gleeful, Tuttle proceeded to explain a good deal more about the Trevane family.

Gordon kept his expression only mildly interested, but when the butler finished speaking, he willingly handed over the bribe. As he left Trevane House, he was busily calculating how long it would take him to reach Castle Romayne.

After he left, Tuttle fingered the money with satisfaction before tucking it away. That was two men in as many days wanting the same information, and both had paid well for it. The first had lit up like a lamp when he'd heard. The second was just a lawyer and not so interested. But interested enough.

Chapter 30

The day's drive from Chillingham to Castle Romayne was blessedly peaceful after the emotional storms of the previous day. Daniel suspected that Jessie was still distressed about her meeting with her father, but that she'd come to terms with his failings as a father and a human being, and was determinedly moving forward rather than collapsing into misery. It was how she had survived—and a good example for him.

There had been some bravado in her lovemaking the night before, as if Jessie needed to declare to herself that she was a free, adult woman. But her responses had been real, and Daniel was male enough to be grateful for his wife's willingness no matter what the cause.

It was late afternoon when Jessie pointed out the window, and said, "Surely that's Castle Romayne? I shouldn't think there are many castles in this area."

Daniel leaned across her to look out her window.

"That looks like the sketch the lawyer showed me. Impressive!" The original castle dated back to Norman times, and it stood firm on a headland above the sea.

"Picturesque but drafty looking," Jessie observed.

"I'm told that a recent Lord Romayne agreed with you and built a modern wing, which we can't see from this angle. Picturesque is all very well, but who wants to live with coughs and colds and the ague all winter?" He patted her hand reassuringly. "If it's unhealthy, we have other places where we can live."

"Too many others! But I expect that after we've seen the castle, we'll have a better sense of how we want to organize our lives."

"It will be nice to have an organized life again," Daniel said ruefully. "My life has been topsy-turvy ever since I inherited all this." He squeezed Jessie's hand. "Though there have certainly been compensations."

She smiled at him, and together they approached their future.

Finally, Castle Romayne. After Daniel helped Jessie from the carriage, she looked around, bemused. "A looming castle by the sea and no living creatures in sight! Do you suppose that it's haunted?"

"Considering how old the place is, almost certainly," Daniel said. "But I'm sure I can come up with a rite of exorcism if any ghosts prove troublesome. As for the lack of people, the London lawyer, Hyatt, said most of the servants were put on board wages until the new lord arrives. There should be a butler and a couple of maids and stablemen around somewhere. Ah, here comes an ostler."

The driver Kirkland had supplied said, "We'll unload your baggage, then take care of the horses, my lord." Jessie suspected that both driver and guard were trained soldiers assigned to this journey for protection, should it be needed. But this far from London, it was hard to take Frederick Kelham's threats seriously. He'd probably given up his hopes for the barony and settled back into his drinking and gaming.

Daniel nodded thanks, then led Jessie up the steps to the castle door. "The closer we get, the draftier this place looks."

"But very, very picturesque."

The heavy arched front door was unlocked, and it opened with an ominous groan. Daniel looked at Jessie, and they both burst into laughter. "Gothic indeed!" he said.

They stepped into a vast entry hall that rose high above their heads and featured a dizzying array of old weapons mounted on the walls in artistic patterns. "Those should be useful if the Vikings attack," Jessie said, eying a circle of battle axes mounted halfway to the ceiling. "But they must be difficult to dust."

"It's gloomy enough that no one will notice a bit of dust," Daniel assured her.

A neatly dressed man rushed into the hall, panting a little. "My apologies, sir! You must be the new master and mistress of Castle Romayne?"

"I am, and you are surely Mr. Pendry?"

"Yes, my lord." Pendry was solid and middle-aged, with thinning brown hair, shrewd eyes, and an air of competence. His voice faintly reproachful, he said, "If we'd known you were arriving so soon, things would be in better order."

"We had a change of plans. I won't blame you for that," Daniel said reassuringly. "Since it's late in the day, could you give us a tour of the living quarters first? And perhaps some general information on the castle and the estate."

"Of course, my lord, my lady. This way, please."

As the butler led them into a passage on the right, Daniel said, "The London lawyer said my predecessor had allowed most of the estate to fall fallow, but I saw fields under cultivation and ready for harvest as we drove in, and sheep being pastured on the hills. Do those lands belong to a neighboring estate?"

Pendry looked pained. "This is a matter you'll need to resolve, my lord. The owner of the neighboring estate said it was a crime to waste good land, so he sent his people in to plant crops in the best of the fields and run sheep on the hills."

"Does he pay rent for the privilege?"

"No, it was a matter of much contention between his lordship and Mr. Trevane."

Jessie stopped breathing. If she were a cat, her fur would be standing on end. Daniel had gone very still, and tension spiked through the roof.

What were the odds? But she'd known Ivo had an estate in this general area. Though his family had sounded large, the murder of a favored young member would not be quickly forgotten.

After a hesitation too brief for anyone but Jessie to notice, Daniel said, "My neighbor is named Trevane?"

"Yes, there are Trevanes all over this area of Dorset. The family is prosperous and between them own a fair amount of property."

Another ghastly new thought struck her. What if the next-door neighbors were Ivo's parents? Though he'd never mentioned family and she had the impression he had no close relatives, she didn't think he'd actually said that. Being young and naïve with no family beside her father, she'd just accepted that Ivo's situation was similar.

For the first time, she wondered if he'd left grieving parents. If there were people who felt as she would feel if she lost Beth . . . ! But she didn't dare ask.

Daniel gave Jessie a swift, sympathetic glance, then distracted Pendry from her white face by saying, "I intend to put the Romayne lands back under cultivation, so Mr. Trevane will no longer feel compelled to use them properly."

Jessie took a deep breath and prayed that these Trevanes were only distant kin of Ivo. She was reminded that Daniel had his own strong emotions about this place when he asked, "I've wondered about the plague that swept through the castle and killed so many Herberts, including my parents. Has it recurred?"

Pendry shook his head, his face grave. "It struck overnight, killed many, and swiftly ran its course. It was all over in a fortnight."

"Is there any idea of where it came from?"

"Based on who became ill first, one of the London Herberts was carrying the fever when he came to the castle. Others quickly came down with it and almost half of them succumbed. The guests of the house party were hardest hit."

"Probably because they had the closest contact with the man carrying the illness," Daniel said, his voice grim. "Swift, inexplicable fevers are a harsh fact of life and someday I believe we'll learn where they come from and how to treat them. But we're a long way from that now."

Hearing the pain in Daniel's voice, Jessie caught his hand for a comforting squeeze. His parents had died here, after all. If they were not the best of parents, neither were they the worst, and this loss was much more recent than anything she'd suffered.

If not for the fever that had killed his parents and the other Romayne heirs, Daniel would never have inherited the title and gone to London to find a wife. That would have made his life much less complicated, but it would have been a sad loss for her and Beth.

They'd been moving through a series of stark stone rooms with few furnishings, but now Mr. Pendry opened a wide door into a corridor filled with light. "This gallery connects to the new house," he explained.

Jessie stepped forward, then halted with a gasp of amazement. The passage had large multipaned glass windows on the side facing the sea, and the view was stunning.

"Ohhh . . . !" she breathed as she moved to the window and stared out. The castle stood on a headland that formed one end of a bay. Below to the right, a long stretch of wide, sandy beach curved around the bay while on the left, the headland fell in a sheer cliff with waves crashing on the rocks. "This is magnificent!"

Daniel stopped beside her, equally enchanted. "A gallery with sea views rather than paintings. How splendid!"

"I've never seen the sea before," Jessie said softly as she traced an irregular curve in one of the panes. "The Severn River at Bristol is impressive, but it's not like this."

He put his arm around her shoulders. "There's nothing like the sea. As Britons, it's bred in our bones. The seas have made us what we are."

With his warm arm around her, she was able to imagine them living here and building a life—if not for the Trevanes.

Daniel said to Pendry, "Are there fishermen in this area?"

The butler nodded. "The local fish are excellent."

"What about smugglers? I've heard that many of the fishermen of the south coast have a secondary career as free traders."

"Some do, it's said," Pendry admitted, his expression turning opaque. Jessie suspected that he bought wine and spirits from the local free traders.

Turning away from the windows, she said, "The gallery is wide enough to be a sitting room. Has it been used that way?"

"Yes," Pendry replied. "Because the gallery faces south, it collects sunshine and warmth all through the year. The seventh baron, who built the gallery, designed it as a conservatory with plants as well as tables and chairs and sofas. His nephew, who became the eighth baron, did not choose to maintain that."

Daniel said thoughtfully, "We should turn this into a conservatory and drawing room again."

Feeling a twist of grief at what she'd lose if she couldn't live here, Jessie turned from the windows, and said to Pendry, "Time to see the new house."

He inclined his head. "If you'll follow me this way."

She took Daniel's arm and they continued through the gallery, though she kept glancing wistfully through the windows. "I could watch the waves all day."

"So could I. Perhaps we can have a light supper here tonight and watch the night sea. Assuming there's any food and someone to cook it in the house?"

"The kitchen maid is a fair country cook, if that would be satisfactory, my lord," Pendry said. "Within three days, the house will be fully staffed if that is your wish."

Daniel looked at Jessie, and she nodded. Though she and Daniel planned to stay only two or three days before leaving to collect Beth, the servants who worked here surely needed more than basic board wages now that Daniel was taking possession and there was ample money to pay them.

"Yes, notify the staff that the house is being opened up again," he said.

They reached the end of the gallery and went through another large door into the new house. It felt welcoming and full of light. Very different from the old castle. The seventh baron, who had built this addition, had good taste. Though the decoration and furnishings were shabby, the rooms were clean and well laid out. As they explored, Jessie decided that the new house was a good size: large enough to live graciously, but not too large.

There were windows everywhere, including the well-lit and well-stocked library. Best of all were the master and mistress's rooms on the upper floor, where the sitting room also had a broad, expensive sweep of glass panes looking over the bay. Entranced once again, Jessie said, "Whoever built this house loved the sea."

Daniel nodded. "The new house is similar in style to Milton Manor. They were built about the same time. Milton Manor doesn't have the sea, but it's much better decorated."

"That can be fixed," Jessie said. Refurbishing these rooms should be done for Daniel's sake, even if most of the time he would come here without her.

His brows furrowed when she spoke, and she guessed that he'd noticed her tension. Tonight, as they ate their dinner and admired moonlight on the dark night sea, they must have a serious talk.

Chapter 31

The efficient Pendry arranged for a small table and chairs to be set up in the gallery. While a burning sun sank into the western sea, Daniel and Jessie shared their first meal at Castle Romayne.

Pendry was serving. As he poured wine for Daniel and Jessie, he said, "The kitchen maid has provided fish stew, fresh bread, and a choice of local cheeses. There will be a warm apple tart for a sweet. She apologizes for such poor fare."

"It sounds very good to me," Jessie said warmly.

"And to me." Daniel sipped the wine and his brows arched. "My esteemed cousin, the eighth Lord Romayne, didn't stint himself when it came to his cellar."

"His lordship had an excellent palate," Pendry agreed as he ladled savory-scented stew into two wide bowls. As he set the first bowl in front of Jessie, he continued. "Word has gone out to recall the servants now that your lordship is in residence. Most live locally. The steward has a house on the estate and will be here in the morning, as will the house-keeper, who has been staying with her daughter in the village."

"I want to meet with him." Daniel tasted the stew. Chunks of white fish and clams swam with potatoes and onions and herbs in a rich, creamy broth. Delicious. The late lord had first-class servants, though Daniel wasn't sure the man had deserved them. No one who knew him had expressed any grief at the man's passing.

"I should go over the property with the house-keeper," Jessie said. "Though she and her staff have done a good job keeping the place clean, there has been much neglect in other ways."

Daniel chuckled. "Neither of us are good with too much leisure, are we? But we're supposed to be on our honeymoon still. If the weather is good in the afternoon, perhaps we can explore the beach. Is there a way down, Pendry?"

"Yes, the seventh baron built a sturdy stairway down to the beach. The stairs begin just below the gazebo that stands on the cliff east of the new house." Pendry set down platters of bread and cheeses. "The sand of the beach is quite firm and good for walking."

"I can't wait to meet the sea face-to-face," Jessie said, but there was a wistful note in her voice, and he suspected the reason why.

"Then we shall do it. Thank you for the information, Pendry." Daniel gestured at the table. "We're well provided for, so you can adjourn to your own dinner if you like."

Pendry nodded thanks and withdrew. When he was gone, Jessie asked, "What was the eighth baron's given name? Calling him your esteemed predecessor is clumsy."

"Alistair. He seems to have been self-absorbed as well as eccentric. But though he neglected the usual country pursuits such as farming his land, he left a fine library and was a good investor." Daniel raised his glass to her. "I thought I'd dislike this place, but now that I've seen the setting and the new house I like the idea of bringing it properly alive."

She clinked her glass with his, but her expression was grave. "It's a fine idea, but I don't think I'll be able to spend much time here if there are Trevanes everywhere. I'm sure they must be related to Ivo." Her mouth twisted. "I didn't think he had any family since he never mentioned any or invited any relations to our wedding. But when Pendry was talking, it suddenly struck me that perhaps Ivo had parents or brothers and sisters who still mourn his loss. Even if the Trevane next door isn't immediate family, he must be a cousin or some such."

Daniel swallowed his wine and carefully set the glass down. He'd been so pleased by the house and its location that he hadn't really thought through the implications of Trevanes in the area. But Jessie had been thinking. "You were called Lisbet then. Is it inevitable that someone will connect you to Ivo?"

She grimaced. "Perhaps not inevitable, but highly likely since my appearance is somewhat distinctive."

Jessie was right. With her stunning beauty, she was a woman people remembered and described. It wasn't all that far from Bristol to the south coast. Connections could be made.

He took another sip of wine and mentally said

good-bye to making a permanent home at Castle Romayne. "I'll need to visit here regularly, but you won't have to come. People will understand that you and Beth need to be at Kelham since she will inherit it."

Jessie gazed out at the night, her face sad. "Surely I can come for a few days a year, just to show people that we aren't estranged."

Even that might be dangerous. "We'll see. Belmond Manor is a pleasant place and near Bristol, so it will be a good home to us for part of the year." Except that Ivo Trevane had died in Bristol. Foreseeing that he'd be spending much of his time at Kelham Hall, he said, "We'll work it out."

And they would. Yet as they continued to chat idly over the rest of their meal, he couldn't escape the fear that Jessie's past would catch up with her. And if she was in trouble, he would be, too.

There was fog the next morning, and even that was lovely, wrapping the house in silky clouds. By the time Daniel finished his session with his new and blessedly competent steward, and Jessie and the housekeeper had worked through every corner of the house, the fog had burned off and hazy sunshine polished the sea with soft light.

After a lunch of ham and bean soup—the head cook hadn't yet returned—Daniel and Jessie set out to explore the beach. The stairway down the cliff was as good as Pendry had promised. The wooden steps were wide and solid, there were railings on both sides, and the whole structure was firmly attached to the cliff.

Daniel went first as a precaution so he could catch Jessie if she fell, but there was no danger of that. She skipped lightly down behind him, the ribbons of her bonnet and her dark red cloak whipping around her in the stiff breeze.

She smiled at him cheerily. "Going down is easy. Climbing back up will be good for our characters!"

"If not for our knees," he said with a smile.

When they reached the bottom of the steps, she took his hand as naturally as breathing and they began strolling down the beach to their right. "What a wonderful place," she said as the sand crunched under their feet. "I assumed a castle would be beastly uncomfortable and this would feel like the end of the world, but it doesn't."

Castle Romayne could so easily feel like home. He watched as a small wave broke on the sand and retreated, leaving a waterlogged twig in its wake. "A pity about those neighboring Trevanes."

"Maybe I should hack off my hair and wear a veil," she said gloomily. "Or would you then be sorry you married me? Would you have looked across a crowded ballroom, seen me, and decided we had to meet if I was average looking?"

He frowned thoughtfully. "You ask difficult questions. Yes, your appearance attracted me, but I've seen other beautiful women who inspired no more than detached admiration. When I saw you, I felt an intense physical reaction in every fiber of my body. If I'd spoken with you and you were a silly widgeon, my interest would have vanished. Instead, the more I saw of you, the more I came to appreciate your warmth and intelligence and character."

"And my problems," she said wryly. "I'm sure you didn't expect them as part of the package."

"A woman who is a blank slate isn't very interesting." His mouth curved up. "You have always been interesting."

She laughed. "You are the most tactful of men, Daniel Herbert. Let's reverse the question. Would I have reciprocated your interest if you weren't so very handsome?"

"Me?" He stared at her. "The most I aspire to is 'presentable' and I don't always manage that. Kirkland's tailor helped my appearance, but I have to be reminded to dress carefully and to cut my hair. There's nothing unusual about my appearance."

"No?" She stopped and swung around to face him. "How about tall?" She reached up to brush a lock of hair from his forehead.

"Broad-shouldered." She swept her fingers across his chest from the point of one shoulder to the point of the other. "And a wide and fine expanse it is."

Her fingertips sketched the lines of his face. "Fine features. Well shaped, thoughtful, serious, but with a lurking bit of humor." She smiled mischievously. "You are altogether delicious."

He felt himself reddening. "You're teasing."

"A little, but I'm also speaking the truth." They'd reached the end of the beach, so she linked her arm in his and they swung around to retrace their steps. "Attraction is mysterious and not easily explained. Being attracted to a person makes us like their looks."

"In other words, I thought you were beautiful because I was attracted to you, not vice versa?"

"Exactly. Though I'm considered good looking,

my looks don't transfix other men across a crowded room."

"If you think that, you haven't been paying attention," he said, amused.

She laughed. "Trying to analyze these things is a futile exercise. Here we are, inhabiting the same marriage, so rather than analyze, we should concentrate on making it work as well as we can."

"Isn't that what we're doing? Talking, exploring each other's minds, getting to the point where we take each other's appearance for granted?"

"Yes, all that plus walking on a beach. *Your* beach."

"*Our* beach. With 'all my worldly goods I thee endowed,' " he reminded her. The tide was going out, widening the stretch of shimmering sand. "Though it still doesn't seem like it's really mine. I never visited here. I don't recall ever meeting Alistair. There is no rational reason all this should be mine."

"The British title and inheritance system isn't rational, but it works," she said pragmatically. "And you will care for this land and these people well, which means the system is still working."

He glanced up at the castle and thought how far he'd come since his first horrified reaction to news of his inheritance. "It works because duty is a powerful force." And because he was learning how he could practice his medical calling while doing his duty.

Jessie nodded. "Speaking of caring for people, the housekeeper, Mrs. Willis, said there's a sizable vacant house in the village that might make a good cottage hospital. She was quite keen on the idea. She also said her daughter has some skill in nursing and would be interested in more training if you open a hospital here."

"Wonderful!" Daniel exclaimed. "We can go look at it tomorrow. Or perhaps this afternoon. It's still early."

Jessie laughed and put a restraining hand on his arm. "Yes, there's time to visit today, but for now, let's enjoy this moment. Our first walk on the Castle Romayne beach."

First, and probably last for quite some time. An occasion that shouldn't be rushed. "Thank you for reminding me to enjoy the moment." He smiled down at her. "I do need to be reminded of such things."

The vast bulk of the castle loomed above as they neared the stone cliff of the headland. Toward the base of the cliff, dark openings of different sizes were visible, often with water splashing inside. "I wonder how deep those sea caves are," Jessie said. "Do you think any of them run all the way through the headland to the other side?"

"Probably Pendry would know. Given that the castle is directly above, it wouldn't be surprising if some of the earlier inhabitants had decided to improve on nature. Perhaps there's an escape tunnel running down to the sea." Daniel squinted against the sun. "The waves have pushed rocks up around the base of the cliffs almost like a path. At low tide, it might be possible to circle around the base to whatever is on the other side."

"Only for someone keen on slipping, breaking bones, and drowning in this place," Jessie said as a larger wave crashed into the rocks, throwing white plumes of water high into the air.

"I'd be able to practice my bone-setting skills," Daniel pointed out.

She laughed. "I should think that setting bones for small boys who fall out of trees would be all the practice you need."

"Small boys are some of my best customers." He brushed a kiss on her forehead, loving the easy bantering between them. How had he become so lucky?

They turned away from the headland and began retracing their steps. In the distance, a graceful fishing boat sailed eastward, its white sails puffed full by the wind. A perfect moment. But such moments were fleeting by nature.

Guessing that the restless unease creeping over him meant this moment was over, he said, "Time we were heading back. I'd like to see that possible site for a cottage hospital."

Before Jessie could reply, a male voice heavy with menace bellowed, "That's her!" The dark sound echoed from the cliff walls as the man added, "Grab the woman *now!*"

The instinct that had kept Daniel safe in the portside taverns of Bristol sent ice through his veins. As he whirled around, he saw half a dozen rough, muscular men pouring from a sea cave, their expressions ferocious.

"Jessie, run back up to the house!" Daniel barked. *"Now!"*

He was between the men and Jessie, and the stairway up the cliff wasn't far behind her. He risked a quick glance over his shoulder and saw that she was frozen in shock. *"Run!* Get help."

He doubted there were enough able-bodied men in

the house to form a rescue party, and there wouldn't be time. But with luck, Jessie might get to safety.

"Out of the way!" roared the leader, a tall man with a dark scarf half obscuring his face. "Or we'll bloody break you in half!"

"If you want my wife, you'll have to get past me!" Daniel snapped.

At the Westerfield Academy, Hindu martial arts were a school passion first taught by the very young, half-Hindu Duke of Ashton. One exercise was for a single student to take on several adversaries at once, and Daniel had been very good at that. Fighting several men simultaneously was like a fierce kind of dancing. Daniel had learned there that an individual had advantages over a group if the assailants weren't trained to work together.

The rules were simple: Close fast, use their numbers against them, strike vulnerable places, and be somewhere else when they strike back. With his knowledge of anatomy, Daniel was particularly good at targeting vulnerable places like soft tissue and fragile joints.

Swiftly he grabbed the leader by the arm and shoulder and hurled him into the man behind. Then he swung to his left and chopped another man's throat with the side of his hand, knocking him to the sand.

A burly fellow tried to tackle him, but Daniel spun away. Kick, punch, slide away. Thank God they weren't armed. Their aim was kidnapping, not murder.

Two men tackled Daniel and he went down, but rolled with it and maneuvered both of them into the path of another man, tripping him as well. As

Daniel shoved the men off him, he saw that Jessie was racing up the steps. But the leader was pursuing her and closing fast.

Daniel fought even harder, scrambling to his feet and driving his shoulder into one belly, then kicking another man in the knee with numbing force. But they were five to one against him. Three of the men tackled him at once from different directions.

Daniel almost went down under the attack, but managed to keep on his feet. Swiftly he kicked one in the groin, then hurled a handful of sand into the eyes of another man. As the fellow gasped, Daniel slammed a crunching fist into his jaw.

His opponent swore furiously. "You fight pretty damned well for a lord!" He accompanied his words with a blow to Daniel's gut, knocking him breathless. One of the other attackers took advantage of Daniel's weakness to knock him to the sand and pin him down. Another man piled on as Daniel fought to free himself.

Above on the steps, the leader caught Jessie. As her bonnet came off to float down to the sand on the breeze, she screamed, "Help!" But the crash of the waves and whistle of the wind drowned out most of her cry.

Still screaming, she went for the leader's eyes with clawed fingers, but he grabbed her around the chest, locking her arms down while he lifted her off her feet. She struggled fiercely as he carried her down the steps to the beach. When she saw how Daniel was pinned down, she cried despairingly, "Daniel!"

With a rush of berserker fury, he broke free and sprinted toward Jessie even though he knew any action of his was futile. As he was recaptured, the man holding Jessie, snarled, "Stop screaming, you bitch! I've got every damned right to carry you off!"

Jessie managed to claw the concealing scarf off his lower face. She stopped struggling, her expression stunned. Incredulous, she gasped, "Ivo?"

Chapter 32

Shocked to her marrow, Jessie stared at the familiar face of the man who held her imprisoned in his arms. The height, dark hair, long nose, and bushy brows were unmistakable, though he'd broadened and looked older and harder. Well, so had she. "It can't be you," she said through numb lips. "You're dead!"

"You didn't quite manage, little Lisbet!" he growled in a familiar voice, not loosening her hold. "You're still quite the tasty little morsel. I'd half forgotten after all these years." He set her feet on the ground and grabbed her backside with one hand, like a housewife checking out the ripeness of fruit. "How about a little kiss for your long-lost husband?"

Jessie kicked him furiously, wishing her half-boots were heavier. At the same time, Daniel surged free of the men holding him. "Let her go, damn you!" he thundered in a voice that could fill a large church.

Before he'd come two steps, one of Ivo's men

bashed him on the head with a stone picked up from the sand. Daniel crumpled to the sand.

Jessie screamed, "Daniel!" and tried to break free of Ivo, but failed once again. "Is he the one you ran off with after cutting my throat?" Ivo asked. "Or a more recent victim of your charms?"

She managed to free her right arm and slapped him as hard as she could. "I wish I *had* succeeded in killing you, you vile, bullying excuse for a gentleman!"

"You've a shrewish tongue on you, Lisbet!" His cheek reddening from her blow, he tugged off his scarf and used it to gag her. His voice dropped menacingly. "I think I'll blindfold you as well. It's more frightening, and I want you to be *terrified!*"

He was succeeding, damn him. She was terrified and not just for herself. How hard had Daniel been struck? His head had been bleeding when he went down.

Ivo had come well prepared, and he efficiently tied her wrists behind her back. One of his men asked, "What do we do with her fancy man? Toss him in the water?"

As Jessie froze, Ivo tied a handkerchief around her eyes, blinding her. "Bring Romayne with us," Ivo ordered. "I don't see why she should do all the suffering on her own."

"Bloody beggar is heavy!"

"There's five of you and one of him," Ivo said callously. "Try not to damage him much." He pinched Jessie's backside again. "Come along, sweetheart. I have a score to settle with you."

He gripped her upper left arm with bruising force and half dragged her across the sand. She stumbled when they came to rough stone. Ivo barked, "Lou, take her other arm so she doesn't break any bones too soon."

Lou took her other arm and the two men managed to keep her upright over slippery, dangerous rocks. Then constriction and dampness. They'd entered a sea cave. Ivo and his men must have come through this passage when they attacked.

"Steps," Ivo said brusquely. "Don't thrash around or I'll let you fall."

Lou's hand dropped away since the stairwell was too narrow for three people to climb abreast. There was barely space for two, and she was squashed into Ivo's side as he marched her up. The stone steps were hollowed out from use. They must be right under the old castle. How many centuries had men come and gone this way?

The only comfort was murmured comments from Ivo's men that suggested they were bringing Daniel along with some degree of care. She hoped that was the case. If he was conscious, he must be cursing the day he met her.

After what seemed like an endless, painful hike, the steps leveled out and Ivo halted. A key turned in a lock; then a heavy door squealed open. Ivo's hard hand shoved between her shoulder blades and she fell hard onto a rough stone floor, bruising her hands and knees.

"Drop his lordship anywhere," Ivo said brusquely. "I'll leave 'em here to sweat." He jerked at the ties binding Jessie's wrists and freed her hands. "Think about what you did, Lisbet," he said gruffly. "While I decide whether or not to leave you here to starve."

As Jessie tore at the gag and blindfold, the heavy

door slammed shut and Ivo locked it behind him. She and Daniel had been left in a crude cell that was apparently carved out of solid rock. A couple of ragged blankets lay in a corner and a narrow, barred window showed sky outside. The sound of crashing surf sounded far below.

Heart pounding with fear, she dropped onto her sore knees by Daniel's crumpled figure. A streak of blood ran through his fair hair, but when she brushed his hair back to examine the injury, his eyes fluttered open.

"A minor concussion." He drew a ragged breath and winced as he felt around his damaged skull. "Nothing to worry about. How are you?"

She managed a smile. "Bruised and terrified, but greatly relieved to know that you're more or less all right. Can you sit up? Do you want to even try?"

He replied by rolling cautiously to a sitting position, wincing again. "Where are we? I missed some of the journey here."

"I think we're under Castle Romayne," she said. "He seemed to be taking us back into the sea cave, then up some stone steps."

Daniel made an effort to stand, and with Jessie's help he managed to clamber to his feet. She wanted him to wrap his arms around her so she could quietly shake for a while, but he turned and limped to the window.

"You're right, this view is very similar to the one from the new house, but lower and a little farther west. The castle is old enough to have dungeons underneath. Over the centuries, escape tunnels and smugglers' hideouts could have been added."

She bit her lip as she watched him silhouetted

against the small window. Rangy height, broad shoulders, and blood matting his blond hair. "I'm sorry," she whispered. "I never imagined that my past would catch up with me in such a ghastly way."

Daniel turned from the window, his face unreadable with the light behind him. "Given how upset you were by that final bloody fight with Ivo, it's not surprising that you couldn't find his pulse. Are you sorry that you didn't actually kill him?"

She hesitated. "I'm glad he isn't dead. It was horrifying to know that I'd killed a man that . . . that I'd loved. But I wish to heaven that he'd never found me and decided to take revenge!"

"He's a very angry man," Daniel said. "Was he always like this?"

"Usually he was talkative and charming, but today he behaved just the way he did when he was drunk," she said. "I didn't smell a trace of spirits on him today, though, so maybe now he's horrible and frightening all the time."

"Can you guess what he intends? He could have easily killed us, but he seems to have gone to some effort to avoid that."

"He wants me to suffer, and you along with me." She swallowed hard, not wanting to imagine what lay ahead. "I'm so sorry."

"No more apologies," Daniel ordered. "Any fault in this situation lies with your husband."

For the first time, the horrifying reality that underlay the events of the day really struck home. "Dear God in heaven!" she whispered, aghast. "If he's my husband, you *aren't*."

"Nor was Philip," Daniel said with cool detachment.

Jessie's mind moved to the next step. "So Beth is illegitimate and not heiress to Philip's title and property."

"No, but she is still the beloved child of you and Philip. Plus, an heiress if not a baroness," he pointed out. "The one good element of this is that Frederick will no longer have a reason to threaten you or Beth."

That was good. Very good. But she felt ill when she looked across the cell at the man who was not her husband. Daniel had given her passion and patience and safety. Only now did she recognize that she had committed herself to him totally, heart and soul. But he was not her husband, and his expression showed the detached kindness and compassion that a doctor, or a vicar, would show to a stranger.

"This is all so *wrong!*" she exclaimed.

"I agree, but the legal and emotional implications can wait for another day," Daniel said coolly. "I'd rather try to escape now, before Ivo returns drunk and armed. Adding alcohol to his existing bad temper is an alarming prospect."

"Escape?" She studied the massive wooden door. It looked very solid and had a strong new lock. "Can a lock like this be picked? Is that one of your many skills?"

"Alas, no. But there is another way out." He was eyeing the window with its heavy metal bars.

"Escaping through the window would be worse than the door!" she exclaimed, appalled. "Even if we could get through those bars, there's a *cliff* out there! With rocks and raging seas at the bottom!"

"The bars are solid," he agreed. "But the wooden

frame they're set in is quietly rotting away from time and damp."

He pulled a folding knife from his pocket and started digging at the frame. Sizable chunks of wood dropped to the floor. "We're more than halfway down the cliff here. Remember how when we were on the beach, I mentioned that a ridge of rocks around the base of the headland looked almost like a crude path? My guess is that the pirates or smugglers who used these tunnels augmented the natural rockfall to create an escape route to the Romayne beach, where they could safely bring a boat in."

She thought of the cliff, the rocks, the waves, the risk of broken bones and drowning—and squared her shoulders. "What can I do?"

He paused in flaking the wooden frame and reached inside his coat to withdraw a flat canvas packet half a dozen inches square and about a half inch thick. He unfolded it and pulled out a small pair of scissors. "Start cutting those blankets into strips. The fabric is heavy enough to tie into a crude rope that we can use to get down to that pathway."

Bemused, she took the scissors. "You carry a medical kit around with you?"

He nodded and turned back to the window. "I've needle and thread and basic bandages and a few other useful things. One never knows when a little surgical work will be required."

"You amaze me," she said as she pulled the blankets from the corner. They were dirty and the edges were frayed, but the material was sturdy. If cut in wide strips, it should be strong enough to support a person's weight. At least, she hoped so. She cut, ripped, then did it again.

It didn't take long to reduce the blankets to broad strips. Jessie asked, "Are you good at knots?"

"I can tie the sort that won't slip," he assured her. "Just a moment."

Muscles straining, Daniel wrenched at the iron bars. He staggered back a step when the crumbling wood surrendered and the welded unit of metal bars came away in his hands, but caught his balance quickly. "Done!"

When removed from the window, the bars and their frame formed a heavy metal grate. As he leaned the grate against the wall, Jessie said, "That was quick!"

"The wood was very bad," he explained. "Your husband isn't a very good plotter."

She bit her lip to keep from swearing that Ivo wasn't her husband. Unfortunately, in the eyes of the law he was.

She moved to the open window and looked out. The drop was sheer and the waves hitting the cliff sprayed high in the air. But there was indeed a very rugged-looking ledge running along the base of the cliff a few feet above the current water level.

She judged the size of the window. "I'm small enough to get out, but can you get your shoulders through?"

"I'll have to go through at an angle, but it can be done."

She looked down again. "We need more rope. I'll cut up my cloak. It's also heavy fabric and it will give us more length."

"Good idea." He began knotting strips of blanket together. He tugged each knot after it was tied, then continued. By the time he finished tying the blanket strips, her lovely burgundy woolen cloak, which she'd worn only twice, was sliced and ready for knotting.

Daniel tied on the pieces of cloak, then tossed her both ends. "Pull as hard as you can while I pull from the middle."

The cell had just enough diagonal length for them to test their improvised rope. "No point in waiting," Daniel said. "Are you ready? I'll lower you down. I think we have just about enough rope to make a loop at one end for you to set your feet in." He tied in the foot loop as he talked.

Jessie peered out the window again, feeling dizzy. The distance seemed twice as far as it had earlier. For an instant, she wondered if it would be wiser to wait for Ivo to return and let him scream off his insults.

No. He was too unpredictable. If he was armed and turned violent, heaven help them. She might deserve to pay for her sins, but Daniel didn't.

She moistened her dry lips. "I'm ready."

Daniel tied one end of the rope to the metal grate, then knotted a loop on the other end. "The grate will make an anchor when I go down. First put your right foot in the loop. I'll lift you onto the sill with your feet outside and hold the rope while you slide out and get a firm grip and both feet in the loop. That should keep you secure as I lower you down. Can you manage?"

Reminding herself that her task was easier than his, she said with as much firmness as she could manage, "I can."

He caught her gaze, his changeable eyes as steely gray as the waves below. "Jessie," he said quietly. "I won't let you fall."

"I know you won't." She wrenched her gaze away, not wanting him to see her fear. She knew he wouldn't let her fall. She would trust Daniel with anything. But she still felt the chilly distance that Ivo had caused between them.

Daniel wasn't her husband. He was more than that.

Jessie stood on her toes to brush a swift kiss on his lips. "Whatever happens," she whispered, "know that I love you."

Then she ducked her head and put her right foot into the fabric loop of their improvised rope. Wordlessly Daniel lifted her and threaded her into the window with her feet outside. She slid her left foot into the loop as well. A good thing she'd worn sturdy half boots for their morning walk.

"When you're ready, slide out and turn around. You can hang on to the sill until you have a firm grip on the rope. All set? You can do this. It will be over in just a couple of minutes."

Suppressing her terror, she nodded and eased herself out the window and into the abyss.

Chapter 33

Daniel kept a strong arm around Jessie until she was dangling over the lethal rocks, her hands locked on the rope in a death grip. No, a life grip. She swallowed hard and tightened her hold until her fingers whitened.

"Here you go," Daniel said, his voice as calm as if he was passing her a cheese plate. "If you want me to slow down or stop, just shout."

Beyond words, she nodded, and he began to pay out the rope. He'd wrapped it around his body so the operation was as secure as humanly possible, but she knew the journey down would live in her nightmares till the day she died. She was sweating despite the cold wind that buffeted and spun her around, sometimes banging her into the rough cliff face.

As she descended, flying spray from the waves spattered icy water over her, growing heavier the closer she came to the rocky ledge that offered a tenuous safety. Dizzily she watched the shiny wet rocks grow nearer and nearer. When she touched down, she promptly slipped and fell because of the slipperiness of the wet rocks, but her grip on the rope spared her from hitting hard.

Heart pounding with relief, she looked up and waved at Daniel high above. Swiftly he pulled up the rope, then lowered it again with his coat and shirt tied to the end. They hadn't discussed that, but she realized he was reducing the width of his shoulders as much as possible. A half inch might make the difference between success and failure.

She removed the garments and waved again. She wanted to call good luck, but he probably couldn't hear her over the sound of the crashing surf. He returned her wave before disappearing for a moment.

Then his feet appeared and he began carefully maneuvering his way out the square stone opening, which now looked far too small. Sickly she realized how much more treacherous his exit was than hers. Not only would he probably be scraping skin to get out, but at the same time he had to maneuver the square metal grate to an angle where it would lock behind the window opening and anchor his descent. If he positioned the grate badly, it would fly through the open square and he'd crash down the cliff.

For the first time since she was a very young child, she prayed. *If anyone deserves your help, God, it's Daniel! Please, please, please . . . !*

Abruptly his torso and shoulders emerged and he was outside, hanging safely from the rope. She began to breathe again.

He came down much more swiftly than she had.

There was blood on the shoulder she could see, but it was fascinating to watch the powerful play of the muscles in his arms and back as he descended hand over hand. He truly was beautiful. Her hero if not her husband. And she really was a wicked woman to think of such a thing under these circumstances!

He even managed to avoid slipping on the wet stones when he reached the bottom. Not caring how disgusted he might be at all the trouble she'd caused, she threw her arms around him and shook, as she'd wanted to do earlier. "Thank *God* you got down safely!" she breathed, her eyes squeezed shut against her tears of relief.

"I think He does deserve much of the credit," Daniel agreed. He patted her on the back as if she were a friendly puppy, then pulled away and reached for his shirt, which she'd put as far from the spray as possible.

As she'd guessed, his shoulders, the broadest part of his body, were scraped raw and were bleeding, but he'd managed to escape. The hardest part was over. At least, she hoped it was.

He pulled the shirt over his head, which made the view less interesting but would help warm him. As he donned his coat, he said, "You're afraid of heights, aren't you? That makes what you did even braver."

She smiled ruefully. "Before today, heights only bothered me a little. Now they *terrify* me!"

"Yet once again, you did what was needed." His smile was friendly rather than intimate.

She'd worry about that later. "I'm not sure how far we have to go around the headland, but if we make good speed, we should be safe on the beach well before it gets dark. Then we call the magistrate!"

"It's possible that Trevane *is* the magistrate, but something must be done about the man. Your attacking him in Bristol the night you ran away was self-defense, but his kidnapping us for his private revenge is a long way outside the law." Daniel studied the rough path they'd have to follow. "The incoming tide is coming in fast and will cover some of this path soon, so it's time we got moving."

She turned and started walking, her right hand skimming the cliff face for balance as she picked her way through the uneven tangle of stones. Some had very sharp edges and her feet slipped into crevasses too often. Grimly she carried on, moving as quickly as she could.

About fifty feet along, the path curved to reveal a sea cave to her right. It hadn't been visible from above, but it was sizable. Higher than a man's head, it disappeared into darkness inside the cliff.

She was about to mention it to Daniel when a howl of fury rang out from behind them. Startled, she turned back around the corner and rejoined Daniel, who was staring up at their former cell.

Ivo Trevane leaned out the window, his expression enraged. "Damn you, damn you, *damn you!* You'll not get away from me this easily!"

"He called that easily?" Daniel said with dry humor.

"He really isn't a very good plotter, is he?" Jessie shivered. "Time to move out before he joins us for more threats and intimidation."

She wanted to run but didn't dare do so on the

dangerous surface. She was at the corner again when she heard a cry of terror.

Jessie jerked around and saw that Ivo had emerged from the window to follow them down. His shoulders must be narrower than Daniel's. But in his haste, he hadn't taken time to place the grate solidly inside the window opening. Now he was looking up as the heavy metal rectangle scraped and twisted inside the cell.

As she watched, appalled, the grate tumbled out the window with shocking suddenness. Ivo dropped like a stone, and his harrowing scream was another horror that would haunt Jessie's nightmares.

His scream ended abruptly as he hit the narrow path. The falling grate clanged down next to him, then bounced into the sea.

Swearing, Daniel took off toward Ivo. Jessie wanted to run the other way until she was home and could bury her head under a pillow. But after an instant, she followed Daniel.

He was already kneeling beside Ivo, who amazingly had survived the fall. Blood was gushing from a long gash on his upper arm. He must have hit a sharp-edged rock. His skull was also bleeding on the same side and his lower left ankle was twisted badly, either sprained or broken.

As Jessie reached him, his eyes fluttered open. "You win, bitch," he breathed hoarsely. "You can leave me here to die and walk away with everything, a real widow this time. You can keep Lord Fancy Pants if you want him. Instead of you dying for your sins, I'm dying for them."

"You are an amazingly unpleasant man, Ivo Trevane," Daniel said in a pleasant voice as he stripped off his cravat. "But don't count on dying yet."

Swiftly he tore the cravat in half and tied one half above the massively bleeding gash in Ivo's arm. Then he pulled a pencil from inside his coat and slid it under the bandage. As he twisted the pencil to tighten the ring of fabric, Jessie realized it was a tourniquet. She'd heard of them but had never seen one.

As the blood flow from the arm slowed to almost nothing, Daniel frowned at the damaged ankle. "With luck, your boot spared you a broken ankle, but I'm guessing there's a bad sprain. I'll have to cut your boot off."

An incoming wave splashed over all three of them. Jessie wondered how close it was to high tide. "Just around that corner, there's a sea cave. It was higher than here and went back into the cliff and there were pieces of driftwood tossed inside."

"That sounds like a major improvement from here." Daniel stood. "Jessie, if I take his shoulders, can you manage his legs?"

"Very well," she said without enthusiasm.

"This will hurt, I'm afraid," Daniel said as he levered Ivo into a sitting position and slid his arms around from the back.

Jessie picked up Ivo's feet. Despite her care, jostling his injured leg caused him to give an agonized cry before he clenched his teeth to cut off the sound.

The next few minutes counted as among the worst of a very bad day. Jessie was moving backward on a wet, stony surface that was treacherous even if she had been moving forward and not carrying anything.

But after a very long quarter hour, they managed to get Ivo to the relative shelter of the cave. A patch of sand was a dozen feet inside, so they set him down there.

Jessie folded onto the sand, gasping for breath while Daniel immediately set to work, loosening the tourniquet cautiously. Since the wound was no longer gushing blood, he cut away Ivo's sleeve and wrapped the arm with a bandage improvised from Daniel's wrecked cravat and Ivo's sleeve. "That should be enough pressure to stop you from hemorrhaging without destroying your arm."

"You seem to know what you're doing," Ivo said grudgingly.

"Because I'm a doctor and I patch up fools all the time," Daniel explained. "I'm going to examine your ankle now. Hope that it's a sprain rather than a break."

"If this is a sprain, I bloody well don't want to find out what a break feels like," Ivo muttered before gasping with pain again as Daniel cut off the expensive boot and probed the injured ankle.

"Romayne, why didn't you just leave me there to die," he asked gruffly. "Would have made your life much simpler, and you'd get to keep her, at least until she runs off again. If you're lucky, she might not try to murder you before she leaves."

"Leaving people to die isn't what I do," Daniel said shortly. "And I suggest that you stop being so insulting about the lady given that I'm patching up your broken body and the process could be a good deal more painful than it is now."

"Lady!" Ivo spat, but he subsided under Daniel's cold stare.

"Jessie, could you take off Trevane's cravat? I need it to bind his ankle."

Not anxious to touch Ivo again, Jessie said, "I can tear fabric from my shift."

"Trevane started all this, so he can sacrifice his cravat," Daniel said dryly. "It will work better, too."

Reluctantly Jessie knelt by Ivo and untied the cravat, then began to unwind the narrow length of linen. He watched her through angry, slit eyes, but didn't say anything. Once it was off, she'd have to confront the scar of the near-lethal stab wound she'd given him, which would be still another bad thing on a very bad day.

She removed the last winding of fabric, exposing the base of his throat—and there was no scar visible. She bent over to see better. A scattering of dark hair, but no trace of scarring. Surely a wound like that would scar?

Struck by an impossible thought, she ripped his shirt down to his waist and looked at the rib area of his lower right side. Another expanse of smooth, unmarked skin.

"Damn you!" she gasped, caught between incredulity and fury. *"You aren't Ivo!"*

Chapter 34

Daniel jerked his head up. "This man isn't Ivo Trevane?"

"I most certainly am!" Trevane said indignantly. "I have a birth certificate at home that will attest to it."

"Well, you certainly aren't the Ivo Trevane I married!" Jessie hissed. "My husband would have had a scar on his throat where I stabbed him." Her finger traced the place. "Nothing! And you don't have a mole here, the way he did." She touched the spot on his bare ribs. "Who are you? My husband's twin brother?"

Trevane started to protest, then exhaled wearily in a resigned sigh. "Brother, but not a twin. I was two years older. We looked so much alike that we were mistaken for twins."

"If you really are Ivo Trevane, what was my husband's name?" Jessie's gaze was burning a hole in Trevane's hide.

"Rupert Ivo Trevane. Half the male Trevanes in Dorset have Ivo somewhere in their names. He did-

n't like the name Rupert, so he often used Ivo when
I wasn't around to confuse the issue." Trevane's
voice had changed, losing the gruffness and sound-
ing more educated.

"In other words, today you are impersonating
your brother, who married Jessie while impersonating you," Daniel said acerbically.

Trevane glowered. "Yes, damn you!"

Jessie frowned. "He never said anything about his
family. I thought he was alone, like me. Why didn't
he invite you to the wedding if you were so close?"

"I had traveled to the Indies on a matter of business. It was months until I returned home. I found
a letter from Rupert saying he'd married a dia-
mond of the first water and he'd bring Lisbet to
Dorset for Christmas if I was home by then." Trevane's mouth flattened to a deadly line. "I was
going to travel up to Bristol to meet you when the
news arrived that Rupert was dead, and his beautiful young wife had killed him and disappeared."

"Did he mention that he married me claiming
he was you?" Jessie asked. "He also claimed that he
owned the Bristol house and that he had an estate
down around here!"

"Both belonged to me as the elder son, but I let
him stay in the Bristol house because he found the estate a flat bore." Trevane frowned. "He liked pranks
and sometimes he did pretend to be me, but surely
he didn't allow you to think that when he married
you."

"Oh, he did!" Voice shaking, Jessie continued. "So
what was the reason for this mad charade of yours? Did
you intend to murder me to avenge your brother?"

Trevane's eyes blazed. "I wouldn't have killed you or your husband. I planned to keep you a day or two and then release you."

"And then what?" Daniel exclaimed with amazement. "You'd just let us go and expect there would be no consequences for your kidnapping and assault?"

"Every magistrate and other important person in this area is related to me," Trevane explained with a smirk. "They'd understand why I wanted to do this before I had you charged and arrested for my brother's murder." His voice broke. " I wanted you to *suffer!* I wanted you to know some of the pain I felt when you murdered my closest kin!"

In a cold rage, Daniel said, "So he was a charming, prankish young fellow and you miss him still?"

"Always," was the whispered reply. Ivo's eyes were haunted.

"Perhaps Jessie can share some of her memories of your brother with you," Daniel said in a voice that cut like a whip. "She can tell you what a vicious brute he was when he was drunk. So vicious that she locked herself in her bedroom nights when she knew he'd come home drunk."

Trevane lifted his head, his eyes furious. "You're lying!"

"Oh?" Jessie spat out. "I was there! You were *not!* Yes, he was charming when he was sober, but he was a monster when he drank!"

"Let me tell you about the night I met her," Daniel said inexorably. "It was the night she killed him. When she appeared in my infirmary that night, her face was so bruised her own mother wouldn't have recognized her. Luckily your dear brother didn't destroy either of her eyes, but it was a near run thing.

"And then there were the bruises around her neck, where he almost strangled her to death. Big, purple bruises that show how her breathing was choked off. Imagine how she felt when she was blacking out from the lack of air, struggling frantically as he threatened to slash her face so no one would ever think her pretty again."

As Ivo stared in shock, Daniel continued, his words slashing like scalpels. "Maybe his intention was merely to mutilate her, but as an experienced doctor, I think it more likely he would have killed her accidentally, then wept bitter tears when he sobered up, because after all, he didn't mean it, which makes it all right, doesn't it? Because he was such a good fellow he'd never kill his wife *deliberately.*"

"No," Trevane whispered hoarsely, not wanting to believe. "He wouldn't have done anything like that!"

"But he did," Jessie said in a hard voice. "I managed to break free and was running for the door when he stabbed me in the back. The scar is so distinctive that Daniel recognized it on our wedding night even though he hadn't recognized my battered, bleeding face." Her voice began to shake. "If not for the kindness of Daniel and his sister, I don't know what would have become of me. I might have died in the streets. Instead, Daniel fixed me up and gave me money and I was able to run away. Because I was a murderess, you know, I had to run for my life."

She turned and yanked the left shoulder of her gown down as far as she could. "See that scar? It runs all the way to my waist. Shall I show you all of it?"

"No," Trevane said in an agonized voice. *"No!"*

His eyes closed and his face twisted as tears leaked from between his lids. After a long, long moment, he opened his eyes. Devastated acceptance was written on every line of his face. "How . . . did he die?"

"When I was struggling to get away, I shoved at his hand with the knife. It swerved into his throat. Right in the place where you don't have a scar." She drew a ragged breath. "So I really did kill him. When I thought you were he, still alive, I was relieved. I never wanted to hurt anyone."

When she stopped speaking, there was no sound except the endless waves. Mouth tight, Daniel used the cravat to bind Trevane's ankle. Then he poked among the pieces of driftwood and found a branch that was long enough and close enough to straight to serve as a staff.

"Let's get out of here. I don't know how much longer the path is to the beach, but the tide is coming in and I really do not want to spend a night in the same cave with you, Mr. Trevane."

Trevane pushed himself to a sitting position. His face was haggard and he looked like a different man. Well, he was a different man now that he was no longer playing the role of his dead brother. "I . . . I'm deeply sorry, Lady Romayne, for what my brother did to you, and what I did to you and your husband," he said unsteadily. "Rupert's death drove me to the edge of madness, and that madness took hold of my mind and better judgment."

"There's a reason why God is reported as saying that vengeance is His," Daniel said acerbically. "He's the only one who knows the whole truth." He put his arm under Trevane's shoulders and hauled him to his feet. "I'll support you with your arm over my shoulders and you can use the staff with your other hand if your arm doesn't hurt too much. How much farther is it to the beach?"

"Not far." Trevane managed to lurch forward with Daniel supporting most of his weight. "The path isn't quite so treacherous the rest of the way. This whole area is old smugglers' quarters. There's a tunnel that leads up to the Castle Romayne dungeons, which was how I got you two there. Our ancestors, Romaynes and Trevanes, did quite a profitable line of business in free trade."

"Do you still?" Daniel asked.

"No, I'm the boring brother." His mouth twisted humorlessly. "I don't ask my people questions I don't want to know the answers to."

As they moved from the cave to the path, Jessie asked, "Mr. Trevane, how did you know who I was? You and I have never met, and I've hidden from my past rather effectively. Daniel and I only arrived here yesterday. How did you realize who I was and put this nasty little plan of yours into effect?"

"I went to school with a nephew of yours, Frederick Kelham," Trevane explained. "He was suspicious of his uncle's death, wondering if you might have poisoned your elderly husband to get rid of him. Somehow he learned that you'd lived in Bristol and he decided to do some investigating of your past. He'd met my brother a time or two and he knew me, so he thought it his duty to tell me who the murderer was."

"Frederick!" Jessie said with loathing. "There is no end to the amount of trouble he wants to make for me and my daughter! But you believed him because he was a man."

"That and the fact that we both went to Harrow," Trevane said apologetically. "He always was a slippery fellow, but when he told me you'd killed my brother—well, I lost a lot of my sanity."

"Losing your sanity seems to be a trait you shared with your brother," Daniel said tartly. The going was indeed easier on this stretch of path, but he'd be very, very glad when they got back to the sand. Then he could put Trevane down and go up to the house and enlist others to finish the job.

"Frederick is a vile beast who threatened the lives of me and my daughter. Of *course* you believed him!" Jessie snapped.

"Mea culpa, Lady Romayne," Trevane said with a sigh. "You seem to have chosen a better husband this time."

"I became much better at choosing husbands after Ivo." She smiled at Daniel with a warmth that almost made up for the rest of the day.

"The end of the trail!" she said with relief as she turned another corner. "Shall I head up to the new house for help while you settle Mr. Trevane on the sand? Someone else can get him up the cliff."

"Exactly what I was thinking." Daniel steered Trevane through the dangerous jumble of rocks mixed with sand that marked the transition from cliff to beach. The sun was setting, a blood-red ball of fire.

Despite her fatigue, Jessie speeded up as she headed toward the stairway up the cliff. She had to be as anxious for this to be over as Daniel was.

A man was charging down the steps to the beach. Daniel squinted, wondering if it was a Romayne servant coming to help.

Frederick Kelham. He was wild eyed and red with rage. "Damn you, Trevane!" he shouted. "You were supposed to take care of that murderess! You promised me you'd see that justice was done!"

Trevane halted, weaving in his tracks. "You can't have thought I'd just murder her out of hand!" he sputtered, aghast. "I wanted to see her humiliated and hanged."

"Why not murder her?" Kelham snarled. "That's what she did to your brother."

Trevane tried to straighten his battered body. "I found out there was more to the story than you told me. No further justice was required."

Jessie, who was halfway between Frederick and Daniel, said sharply, "You've spread enough lies about me, Frederick! How would your fashionable friends feel if they knew what a disgusting, greedy liar you are? If you ever threaten me or mine again, I'll find some way to take you to court and into bankruptcy!"

"You *bitch!*" Face contorted with rage, Frederick pulled a pistol from his coat and cocked it, holding the hilt in both hands as he aimed at Jessie at point-blank range.

Her jaw dropped as if even now, she couldn't think such a thing of Philip's nephew. "You really *are* mad!"

Daniel abandoned Trevane to his own devices and

sprinted toward Frederick, knowing he wouldn't be able to reach the bastard before he fired.

Jessie tried to dodge away, but the barrel of Kelham's pistol followed her. Oh, God, he was squeezing the trigger. . . .

A shot exploded through the twilight, echoing from the cliffs and driving a flock of gulls screaming into the sky.

No, no, noooooooo! A primal howl started in Daniel's heart and rose to the heavens, threatening to shatter him into anguished pieces.

But it was Frederick who crumpled to the ground, not Jessie. Frederick's blood that stained the sand. Someone else had fired.

Heart pounding, Daniel halted and scanned his surroundings. Salvation was a man with pale blond hair who was now racing down the stairs three steps at a time. A rifle angled down at his side with a wisp of smoke trailing from the barrel.

Gordon. Praise be to all the saints, *Gordon!*

Daniel reached Jessie and she hurled herself into his arms, shaking as if she'd break into pieces herself. He enveloped her in an all-encompassing embrace, scarcely able to believe that she was here and alive.

Slowing his pace, Gordon crossed the sand toward them, as travel stained as when they'd last seen him at Milton Manor.

Holding Jessie tight, Daniel said, "I approve of your timely arrival, but how?"

"I was lucky. I'd almost finished my interview with the butler at Trevane's house in Bristol when I asked the right question and increased my bribe. He immediately told me that it was a younger brother who died, one who liked to pretend he was the heir," Gordon explained. "I also learned that someone had been asking the same questions I was a few days earlier. I thought you should know, but I didn't expect the situation to have become so dangerous so quickly."

"Neither of us would have guessed," Jessie said in a thin voice. "Thank God you arrived when you did!"

Gordon knelt by Frederick Kelham's body and did a quick check for signs of life. Rising to his feet, he said, "That's one villain who won't be bothering you again, Lady Romayne." His gaze moved to Daniel. "I charge more for saving client's lives."

Daniel almost laughed. "Send me an invoice. I won't quibble about the price."

Gordon returned a faint smile. "You get your wife up to the house. I'll take care of matters here." He turned to Trevane, who had managed to limp along and join the group. "Are you the real Ivo Trevane?"

"For my sins, yes." Trevane's voice was a croak.

Gordon said, "Send down every male servant in the house, Romayne. Then I trust that very efficient butler of yours will find me a bed and tomorrow morning you can tell me what the devil's been going on here!"

"I can give you a start on that," Trevane said as he folded wearily onto the sand.

More than happy to leave Gordon in charge, Daniel guided Jessie toward the staircase. "I'm glad you're my wife again. I was contemplating whether you could get a Scottish divorce from Trevane. And if so, would you marry me again?"

"Of course I would! Would a Scottish divorce have been possible? I find that retrospectively comforting."

"I'm not sure, but I certainly would have found out." Arm in arm, they tiredly began climbing the steps. He gave exhausted thanks that there were railings on both sides, since they were useful in hauling tired bodies upward.

"I'm so sorry, Daniel. My sordid past could have got you killed tonight," Jessie said in a constricted voice. Her head was bent and her hair falling every which way, obscuring her face.

"Is this the end of it?" he asked with weary humor. "No more resurrected parents or husbands or murders or murderous relatives?"

She gave him a tired smile. "Not that I know of. But I certainly didn't expect this, either!"

Panting, they reached the top of the stairs. By unspoken agreement, they headed for the gazebo and folded onto the wide, comfortable wooden bench inside. The gazebo was an elegant structure with a wall to act as a wind break on the side facing the new house. Daniel sat and pulled Jessie into his lap. Limp as a silk scarf, she cuddled against him, her head on his shoulder and her arms around him.

For long moments, they simply breathed together, regaining their strength and appreciating the fact that they were alive and well. Daniel finally broke the silence when he summoned the courage to ask, "Did you mean it when you said you loved me?"

She tilted her head back and caught his gaze, her aquamarine eyes transparent with truth. "With all my heart and soul," she said quietly. "With you, I've found more passion than with my first husband, as much trust and kindness as with my second, and those qualities are allied with a warmth and intelligence that is all your own. I love you, Dr. Daniel, in all your aspects."

Warmth flowered deep inside him, dissolving all the doubts and pessimism he'd felt when they first met. "I thought that I could never love with as much power and passion as when I was a youth," he said equally quietly. "I love you, Jezebel Elizabeth Braxton Trevane Kelham Herbert. I must have had a premonition of this when I first saw you across a crowded room. I just wasn't wise enough to realize that I could love again."

In the red glow of sunset, Jessie was the most beautiful creature he'd ever seen. An earthy goddess with endless resources of passion and loyalty. He kissed her with all the love and tenderness he'd discovered.

Coming up for air, Jessie said breathlessly, "It's perfectly obvious why I would fall in love with you! Julia and Mariah were quite firm on that point. But with my tarnished past, what do you see in me?"

"All the difficulties you've survived have made you who you are. A woman of strength and wisdom." He brushed back her hair. "You bring me passion and joy, Jessie. Both qualities were sadly lacking in my life. I can imagine no greater gift."

She pressed her cheek into his stroking hand. "You already had those qualities. I'm glad if I helped you find them."

Realizing that it was time for an overdue revelation, he said, "You're the first woman I've ever lain with, Jessie. Rose and I had discovered each other's bodies with all the passion of youth, but only to a point. After she died, I buried that part of myself. I couldn't imagine loving again, nor could I use a woman without love. I thought I'd live the rest of my life celibate as a medieval monk."

"That would have been an appalling waste!" Her eyes shot open like a startled kitten's. "I would not have guessed that from your lovemaking. Though knowing the honor in your soul, perhaps I should have known you would not take mistresses casually."

"As a doctor, I know quite a lot about bodies, and how to touch them," he explained with a wry smile. "It was a great delight to experience the pleasures as well as the pains." He leaned forward for another kiss that swiftly turned scorchingly intense.

She melted against him as the kiss went on and on and on, accompanied by whispers of laughter and passion. When it finally became too cold to linger any longer, Daniel reluctantly set her feet on the marble floor of the gazebo and stood. "Time to go into the house and tell Pendry that help is needed below."

She nodded and linked her arm in his and they ambled toward the new house. He asked teasingly, "Does this mean I'll be able to see that red dress again?"

Laughing, she said, "You will, sir. But there will be nothing so complicated as that tonight!"

So he kissed her again. Who needed a stunning red gown when he was married to the most beautiful woman in the world?

Epilogue

Breakfast in the gallery had become a regular custom after Daniel, Jessie, and Beth settled into Castle Romayne. Jessie had suggested it rather firmly, and Daniel had come to love these quiet intervals with his wife as they talked about the day ahead. With Jessie's guidance, he'd become much better about savoring life's simple joys.

Jessie emptied the teapot by topping up their cups. "I never appreciated weather so much before. No matter how wild or serene the sea is, the view here is magical."

"And today it's serene," Daniel agreed. "I'll be spending most of the day at the hospital, training the new nurses in the morning and opening the infirmary in the afternoon."

"A worthy day." Jessie made a face. "It's my day for balancing the monthly accounts. Equally worthy but far less interesting."

They shared an intimate smile. Daniel's hope of a wife who could manage all his business interests had been fulfilled better than he'd dreamed possible. It had taken her less than three months to take firm hold of his personal inheritance from his father and the Romayne properties. The Kelham estates she'd already had under control.

Peace was interrupted when a muddy Beth galloped into the gallery, accompanied by three equally muddy village children who shared her lessons, all of them clutching golden flowers. "Daffodillies!" Beth proclaimed triumphantly as she offered Daniel and Jessie a handful each.

"They're lovely." Jessie buried her face in the blossoms, emerging with a pollen-dusted nose. "Spring comes so early here on the south coast."

Beth's nurse, Lily, and the young governess they'd hired entered the gallery at a slower pace, though with muddy shoes of their own. "Sorry, my lady," Lily said apologetically. "We were heading to the kitchen to put the daffs in water, but the little ones got away from us."

As Jessie laughed, Daniel said, "The first flowers of spring are worth some exuberance." He kissed Beth's rosy cheek. "Now off with you all! Lily can drop you into the horse trough to wash off the mud, and then on to lessons."

The giggling children were rounded up and escorted out just before Pendry entered with a silver tray holding the morning post. It was neatly divided into two piles, his and Jessie's. After the butler left, they looked through their letters, which was another part of the daily ritual.

"Here's a letter from Julia," she reported. "They'll

want me in Kent for the opening of the Canterbury Zion House next month. That will fit in nicely since we were going to go there in April anyhow."

Daniel opened a letter from his sister first. "All is well in Kirkland country," he reported, "and my nephew is a paragon of infant beauty and brilliance." He glanced up, his eyes crinkling at the corners. "Laurel adds that she is joking, but nonetheless, the brilliance and beauty are entirely true."

"She'd be an unnatural mother if she didn't believe that." Jessie patted her slim waist, which didn't yet show the miracle within. "Our offspring will be equally brilliant and beautiful." She glanced at Daniel. "You're beaming."

"I can't help it," he confessed. "Procreation may be the most common of human miracles, but it's still a miracle." Still smiling, he slit the seal on his last letter.

His smile vanished. "Jessie." When she looked up inquiringly, he said, "Your father is dead. He passed away in his sleep. Apparently his heart gave out."

She pressed a swift hand to her mouth, her eyes shocked and vulnerable. "As . . . as you predicted."

"At last he's at peace," Daniel said quietly.

She sighed. "I can't really mourn a man who was never my father in any good way. Who wrote the letter?"

"His housekeeper, Miss Ludley. Being a woman who knows her duty, she thought you should know." Daniel glanced at the date. "The funeral took place yesterday."

"So I'm spared the hypocrisy of attending and pretending I'm grieving," she said dryly. "I'm a good actress, but not that good."

Daniel read the final paragraph of the letter. "Miss Ludley says rather aggressively that your father left her all his possessions. Do you think that's likely?"

"Perhaps. She is probably the only person who truly mourns him. I won't challenge her statement. She was a poor spinster and would have been in dire straits if my father hadn't hired her as a house-keeper. My father wasn't a rich man, but I'm sure he left enough to give her a comfortable life."

"You may take pleasure in the knowledge that your graciousness will surely infuriate her." He hesitated, then added, "How do you feel? I've observed that it's often more difficult to deal with the loss of a bad parent than a good one."

Jessie pursed her lips, then nodded. "That's it exactly. As long as my father was alive, there was a chance that he'd summon me to his deathbed and apologize for his behavior and say that he really did care for me. Now that I say that aloud, I know how foolish the hope was." She drew an unsteady breath. "But it was real and now it's gone."

"The loss of hope is always sad, but I suspect your mother will just be relieved."

Jessie's brow furrowed. "She certainly will! Does this mean she's no longer a bigamist?"

"I suppose so, but her marriage to George Lester is still invalid because it was performed when she had a living husband," Daniel replied. "You've been secretly corresponding with her for months now. Will she care about the invalid marriage as long as she knows your father can't show up on her doorstep breathing fire and brimstone?"

"She'd rather be married all right and proper," Jessie said with conviction. "She wants to publicly acknowledge that I'm her daughter and she's desperate to meet Beth. But until now, she's been terrified that doing so might cost her everything she has."

Daniel considered. "I could marry her and George Lester very quietly, but she'd have to tell him the truth first. Do you think he'd be horrified and put her aside if he knew she's been lying to him all these years?"

"From what she says in her letters, he dotes on her, so he'd probably be horrified, but more interested in correcting the situation than in destroying his family." A wicked spark showed in Jessie's eyes. "She could tell him a version of the truth and claim that not long after Cassius Braxton threw her out, she heard he'd died. She believed that or she wouldn't have married George. Only now that he's really dead does she realize that she was an accidental bigamist."

"Shock! Horror! Collapsing into George's comforting arms with wails of distress!" Daniel said with a grin, easily able to visualize the scene.

"Through Braxton's death, she also learns that her daughter survived," Jessie said, getting into the spirit. "Joy! Bliss! Better yet, her long-lost daughter is married to a vicar who can quietly legitimize her marriage to George and no one else need know the awkward truth!"

"Perfect. When you write her about Braxton's death, will you suggest this?"

Jessie caught her breath, eyes shining. "Better yet, I'll suggest that she and George celebrate the discovery of the long-lost daughter and her vicar husband with a renewal of their marriage vows. A proper wedding with all her family there. Only she and George and you and I would know that it would be a true marriage, not a renewal of vows. Is that possible?"

Daniel laughed. "I'm not sure that Church law covers a situation like this, but why not? No one would be hurt by it, and it could be explained as a celebration to welcome you and Beth into her other family."

"Then I'll suggest it." Jessie joined Daniel's laughter. "Because I do know that my mother and George love a good time!"

April 1814

The parish church of Saint Helen Bishopsgate was not in fashionable Mayfair, but firmly planted in the City of London, the heart of London's business community. The grand Gothic structure resonated with the music of its famous organ, and brilliant spring sunshine poured through the windows. It was a perfect setting for the renewal of wedding vows.

In the church foyer, Jessie bent to kiss Beth's curls. "Time to march down the aisle, little finch. You're an experienced carrier of flowers now, so show everyone how it's done."

Beth giggled, then firmly grasped the handle of her flower basket in both hands and stepped into the church. Her gaze was fixed on her Daddy Daniel, who stood at the altar. In his clerical robes, Daniel looked like a particularly handsome saint who would dispense warmth and forgiveness to all who needed it. He certainly had given that to Jessie and Beth.

Waiting at the altar were George Lester and his best man, a friend and colleague of many years. A practical businessman, George had accepted the news that his marriage wasn't legal with surprising calm, and had entered gleefully into plans for the supposed renewal of vows celebration. Not only would it be a jolly party, but a chance to show off his beautiful new stepdaughter and her lordly husband.

Resplendent in cream satin, Jessie's mother whispered, "I'm as excited as if I was seventeen again!"

"You should be," Jessie said as she straightened her mother's bonnet. It was the sort of thing a bridal attendant was supposed to do. She'd been delighted when Elizabeth had asked her to stand as witness. "This time you're marrying the right man."

Her mother laughed, tears in her eyes as she gave Jessie a hug, knocking her bonnet askew once more. "Oh, darling, I'm so happy to have you in my life again! You're the best thing that ever happened to me."

"No, George is," Jessie laughed as she returned the hug, then stepped into the church to follow Beth down the aisle.

As she walked solemnly forward, she gave a special smile to her new-found half siblings. The two boys and two girls resembled George more than Elizabeth, and they had his good nature and practical good sense. They'd been delighted by the discovery of a half sister who was not only a baroness but had given them an adorable niece.

Old Mrs. Lester had a satiric glint in her eye and Jessie suspected that she wasn't entirely convinced by the "renewal of vows" story, but she was as practical as her son. What mattered to her was that Elizabeth had produced four healthy, intelligent grandchildren.

Jessie raised her gaze to meet Daniel's. He gave her a wicked smile that promised they'd have a very private celebration of their own when they retired for the night.

Because, thank the Lord, Daniel was not always a saint!

Author's Note

Yes, there really are a (very) few peerage titles that can be inherited by a female. I used the same plot device, a barony of writ, in my early traditional Regency, *Carousel of Hearts*. It's great fun to turn the male hierarchy on its head!

Medical practitioners were classified differently in Regency times. Physicians were gentlemen and well educated, and they were called "Doctor." Surgeons were descendants of barbers and butchers and other vulgar folk who used knives and handled human bodies. They were not considered gentlemen and were called Mister, though by the Regency, schools of anatomy existed to train surgeons. In Britain, surgeons are still called Mister even though they're highly trained medical school graduates. Tradition!

Certainly it was possible for one person to have a range of medical skills, particularly if they lived in an isolated area and there was no other source of medical aid available. My Lost Lords midwife, Lady Julia, had become such an all-purpose practitioner in her remote village in Cumberland in the far northwest of England. The same is true of Daniel, since he would always do his best to help someone in need. I usually call him a doctor for the sake of reading simplicity.

Cottage hospitals began to appear in this period, and establishing more of them is an activity that will suit Daniel right down to the ground as he proves that he can be a doctor as well as a lord. And now, by the power invested in me as a writer, I grant Daniel and Jessie happily ever afters!

You are cordially invited—to fall in love . . .

THE LAST CHANCE CHRISTMAS BALL

Mary Jo Putney

Jo Beverley

Joanna Bourne

Patricia Rice

Nicola Cornick

Cara Elliott

Anne Gracie

Susan King

Christmas 1815. **Upstairs and downstairs, Holbourne Hall is abuzz with preparations for a grand ball to celebrate the year's most festive— and romantic—holiday. For at the top of each guest's wish list is a last chance to find true love before the New Year . . .**

A chance meeting beneath the mistletoe, a stolen glance across the dance floor—amid the sumptuous delicacies, glittering decorations, and swell of the orchestra, every duchess and debutante, lord and lackey has a hopeful heart. There's the headstrong heiress who must win back her beloved by midnight—or be wed to another . . . the spinster whose fateful choice to relinquish love may hold one more surprise for her . . . a widow yearning to glimpse her long-lost love for even one sweet, fleeting interlude . . . a charming rake who finds far more than he bargained for. And many other dazzling, romantic tales in this star-studded collection that will fill your heart and spice up your holidays this October!